THE CHARCOAL HOUSE

GILLIAN JACKSON

BLOODHOUND
— BOOKS —

First published in 2023 by Bloodhound Books.

www.bloodhoundbooks.com

Print ISBN: 978-1-5040-8596-0

This book is dedicated to two of my greatest encouragers, Rita Wilkinson, a lady I met when speaking at a WI meeting who has been a constant source of encouragement. Thank you, Rita for your support.
And also, at the other side of the world, Kelly Ferret, a lady whose enthusiasm and messages lift my spirits. I'll try to write more quickly for you, Kelly!

ALSO BY GILLIAN JACKSON

The Pharmacist

The Victim

The Deception

Abduction

Snatched

The Accident

The Shape of Truth

CHAPTER ONE

At the sound of the front door opening, Emma Porter jumped, snapping shut the wooden box which held the remains of her once-extensive collection of artist's materials. A couple of white charcoal highlight pencils and a few stumps of willow charcoal were all that remained, bits and bobs rattling around inside as she stuffed the box into the back of her wardrobe.

The sketch pad, falling from her knee in her moment of panic, held the result of the last hour, a dark representation of a house – a depressing place with no lights within and a heavy door to keep visitors out – or to keep Emma in?

The image held no warmth or colour, no wrap-around garden with riotous displays of flowers, no trees for birds to perch in and sing, simply a muddy path winding up to the shadowy house. Why she'd sketched such a place was a mystery, even to herself. Perhaps it reflected her current mood, dark and gloomy, without joy or hope. Quickly she slid the pad into a large manilla envelope and tucked it behind the box in the wardrobe. Emma stood, trembling, and swallowed hard as she went downstairs to meet him.

Life hadn't always been this way for Emma, and her paintings were previously very different from the charcoal house. Emma's talent had exhibited itself when as a young girl, each image reflected her enthusiasm for life. Landscapes and seascapes were her preferred themes, but always with a house secreted somewhere in the picture – a tiny beach house half-hidden by sand dunes or the shingle roof of a cottage nestling at the edge of a forest.

Colour had previously defined Emma's paintings. Glorious arcs of cerulean-blue skies or sweeps of emerald sea clothed with peaks of white frothy foam. She possessed a gift for capturing beauty, replicating nature and communicating the splendour of a moment in time. Sometimes the scenes were painted from an inside perspective, looking out, with window struts or billowing curtains framing the distant view. To Emma, placing a house in each picture gave it ballast, a solidity and a place of safety, but that was before – another life. Emma Porter was now Emma Beecham, married to Simon, and a shadow of her former self.

Emma and Simon's first meeting was at a bus stop as she sheltered from the elements beneath her umbrella. But the lashing rain, blown almost horizontal by a gale-force wind, whipped the flimsy umbrella from her hands, turning it inside out as it bounced back along the street. As Emma wavered over whether to chase it and risk missing the bus or abandon it altogether, a car pulled up ten yards away and a man jumped out to retrieve the useless umbrella. He ran towards her, a knight in shining, if somewhat soggy, armour.

'Thank you, but you really shouldn't have bothered.' Emma smiled shyly, noticing the man's vivid green eyes set in a pleasant oval face and his sandy-coloured hair darkening as the rain plastered it onto his head.

'I could hardly leave you without this, although I think it may be beyond repair.' The man fiddled with the bent spokes, concentration creasing his brow.

'Thanks for trying but you'd better get back in the car before you drown.' Emma laughed, hoping mascara wasn't running down her face.

'Look, you're soaked. I know your mother probably warned you about getting into a car with a strange man but can I give you a lift?' He held his hand out. 'My name's Simon Beecham, so we're not exactly strangers now, are we?' A lopsided smile convinced her.

'Emma Porter,' she replied, taking his hand in her own rather wet one. 'And thank you, a lift would be wonderful if you don't mind me dripping all over your car?'

Simon hurried back to open the passenger door. 'I should've asked where you live. I hope it's no more than fifty miles, although I *have* finished work for the weekend.'

That crooked smile again. He was achingly handsome, even soaking wet, and she liked his gentle teasing. Emma jumped into the car, reciting her address and promising it was less than a couple of miles away.

Relaxing into the leather seat, feet numb and teeth chattering, the warmth began to thaw Emma through. As the journey lasted only fifteen minutes, there was little time to talk. Simon chatted briefly about his job as a claims manager at a large insurance company and Emma reciprocated with information about her work as a receptionist at the local dentist.

'Hmm, not the most popular venue in town.' He grimaced. Emma had probably heard every dentist joke going but would happily listen to more from this man. In fact, the journey was far too short for her and as they pulled into her parents' driveway, Emma had decided she'd like to know Simon Beecham better.

'Can I offer you a coffee? *Your* mother probably warned you about fast women, but my mum's at home – you'll be perfectly safe!'

Simon threw his head back and laughed as if she was the most entertaining woman he'd ever met. 'I'd love a coffee if you're sure your mother won't mind?'

'Not at all. She'll be grateful you rescued my umbrella – and me.'

As expected, Mrs Porter made a fuss of Simon, thanking him for his kindness and leading him to the kitchen to put the kettle on while Emma ran upstairs to change. Her shoulder-length brown hair was beyond repair, a quick towel dry and a brush through would have to suffice, and her make-up was a mess.

After changing into jeans and a jumper, she did a quick repair job on her face before running back downstairs to find her mother and Simon chatting like old friends, his coat drying next to the radiator with steam rising from it. Emma was struck by the contented domestic scene. Simon turned and looked appreciatively at her.

She sat at the kitchen table. 'Any coffee left for me?'

Margaret Porter turned to her daughter. 'Of course, love. Simon was just telling me what happened to your umbrella. It's a good job he was passing.' Emma fully expected her to give an exaggerated wink as she poured the hot coffee before tactfully leaving the young couple alone.

There are times when you meet someone and click immediately, which was how Emma felt about Simon. Conversation flowed as if they'd known each other for years and he appeared as reluctant to leave as she was to let him go. Before venturing into the rain, Simon asked Emma out to dinner, an invitation she accepted without hesitation.

The next few months passed in a dreamy whirlwind as Emma grew more and more dazzled by Simon's attention. He was nine years older, thirty-two to her twenty-three – and to her mind mature and attractive. He regularly surprised her with small gifts, the first of which was an umbrella, *a sturdy industrial-strength one,* he announced, and she'd laughed. Each date was planned with an almost military precision and thoughtfulness with the effect of impressing Emma, who found herself rapidly falling in love.

As Simon's office at Johnson & Co Insurance was near to the dental practice where Emma worked, he fell into a pattern of picking her up from work each evening, and she no longer caught the bus as she'd always done. The first time Simon ventured into the dentist's surgery to wait for Emma, the other receptionist, Fiona, and the dental hygienists flirted outrageously with him, which he took in good humour. As Emma grabbed her coat, her colleagues whispered how lucky she was to have such a gorgeous boyfriend. She nodded in agreement, drinking in their comments. Emma happily took Simon's arm as they left together.

Margaret and George Porter readily accepted Simon – he made Emma happy, which in their eyes was the chief requirement for any prospective son-in-law, and they cheerfully welcomed him into their family. Emma had been a much-wanted baby who hadn't arrived until the couple had almost given up hope of becoming parents. From the moment of her birth they'd loved her unconditionally and in return, Emma adored them and enjoyed an idyllic, carefree childhood under their protection.

When Simon proposed, her parents expressed only a slight concern that the couple had only known each other for a few months, but their daughter was so much in love that they soon celebrated with them. Emma was no longer a teenager – they accepted that she knew her own mind and raised no objections. The addition of a son-in-law would enrich their lives and hopefully there would be grandchildren all in good time.

As expected, nothing was too much for the big day and Emma needed to rein in her parents; they were in danger of going overboard with the wedding and reception plans. But the family delighted at organising the perfect day – it was a magical time.

Being an only child, leaving home would be a bittersweet experience for her, Margaret and George, but Simon was Emma's choice. She convinced them he was the one to make her happy.

Emma Porter thought she was living in a fairy tale – a feeling which lasted for a blissful year – until she became Emma Beecham.

CHAPTER TWO

Simon growled, angry yet again with his new wife. 'You're not Daddy's little princess anymore! You live with me now – we're married, remember – and money's too tight to be wasted on rubbish!' Each syllable of this last phrase was emphasised by his finger rhythmically tapping on Emma's forehead as she stood, frozen to the spot. Then in a heartbeat, his mood changed and Simon pulled his wife towards him, laughing, embracing her in a bear-like hug until she could hardly breathe.

'Don't make me get cross with you.' His voice sounded more rational, surprisingly gentle even. 'I love you, Emma, and only want what's best for you, but just because your father spoiled you doesn't mean I will. I'm the one who'll look after you now, and you know how much I love you, don't you?'

Emma smiled half-heartedly while attempting to wriggle free from her husband's grasp. It was true he often reminded her of his love but it was a love which seemed to have changed since their wedding, or at the very least was manifesting itself in different ways, ways which Emma hadn't expected. Yet he could be generous at times – if she'd pleased him.

Simon turned to leave the room – the matter closed. There

would be nothing more said on the subject – Emma recognised the pattern. Perhaps he was right. She was no longer a child at home with her parents but a married woman who would have to accept that her husband was now the one to make all the decisions.

Busying herself in the kitchen and enjoying being in control there at least, Emma reminded herself that a few settling down problems were to be expected – married life was bound to be different from being a singleton living at home with her parents. Maybe she and Simon should have discussed practicalities in more detail before the wedding, but being young and in love perhaps her view of marriage was somewhat naïve.

In hindsight Emma could see that this latest incident was her fault. It had been thoughtless to buy the glossy magazine and a new mascara – it gave Simon something else about which to be annoyed. Being without the kind of disposable income Emma had enjoyed when single was another change to become accustomed to – and her impulse buying would have to be a thing of the past. It wasn't worth provoking Simon's anger over such trivial matters, and it was only fitting he should handle their finances, after all, he was the one who worked with figures. Emma hadn't even realised she wasn't good with money until her husband pointed it out.

If Emma was completely honest with herself, the money issue did niggle at the back of her mind. It made her feel incompetent and embarrassed that Simon should have to look after their finances. A small part of her thought her ineptitude was due to being kept in the dark regarding money issues. Wouldn't she manage better if she knew more of their financial position? Emma didn't even know how much Simon earned, he'd never told her, and after a while it seemed too late to ask. Maybe most wives were happy to leave the financial side of marriage to their husbands, Emma didn't know, and there was no one to ask for advice without being disloyal. If she discussed it with anyone it might suggest a lack of trust in Simon. And he did look after her, didn't he?

But it was no good wishing to be more in the loop, Emma had inadvertently handed over all control to Simon and now it was too late. Before their wedding, Simon arranged to visit the bank and open a joint account. Using the surname Beecham for the first time was a novelty, and Emma finally felt grown up – she was starting a new life as a married woman.

At the bank, Emma thought the girl attending to them in the tiny cubicle glanced at her with envy as she sat beside her handsome fiancé and a warm inner glow flooded her body. But it came as a surprise when Simon instructed the girl to close Emma's current account; she'd mistakenly thought it would remain open for her salary to be paid into as usual. It also held her savings of about £16,000, which Simon asked to be transferred to the new account. He'd winked and smiled at Emma's confusion, so she dutifully signed the paperwork to close her account without a word and, by default, agreed to have her salary paid into their new joint account.

Afterwards, Emma felt foolish for accepting the situation without question and tried to convince herself that it was simply another adjustment to adapt to. And as she possessed a debit card for the new account, there was no problem, was there?

Yet at times Emma wished Simon would discuss their finances with her instead of fobbing her off with statements like, *There's no need for you to worry about money. I've got everything in hand,* remarks which made her feel stupid and petty for having asked.

And then there was the house they were living in, something else which wasn't quite what Emma had expected. Like all brides-to-be, dreams of a cosy new home filled with love and the memories they'd make in their early days of wedded bliss filled her mind. She anticipated shopping trips together for furniture and items to decorate their home, colour schemes and wallpaper featured in her daydreams and Emma couldn't wait to begin house hunting. Simon had other plans. He proposed renting for a couple of years while saving everything they could, a strategy he insisted would give them a good-sized deposit to put down on their perfect home and place them in an excellent position to negotiate a reasonable price on the property of their choice. It made sense, or so Simon said.

The stark reality of their first home together was a drab, pokey rented house – not Emma's ideal home by any stretch of the imagination. The only perceivable attraction was that it was cheap, which seemed a priority to Simon, less so for her. The place was an embarrassment, so awful that Emma hardly dared to imagine what her parents would think. The house came furnished, which Simon counted as another plus, yet she longed to buy their own furniture. He did concede on the bed and allowed her to order a new one as the previous tenant was an old lady whom Emma feared may have died in their present bed, an assumption which sent shudders down her spine.

Ugly damp patches appeared to be growing on the bedroom ceiling, which returned as quickly as Emma could spray them with mould remover. The windows didn't close properly, allowing a constant draught to blow through the house. What it would be like as they neared the winter months, Emma couldn't imagine – it would cost a fortune to heat, false economy, surely? Yet Emma didn't dare say so to Simon. He appeared content to live there and she consoled herself with it being only a temporary situation.

When the house dragged Emma down, she dreamed of the day they could begin searching for their forever home. If she had free rein, they'd visit local estate agents every weekend and sneak a look on Rightmove's website daily. Simon frowned at any such suggestion, warning her not to look until they were in a position to proceed with a purchase. Yet Emma could still dream couldn't she?

Perhaps it had been foolish to imagine moving into a perfect new home immediately after their wedding. Even with the £10,000 wedding gift from her parents, Simon insisted they wait to buy and that renting was the sensible option.

CHAPTER THREE

Margaret Porter beamed as she spotted the green Nissan Micra from the kitchen window as it pulled into their drive. Quickly she dried her hands, shouting to her husband. 'Emma and Simon are here, love!'

Margaret hadn't seen their daughter since the wedding day and was excited to hear all about the honeymoon and relive the wedding with Emma. Almost sprinting to the door, Margaret reached it before her husband, but was surprised to see that Simon was alone.

'Hello!' Simon climbed out and smiled at his mother-in-law, who struggled to hide her disappointment.

'Oh, hi, isn't Emma with you?'

Simon strode confidently past Margaret and into the hall. 'No, she's unpacking and catching up with the washing.'

'Of course, she must have plenty to do.' It did strike Margaret as strange that Emma would choose housework over a Saturday morning visit home, but she dutifully offered coffee to Simon, who accepted readily.

When the three of them were seated in the lounge, coffee in their hands, Margaret was bursting to ask, 'How was Portugal?'

She'd spoken only briefly on the phone with her daughter since their return, when Emma was in a hurry and unable to talk. How Margaret wished her daughter was there now for a good old natter.

'Fine.' Simon took a sip of the hot drink.

Fine. Margaret was taken aback; what kind of word was that to describe your honeymoon?

'Actually, Emma doesn't know I'm here this morning. I thought it best not to distract her from her chores and I want to discuss a little business with you, if I may?' His words were primarily addressed to George, and Simon glanced at Margaret as if he expected her to leave the room – she was too surprised to hear that Emma didn't know he was there and didn't notice the hint – surely their daughter should have been visiting them too?

When he realised that Margaret was staying put, Simon cleared his throat and commenced speaking.

'As you know, George, my background is in finance and latterly with insurance. I've been making plans to move on, to better myself.' He paused and looked from one to the other, clearly expecting them to be impressed with such ambition. 'I intend to start up as an insurance broker on my own, an independent company. I've gone about as far as I can with Johnsons and feel the time and the market is right.' He coughed again and paused for a few moments. Margaret wasn't fully concentrating, still upset about Emma being left in the dark.

'Naturally,' Simon continued, 'I'll need finance, and that's where you can benefit too, as a backer perhaps, or a sleeping partner if you'd prefer. When the business takes off, it'll be financially beneficial to both of us.' Simon smiled as if he'd handed George a gift, waiting for him to unwrap it with excitement.

Instead, George Porter raised one eyebrow and spoke

slowly, his words measured. 'I wasn't aware you had financial qualifications, Simon, let alone such aspirations.'

'Ah, well yes... but I've had experience working in finance for years.'

'And you say there's no chance for furthering your career at Johnsons,' George persisted.

'I dare say I could climb further up the ladder, but quite honestly, Johnsons is on the way out – they're living in the dark ages – falling behind in today's competitive market.'

'Really, I always thought they were a good, solid company. Family run, aren't they?'

'Yes, and that's half the trouble. They won't change their practices to compete in today's more aggressive market. They're too soft with claimants; they don't investigate fully and settle too many petty little claims.'

'They sound like an insurer I'd be happy to do business with.'

Simon tilted his head to one side and looked condescendingly at his father-in-law. 'With respect, George, you might be an excellent surgeon, but you haven't got half my experience regarding financial matters.'

George drew in a deep breath before speaking again. 'So, what do you envisage my role in your little scheme?'

Simon looked smug. 'Naturally, I would expect to do all the work. I simply wanted you to have the opportunity of investing; after all, this is your daughter's future as well as mine.'

'And do you have a figure in mind for this investment?'

'Initially, I was thinking of a ballpark figure of, say, £80,000.'

Margaret gasped then tried to cover her reaction with a cough. She glanced at her husband but found his expression unreadable.

Simon continued. 'The initial problem will be getting start-up capital from the bank. I'd probably need a similar amount from them as well, but as you know, Emma and I don't own a property yet, so I thought perhaps you would allow me to use this house as collateral for a bank loan?'

George's face was turning red. He maintained silence for a few moments while Margaret sat, open-mouthed, wondering if she'd misheard the whole conversation. Did their son-in-law of only a couple of weeks just ask them for an £80,000 loan and to offer up their home as collateral?

'I presume you've brought a business plan for me to see?' George spoke quickly, more forthright.

'I haven't quite finalised the plan yet, but you know me, I'm more than capable of pulling this off. So what's the problem?'

'The problem is, that to make any investment, even with you, I would want to see a detailed business plan with projections of income and expenditure, which I would then pass on to my accountant and financial advisor to seek their opinion.'

Simon's nostrils flared. 'Look, George, we're family now; you don't have to bring in accountants and financial advisors. Hell, with my experience I can even take over your financial affairs for you if you like. Why pay someone else, someone outside of the family?' His eyes were wide as if surprised that his new father-in-law wasn't simply writing him a cheque on request.

George took a deep breath. 'Come back to me with a business plan, and we'll talk then, although I can tell you for a start that this house would not be on the table to use as collateral.' George was firm and more civil than Margaret expected. It was taking her considerable effort to maintain a polite demeanour.

'But why? It'll all be Emma's one day?' Simon persisted.

George stood. 'I think perhaps it's time for you to leave. Tell Emma we've missed her, will you, and we'd like to see her soon?'

'Actually, I'd rather you didn't tell Emma about this little meeting – you know she doesn't have much of a head for finance and I don't want her to worry.' Simon stood, taking the hint to leave.

Margaret finally found her voice and moved ahead of the two men to open the door. 'Just tell her we're looking forward to seeing her.'

When Simon left, Margaret refilled their coffee cups and the couple sat staring at each other, incredulous. Margaret spoke first. 'Did I just imagine that conversation?'

George shook his head. 'No, you didn't. Simon seemed to think his request was reasonable – I can't believe the man's nerve. He expected us to greet his half-baked idea with enthusiasm.'

'And apparently Emma knows nothing about it. Surely she wouldn't have let him come asking for money if he'd told her?'

George stroked his chin, unable to process the morning's visit from their new son-in-law. 'I don't know, but there's something off about it all and I'm astounded to say the least. Do you think we could have misjudged him? Maybe I should ring Emma and have a word with her before Simon gets home?'

'Oh, no, don't! They've just come back from their honeymoon. Let her enjoy their time alone together and maybe I'll ring her tomorrow. Simon might think it over and realise how ludicrous his request is.'

'There's no way I'll be investing any money in such an ill-conceived scheme. I thought he was settled at Johnsons; they're a well-established company. Why ever would he want to take the risk of setting up alone when he has such limited experience and no formal qualifications?'

'And he didn't want to talk about the honeymoon, how strange. I don't like this at all. Let's hope we get the chance to speak to Emma soon.'

CHAPTER FOUR

Emma longed to see her parents, yet after the honeymoon, Simon found plenty of reasons why she couldn't visit them. Reluctantly she agreed that they were busy with being back at work and settling into their new home but she was uncomfortable with the situation. Even while they were away in Portugal whenever Emma suggested ringing home, Simon grumbled, hinting that his company should be sufficient, an argument she could hardly dispute as they were on honeymoon.

Two weeks after their return, Emma invited her parents to her new home for a meal. It would be the first time they'd been together since the wedding, so there'd be plenty to talk about and Emma was excited at the prospect. Simon raised an eyebrow at the news of the invitation which she laughed off, telling him he'd enjoy the evening and she would cook something special.

The 'something special' was a leg of lamb, a modest one, Emma thought, but its price angered her new husband and provoked what she later thought of as their first row. Shocked and dismayed that Simon could be so petty about cooking a simple meal for her parents when they'd been so generous,

Emma's anticipation of the evening was ruined. Her only hope was that Simon would snap out of his mood before her mum and dad arrived. The last thing she wanted was for them to pick up on her husband's frostiness.

Simon had continued the habit of picking Emma up after work, a practice which, although initially exciting, now seemed rather binding. Secretly Emma would have much preferred to go back to getting the bus. The bus ride home was always enjoyable, relaxing, and an excellent opportunity to switch off and unwind after a busy day. Yet Simon maintained it was quicker and cheaper to pick her up.

On the evening of her parents' visit, Emma could sense Simon's mood as soon as she stepped into the car. It was no more than she'd expected; he'd made it clear how unhappy he was about the evening's arrangements.

Emma matched his silence rather than risk saying the wrong thing and aggravating his temper and as soon as they were home, she jumped out of the car and ran towards the house. A delicious smell of minted lamb wafted through the tiny rooms as she opened the front door; she'd set the timer so the oven would turn itself on mid-afternoon.

Unfortunately, nothing seemed to improve Simon's ill temper. He went upstairs to change without comment while Emma parboiled the potatoes ready to roast around the lamb. She'd prepped the vegetables before leaving for work and a trifle she'd made the evening before was in the fridge, ready to serve for dessert. Emma had managed to brighten up the kitchen table yet her husband's mood dulled the pleasure she took from using the beautiful new dishes and tableware they'd received for wedding presents.

Emma wasn't an accomplished cook, although capable enough. Her mother had taught her the basics as a child and a roast dinner always proved successful, but it wasn't the food that concerned Emma as she went upstairs to change. Simon hadn't spoken to her since they'd arrived home, not even popping his head around the kitchen door to see what she was doing or offering to help, and now he was in the lounge, feet up, reading the paper. He didn't even move to answer the door when the bell rang, and Emma ran downstairs to welcome her parents without the pleasure she would normally have felt. She couldn't understand why Simon appeared reluctant to see them.

'Mum, Dad! Come in...' She forced a smile, hugging them warmly as they entered her home. 'Simon, they're here!' she shouted needlessly; he must have heard their arrival but took his time to greet them with what Emma felt was a cool, insincere welcome.

'Something smells good.' George inhaled. 'Your mother's been starving me all day!'

Margaret poked him in the ribs. 'Oh, George, don't. Can I help, love?'

'It's all ready, Mum. I thought we'd eat in the kitchen. It's much cosier.' Emma led them to the tiny table in the corner of the kitchen. In reality, there wasn't an alternative as they didn't have the luxury of a dining room. Her parents took her lead and followed enthusiastically. For one awful moment, Emma thought Simon was going to return to the lounge, yet after standing in the lobby and staring at his wife for a moment, he tailed them through and took a seat at the table.

The meal was delicious and the Porters complimented their daughter. However, the conversation was sadly stilted. Emma knew she was talking too much, answering questions about their honeymoon with a brittle and forced brightness, aware of Simon's eyes upon her, attentive to every word. If her parents picked up on anything amiss, they hid it well, although at one point Emma noticed a look pass between them when Simon answered yet another of their enquiries with just a single word reply. Each time he was spoken to, he seemed to lift his chin a fraction with an almost arrogant air before replying. It was a trait Emma hadn't noticed before and one she instantly disliked.

Little was mentioned about the house in which the young couple lived. Although they'd not visited before, Emma didn't offer to show her parents around, embarrassed at the shabbiness of it even though she'd attempted to make it comfortable and it was as scrupulously clean as ever. Her parents tactfully didn't ask for a tour. Simon had declined all offers of help to move in before the young couple left for their honeymoon and Emma was sure they now realised why.

At the end of the evening, George and Margaret Porter left with hugs and thanks, perhaps a little sooner than Emma would have liked, but to her embarrassment, Simon took delight in reminding them all they had work the following morning.

When her parents were gone, Emma burst into tears, the strain of the evening catching up with her and upset that Simon hadn't been at all welcoming. She blurted out how disappointed she was that he hadn't made more of an effort and explained how much she'd missed them – but surely he knew.

Simon remained cool, his expression inscrutable. 'You should have asked me before inviting them here.' His words stunned her, as did his harshness.

'But you knew I was planning to have them over for a meal – I've talked about it since we came back.'

'In future, I'll be the one to decide who visits us and when.'

Emma was astounded. 'But they're my parents! Surely they don't need an invitation to come and see us?'

Simon took a deep breath and steered his wife to the sofa. Then, with his voice calm and those green eyes almost boring into her, he pointed out how such a close relationship with her parents was unhealthy for someone of her age. He said they needed time alone to cement their marriage and regular contact with her parents would hamper this.

Emma sat motionless, speechless as she listened to her husband's lecture, trying hard to understand his logic; she felt more than able to devote time to her husband and parents. It didn't have to be a choice between them, did it?

Emma attempted to express this, to explain her point of view, but as she looked at her husband she knew he wouldn't listen to reason. Those green eyes she'd found so stunning when they'd first met now seemed icy as he stared back at her. It appeared his mind was made up and Emma, upset and confused, said nothing more.

Simon told her she could visit Margaret and George only once a month in future, and it seemed he interpreted her silence as acceptance. It was a compromise, he said, and as for inviting them again for a meal, he spent an inordinate amount of time explaining how it would set a precedent and give them expectations of such events becoming regular. Although utterly unhappy with Simon's decisions Emma felt unable to argue against him. How would she explain this to her parents?

When his lecture was finished, Simon went upstairs to bed while Emma, in a daze, cleared up. An uncomfortable heavy feeling settled in her stomach, making her quite nauseous.

During the night, her husband's rules threaded through Emma's mind, robbing her of rest. Simon snored peacefully while she wondered if she knew this man beside her – he was so unlike the fun-loving person she'd first met.

The following morning, as Simon dropped Emma outside the dentist's surgery, he reminded her to ring her parents and tell them what they'd decided. Emma maintained her silence, fuming inwardly at his choice of words; *they* hadn't decided anything. It was Simon's decision yet she was the one forced to implement it.

Needing to get it over with, Emma rang her mother from the staffroom before starting work, stumbling over her words and finding it hard to explain and totally embarrassing. Margaret was understanding and spoke after only a slight hesitation.

'Simon's quite right, dear, I understand. You need time to settle down as a couple. Dad and I don't want to intrude.' Yet Emma could sense the underlying disappointment in her mother's reasonable, carefully chosen words. Ending the call with a heavy heart, Emma tried to swallow her distress. She blew her nose, dried the tears from her eyes and purposefully pushed thoughts of Simon from her head.

CHAPTER FIVE

Over the following few weeks, Emma made several attempts to change her husband's mind and appeal to his softer side, yet he stubbornly refused to allow her more time with her parents than the allotted monthly visit. The situation caused distress to Emma and her mum and dad, yet she remained powerless to make Simon understand. It had all been an unwelcome revelation – Simon had changed from the man she'd fallen in love with to someone she no longer recognised. Initially, the changes were minor, some hardly perceptible, but others came as a shock.

Simon also dictated that time to herself was no longer acceptable; browsing around the shops in town or meeting friends for coffee at the weekend, a source of pleasure to Emma, became a thing of the past. Simon strongly disapproved of frittering time and money away on coffee dates, maintaining it was so much cheaper to have coffee at home. He reminded his wife they'd married to be together and not to waste their free time with friends.

A niggling uncertainty gnawed at the back of Emma's mind, a vague impression of being trapped. It was a hollow, unwelcome sensation that she tried hard to dismiss and couldn't articulate to her husband or anyone else. Guilt similarly hovered at the edges of her mind – wouldn't any girl be delighted to have a husband who was so protective and wished to keep her exclusively for himself? Wouldn't anyone else kill for someone to love them in such a way? So, where was this unease coming from?

Time no longer seemed to be her own, was this what being married meant? It was bound to take a while to adjust to a new pattern of life – marriage was just not what she'd anticipated. Emma would have to content herself with keeping in touch with her friends by phone, not quite the same but she clung to the hope that Simon would change his mind when he realised how meaningful these friendships were to her.

One morning, intending to catch up with an old school friend, Emma took out her mobile phone to discover that all her stored numbers had disappeared. Frustrated about how this could have happened, she searched through the phone settings. It was a simple phone, used only for calls and texts, nothing complicated – Simon insisted more could go wrong with expensive iPhones – but all her contact numbers had vanished completely.

It would be quite a chore to collect them again and it would take time. Hopefully, her friends wouldn't think she no longer wanted to keep in touch – it was difficult to find the opportunity to ring for a chat without Simon commenting on her wasting time and money on gossip. Still, it was her fault; she must have somehow pressed the wrong key and deleted the numbers by mistake.

Pushing open the heavy glass doors leading into the dentist's surgery, Emma took the vacant seat behind the reception desk, turned to her colleague, Fiona, and explained what had happened.

'Give me your number again so I can put it back in my contacts,' Emma asked.

'I'll ring you, and you can just save it; it'll be easier.'

'Thanks, that's great.'

The day's first patient arrived and Emma buzzed through to the dentist to let him know. As the waiting room filled up and the phone rang constantly, the mobile phone incident was forgotten as Emma became immersed in the work she loved. As one of two receptionists working for six dentists and two hygienists, her days varied with endless new people to meet, and the social side of the job was excellent. The dentists were a mixed bunch but all easy to work for and Fiona and the dental nurses were all firm friends.

Perhaps it wasn't a challenging career with prospects but Emma enjoyed the work, which to her was the most important factor. It also left her free time open for painting, the other love of her life – until she'd met Simon, of course. Emma's ultimate ambition was to turn her love of painting into a career so an undemanding nine-to-five job was perfect, leaving plenty of time for her hobby.

However, painting was something else which had been on hold since the wedding, with her materials stored away until they found their perfect home. Simon encouraged her talent during their engagement and promised to find a house with a studio and plenty of light to enable her passion. Yet since returning from their honeymoon, he'd frowned each time she took out her sketchbook in the evenings, asking if she had nothing more productive to do than draw pictures. It became easier to stop sketching altogether to avoid his caustic remarks and Emma looked forward to moving when she could again take up painting in a perfect, designated space.

It occurred to Emma that Simon might be more relaxed and revert to his old self once they found a permanent home. Could this pressure be weighing on his mind and altering his once-cheerful personality? Had Simon changed so much since their wedding, or were her expectations too high? Before they were married, they'd done fun things together at weekends, simple things like driving to the coast with a picnic or walking through the woods.

They'd laughed together too. Simon was attentive and worked hard to please her as if her happiness was important to him. Was she so wrong to expect a little of the same consideration now, or was there another underlying reason? If he was concerned about providing for her, perhaps that could explain his behaviour change – maybe she should be more sympathetic and work with him.

Simon hadn't had an easy childhood and shared very little of his early life with Emma. She appreciated how difficult it was for him to talk about, but from the little he'd told her, she knew he'd grown up in care and not always happily. Emma, in contrast, had been blessed with all the advantages of a loving family and a comfortable lifestyle. Did Simon perhaps feel under pressure to match up to what her parents had always provided? Emma pondered these thoughts throughout the day and decided to try to understand her husband more, to learn why he acted as he did. But this resolve was short-lived as the evening again threw her into confusion, leaving her thoughts reeling.

Simon picked her up as usual from work and as it was Friday they made their way to the supermarket for their weekly shop. Emma could sense her husband was in a mood yet didn't know why.

'Did you have a good day at work?' she asked brightly in an attempt at conversation.

'Not particularly.' The answer was flat, monotone.

'We've been rushed off our feet today. Everyone seems to

want an appointment at the moment and with the nearest dentist to us retiring there's been dozens of requests to join the practice.'

Simon didn't seem in the least bit interested so Emma reverted to silence for the rest of the journey, on edge, as she often was when he was in one of his moods. Shopping used to be an enjoyable experience but Simon didn't like to waste his time doing something as mundane as buying their food for the week. Offering to do it herself proved not to be the solution either. He rejected the idea entirely when she'd suggested it; Simon clearly didn't think she would stick to his list, and the list must be obeyed. Emma knew what she'd like to do with the list but as with everything else it had become so much easier to go along with her husband's wishes.

Arriving at the supermarket, Emma reminded herself of her resolution to attempt to understand where Simon was coming from and dutifully walked beside him reading the list while he pushed the trolley. It was the usual order of their task, and Simon stacked the items in the trolley – she was deemed unable to pack things in the proper manner.

The store was busy and the queues at the tills frustratingly long. Simon almost sprinted to get a place in a line before another customer, leaving Emma somewhat embarrassed. She smiled a weak apology at the other shopper before waiting beside her husband, who was clicking his tongue at the elderly lady in front of him who wasn't fast enough to load the conveyor belt for his liking. Emma wished the ground would open up and for her to disappear into it. He was so impatient. When the shopping ordeal was over, they joined the slow-moving Friday evening traffic and headed for home.

Turning into their road, Simon announced that Emma would have to put the groceries away on her own as the oil light on the car was flashing and he wanted to check the oil and water. Perhaps, she thought, this could be the cause of his present bad mood.

'Okay, I'll do it and then I'm off upstairs for a quick shower before we eat.'

Simon didn't even help her carry the bags inside but Emma didn't care. It was quite a relief to get away from him when he was in one of his moods. Her own company was preferable.

After ten minutes in the kitchen, she dashed upstairs for a shower. It was heaven, standing under the hot water, letting it caress her tired limbs and aching back.

Emma was glad to have taken the time to put a casserole in the slow cooker before leaving for work that morning, she was weary after their shopping expedition and a tasty meal and glass or two of wine might just soften Simon's mood.

Pulling out jeans and a sweatshirt from the wardrobe, Emma sighed. These days weekends were anticipated with mixed feelings. Saturday mornings in town used to be fun, meeting friends for coffee or rummaging in the shops with her mum for bargains, yet things were very different now, a fact she supposed she'd have to get used to.

'Emma!' Simon's voice sounded icily sharp as he called her name.

'Coming,' she replied, hurrying down the stairs to find him standing in the kitchen surrounded by their shopping – still in the carrier bags.

'I thought I told you to put these away,' he growled. 'This ice cream's melted. It's ruined!'

Emma stared around the tiny kitchen in disbelief. 'I did put it away – I'm sure...'

'Don't be silly. I suppose the goblins got it all out again, eh? Honestly, I can't trust you to do anything right.'

Emma was stunned, convinced she'd put everything away before her shower, but here it was, still in the carriers with

Simon staring at her waiting for an explanation. She could think of nothing to say except, 'Sorry, I'll do it now.'

Her husband left her alone in the little kitchen as she unpacked the bags, tears stinging her eyes. As she was placing each item in its rightful spot Emma was sure she'd only just completed this same task, a certainty that brought her total confusion. How did the groceries get back into the carriers if she had done it?

Emma tried not to think too deeply about this incident. Maybe her husband was playing a trick on her? If so, it certainly wasn't funny, or had she really been so distracted that she'd left the shopping in the bags?

When the kitchen was tidy Emma went into the lounge where Simon sat with his feet up, reading his paper.

'I've done it.' She was determined not to apologise again yet still expected a tirade from Simon about her carelessness, but his mood appeared to have lifted.

'Don't worry about it now, we'll have a nice cosy evening together and an early night, shall we?'

The prospect of an early night made her sigh, knowing precisely what Simon expected of her. He was giving her the chance to *make it up to him*. Not for the first time, she wondered if marriage was like this for everyone.

CHAPTER SIX

'Morning, Emma,' Fiona sang chirpily the following Monday but seeing her friend's face, her look changed to one of concern. 'Are you okay? You look miserable – bad weekend, was it?'

Emma, lost in thought, mentally shook herself and attempted a smile, but the worry was still etched on her face.

'I'm fine, thanks.' Her reply was quiet, subdued. 'Have we got a busy day again today?'

Fiona's enquiry was deflected for the time being but later when they took their lunch break she asked again, 'Was it a bad weekend?'

'What?' Emma looked up, startled by the repeated question.

'You look as if you have the cares of the world on your shoulders.' Fiona laughed. 'Damn it, I sound just like my mother!'

'I'm sorry, I'm just a little tired.' Emma's face was pale, her eyes set in dark circles, giving Fiona more cause for concern. A young, newly married girl should be carefree and happy. It hadn't gone unnoticed at work that Emma no longer fitted that description, and her colleagues wondered what had transpired to bring about the change.

'I can see. You haven't seemed yourself these last few weeks, Emma. I don't want to pry but if you'd like to talk, you know I'm here for you.'

The two covered for each other on reception, so finding time to talk wouldn't be easy, but whether prompted by the empathy in Fiona's voice or the look on her face, Emma suddenly released the tears which had been threatening to spill all weekend.

'Hey.' Fiona instinctively moved closer, sliding an arm around her younger friend's shoulders. 'What's all this about?'

'I'm sorry.' Emma sniffed. 'You must think I'm a right idiot.'

'Hey no! I'm just concerned for you. We've time for a quick coffee before surgery opens again. Come on, let's go to the staffroom.' She led the way with Emma dutifully following, relieved that someone was concerned enough to listen.

As Fiona placed a cup of hot coffee in her hands, Emma apologised again. 'I'm so sorry. I don't know what's the matter with me these days. I know how fortunate I am and I should be ecstatic – but I'm not. It's probably just the changes. I seem to be struggling with being married, which is stupid as I love Simon, but things aren't how I expected them to be.'

'You've been married what, two, three months?'

'Four months. Early days, I know. It's probably just the honeymoon period wearing off.' She gave a forced laugh which didn't appear to convince Fiona.

'Hell, I've been married for two years and we're still in the honeymoon period. Of course, there's been the odd spat but it adds a bit of excitement, especially in the making-up!' Fiona looked at Emma with concern. 'Tell me about Simon. I know he's gorgeous but is he all you expected him to be?'

'That's the problem – he seems like a different man to the

one I was engaged to – as if the wedding changed everything. But it's probably me. Maybe my expectations are too high.' Her words were flat, almost apologetic. Fiona didn't press for details or bombard Emma with questions, but she was clearly troubled by the girl's apparent sadness.

'What about your parents? Can't you talk to them, get their take on Simon?'

'I don't actually see much of Mum and Dad anymore.'

'But surely you could make time? Life's busy, I know, but you should always keep in touch with family and friends.'

'Tell Simon that, will you!' Emma immediately regretted her words and, feeling disloyal to Simon, she tried to explain. 'I'm sorry, that sounded awful. He's a good man and does his best to take care of me, yet I sometimes feel he wants me to the exclusion of everyone else. He seems happy for us always to be alone. Simon has no family, you see, so he can't understand how important mine is to me.'

Fiona pressed on. 'He must have had some kind of family once?'

'No, none that he can remember. He was brought up in care and moved to several different foster homes, none of which worked out for him. He doesn't like to talk about his childhood, it brings back some rather bad memories, you know?'

'But you'd think he'd be glad to be part of your family. Your parents do like him, don't they?'

'Oh yes, Mum and Dad were delighted when I found someone who made me happy. At first, he seemed to fit in so well. It was only after we married that he decided I shouldn't see so much of them.'

Fiona frowned. 'Perhaps he'll come round in a little while. Being married isn't always plain sailing – it takes adjustment and a little compromise on both sides. We've got to get back to work now but you know I'm here for you if you need someone to listen, don't you? So come on, grab your coffee and we'll open the shop up, shall we?'

'Thanks, Fiona. It's helped just to be able to talk. I sometimes think I'll burst with all these thoughts spinning around my head. I'm sure you're right and things will eventually sort themselves out.'

They returned to reception just in time to book in the first of the afternoon's clients who arrived early. Emma's mind was diverted from her home life for a while as Fiona tried very hard to keep the mood light. Emma was grateful for such a good friend.

CHAPTER SEVEN

At lunchtime on Tuesday, Emma couldn't find her purse and as they were collecting for one of the dental nurses who was soon to go on maternity leave, she wanted to put in her contribution.

Emma muttered to herself, digging deep into the corners of her bag. Her purse was always with her; if she changed bags, she was sure to swap it over with her mobile phone. She felt lost without either item.

'I'm sorry, Fiona, I must've left it at home. Can I give you mine tomorrow?'

'No problem.' Fiona smiled but Emma felt she was letting the side down and knew Fi wanted to shop for the gift during her lunch break.

'Could you sub me ten pounds?'

'Of course I can. That's great, Emma. We'll have nearly a hundred pounds. I'm going to enjoy spending so much money on baby things!' Fiona beamed.

Emma smiled, trying to put the incident out of her mind and concentrate on work. She'd have to clear spending so much on a gift later. Simon wouldn't be happy but Emma would face that if he found out. More concerning was how she appeared to be doing some stupid things lately, first the shopping and now this – it simply wasn't like her.

As usual, Simon picked her up after work, and Emma decided not to mention the missing purse. It must be at home. She hadn't been anywhere other than work so there was no need to upset him. However, Simon stopped outside a newsagent's shop.

'I didn't have time to get my paper today. Would you pop in to get one for me?' he asked.

'I, er, I haven't got any change... have you?' she dithered.

'No. Use a note and then you'll have some change.'

Emma could feel the colour flush to her face. Why such a silly situation should make her feel like this was beyond her. She was like a child trying to hide a misdeed. 'I've left my purse at home.'

'What? Are you sure? Have you lost it somewhere outside? Your bank card's in it, isn't it.'

'Yes, but I'm sure it's at home. I must have forgotten to put it in my bag, that's all.' Emma tried to make it sound as if it was no big deal but Simon clicked his tongue in annoyance and drove away a little too fast.

'What about your paper?'

'It's more important to find your purse! You don't seem to realise how serious this kind of thing is, Emma. Your mind's anywhere but where it should be these days.'

Emma sat silently during the rest of the journey home, feeling like a naughty schoolgirl. When they arrived, Simon raced into the house as if it was on fire.

'Where did you leave it?' he demanded.

'It'll be upstairs in the cupboard by my side of the bed.' She ran ahead hoping to put her hands straight on it, but a sense of panic overwhelmed her when it wasn't on the shelf with the bag she'd used the previous day. Scrambling about, she looked under the bed and anywhere else it could be.

'Have you found it yet?' Simon's voice was loud and harsh behind her, making her jump.

'No, but it must be here somewhere.'

Simon pulled open all her drawers and the wardrobe, rooting angrily among her possessions. Emma felt strangely resentful but was too afraid to ask him to stop. Finally, after several minutes of frantic searching, he slammed the wardrobe door shut with such ferocity that the whole room rattled.

'I'm going down to ring the bank,' he barked. 'That's if it's not too late, anyone could use those cards.'

'But I'm sure it'll be here somewhere. I can't have lost it outside.' Tears were pricking the back of her eyes.

Simon's eyes narrowed with fury. 'How do you know someone hasn't stolen it at work?'

The suggestion shocked her. 'I always put my bag in the staffroom, the public can't get in there and my colleagues certainly wouldn't take it.'

'Honestly. Sometimes you're so bloody naive!' With those words he slammed the bedroom door and went downstairs to phone the bank.

Emma sat on the bed, fighting back tears. She was usually so careful and had no idea what could have happened to her purse. Maybe Simon was right and it had been stolen, but she couldn't bear the thought of it being someone at work. Yet it was her husband's reaction which was more upsetting. Didn't he realise she felt bad enough without his anger adding to it? A little support and understanding would have been nice.

After a while the sound of Simon banging around in the kitchen prompted Emma to go down to begin their evening meal before he found another reason to grumble. When she reached the top of the stairs, Simon was shouting her name from the kitchen, so she hurried down to be greeted by a steely glare.

'Open the fridge,' he ordered.

'What?'

'Just open the damned fridge!'

Emma did, and found her purse in full view on the middle shelf. She didn't know what to say but Simon got in first.

'What were you thinking about? I'll have to go and ring the bank now to tell them you've found it. How will that make me look? You can be such a bloody idiot sometimes!'

Emma burst into tears – stunned, and with genuinely no idea how her purse came to be in the fridge. With a look of disgust on his face, Simon turned abruptly, leaving her alone while he stomped back to the telephone.

Perhaps she'd done it in a moment of distraction? Her mother always said her mind was rarely on the job at hand, that she was a romantic with her head travelling down one of the winding pathways in her paintings rather than focusing on what she was supposed to be doing – but her mother laughed as she spoke the words, loving Emma's dreaminess and proud of her daughter. Why couldn't she expect more understanding from Simon?

The evening passed in an atmosphere of icy silence. Emma cooked their meal and they ate without conversation – she felt too weary to make an effort even though Simon would expect it of her. Why could he not laugh at the absurdity of the situation instead of turning it into a full-blown drama? Surely everyone has those moments when they do stupid things, but nothing was spoiled and it really was quite funny, wasn't it?

Standing at the sink washing the dishes, Emma heard Simon come into the kitchen but was reluctant to turn and face him. Instead, she reached for the bleach from beneath the sink and began vigorously cleaning the bowl.

'Leave that,' Simon told her. She stopped yet still didn't turn round. He stepped towards her, circled his arms around her waist and pushed the hair away from the back of her neck, kissing her warm skin.

'You've been a silly girl again, haven't you? But it's all right. I'll look after you – whatever happens. Why don't you go and have a nice bath and I'll be up soon for an early night? You can show me how sorry you are then, can't you?'

Emma's skin felt chilled. *What the hell does he mean, 'whatever happens'? Is he trying to make out I'm going senile or something?*

Rather than make an issue of it, Emma turned to go upstairs, knowing precisely what Simon wanted and resigned herself to it.

CHAPTER EIGHT

'Are you okay?' Fiona asked Emma the following day. It felt like *Groundhog Day* as she spoke, but Emma looked worse than ever. 'What is it? Would talking about it help?'

The two were again having a quick coffee before work while the staffroom was quiet, only they occupied it. Fiona had sensed that all was not right with Emma and Simon and had been surprised at some of the things Emma related during their last little chat. It seemed to Fi that Simon was more than a little controlling. Emma's eyes filled with tears.

'Hey, don't get upset. Whatever's wrong can be sorted, you know.' Fiona knew the words were inadequate even as they left her lips but unless Emma confided a little more, she didn't know how she could help.

'I'm sorry, I don't mean to be such a misery all the time. Forget it, Fi, it's nothing.'

'From your expression, it doesn't look like *nothing*. Perhaps sharing will help?'

'Oh, Fiona, I feel like I'm going insane sometimes. It's hard to explain – I've got everything I ever wanted, yet I feel so miserable. And I think there must be something wrong with me.

I'm doing such stupid things and then don't remember doing them.' Emma related the incident of losing her purse and finding it in the fridge.

'But that's hilarious.' Fiona laughed. 'We all do crazy stuff at times, it doesn't mean you're going mad.'

'It might be funny if it was the only thing. Remember when I managed to delete all my contact numbers from my phone? I don't know how but they were in there one minute and then they weren't! It took me ages to get them all again.'

'Oh, I often send texts to the wrong people; it's embarrassing but surely not the end of the world?'

Emma frowned. 'Simon gets so cross with me when I make a mistake and I have to make it up to him, you know... to get back in his good books again.'

Fi's expression changed from mild amusement to concern. Did Emma mean she had to have sex to appease her husband?

'I thought being married would be wonderful, our own home and doing things together, but more often than not I don't want to do things with Simon. He's always there and sometimes he makes me feel like I'm suffocating – and then the guilt sets in – it's so confusing! Do you think it could be some kind of breakdown? I should be happy, yet I want to run away and hide. I miss Mum and Dad so much too, is that natural?'

'Of course it's natural. I was surprised the other day when you told me you didn't see them very often now. I see my mother all the time and I don't particularly like her! Perhaps you should make an appointment to see your doctor, maybe you're a bit depressed with all the recent changes, or you could try having a little chat with Simon to explain how you feel.'

'Huh, I've tried but he's impossible and won't budge. He keeps reminding me I'm his wife now and he has to come first.'

Fiona was stunned; it was like something out of the Dark Ages. Her Kev wouldn't even think such a thing let alone say it. She hardly knew Emma's husband so it was difficult to grasp the situation, yet she was already beginning to dislike the man. 'Have another try, Emma. He might be surprised to learn how you're feeling and a few gentle pointers might do the trick.'

'I wish it was as simple. Simon was different before we were married, treating me like a china doll, you know? Spoiling me with little gifts and things, but it's all stopped completely. He likes his own way and expects me to do all the running, yet he doesn't let me out of his sight except for work. I'm sorry, I shouldn't be moaning on at you.' She stood to return to reception and Fiona followed, feeling that perhaps all she could do for Emma was to be there for her and offer a shoulder to cry on.

Another incident occurred that night, something else to shake Emma's confidence and make her wonder if she was going mad. She flinched on hearing Simon shouting her name from upstairs, his voice clearly indicating annoyance about something. Her stomach clenched – what could be wrong now? They'd only been home for a few minutes. Then, at his second, more urgent shout, Emma quickened her step, almost tripping over the stairs on her way up, anxious not to upset Simon any more than it appeared he was already.

'What is it?' she asked, entering their bedroom. For one awful moment Emma thought they'd been burgled.

'Look at this mess! Why the hell didn't you make the bed before we left for work this morning? It's too much, having to come home to this.'

'But I did – or I thought so.' Emma couldn't believe what was in front of her. It wasn't only the bed, the whole room looked in disarray with drawers half-open and her dressing gown and nightshirt thrown across the ottoman.

'I'm sure I...' Tears pricked the back of her eyes. She blinked them away, not wanting Simon to see how confused she was. They hadn't been burgled – the room had simply not been tidied as it usually was. It was invariably part of Emma's morning routine to make the bed before going to work, yet thinking about it now, she couldn't remember doing it. But it was like locking the door; if you thought about it, you couldn't always remember the actual motion of doing so but if you went back to check, it was always locked.

'I'll do it now – it won't take long.'

'That's not the point. It's just further proof that you're losing it, Emma. Do I have to see to every little detail in this house?'

'It's only an unmade bed.' Attempting to defend herself and make light of the situation, Emma was surprised at how much her legs were shaking.

'Don't you dare speak to me like that. I put up with enough as it is! All I ask is for you to keep the household running smoothly. I'll make the bed – you go down to start dinner!'

Emma returned to the kitchen, her legs barely supporting her as it suddenly dawned on her – she was afraid.

Afraid of Simon, of her own husband!

A few minutes later when he came downstairs, Simon went straight to the lounge to put on the early evening news. Emma continued making the meal, fighting the desire to get out of the house, to walk or even run – anywhere. Realising she didn't want to face Simon again, it struck her like a physical blow; *she didn't love him anymore!*

What was happening? Emma had been so much in love when they married, full of hopes and plans, but things weren't as she'd imagined. In truth, she no longer wanted to be with

Simon, a thought that both surprised and scared her. But this was a marriage. They'd made promises which she took seriously – these feelings shouldn't be happening. So what was wrong with her? Was she losing her mind, doing such stupid things?

Perhaps it was insanity, so Simon had every reason to chastise her. Maybe she did need him to look after her – was he right after all? Emma was engulfed in a dense fog of fear and uncertainty.

CHAPTER NINE

Emma made an appointment to see her GP as Fiona had suggested. She was generally never ill and couldn't remember the last time she'd visited the surgery, yet it was worth a shot. Maybe she was run down, a vitamin deficiency perhaps and he could give her something to make her feel better? The appointment meant a change of lunch hour but food didn't taste quite the same at the moment and apart from a piece of toast, Emma hardly ate at all most days until the evening when she cooked for Simon.

Fiona happily covered for her, glad her friend was taking her advice. Then, crossing her fingers, she gave Emma an encouraging smile as she left to go to the surgery.

It was only a short walk. There was a chill wind although the sun was shining and Emma enjoyed being alone in the fresh air. Midday was quiet at the surgery as some of the doctors had begun their home visits. Dr Chakrabarti, however, made appointments up until twelve-thirty and his last patient of the morning was Emma Beecham.

'Emma, it's been a long time. How are you, my dear?' A wide smile accompanied his words as his arm directed her to a seat. He was a small, tidy man with a shock of thick black hair and large, warm brown eyes set into a broad face. His smile was infectious, revealing a row of perfectly straight white teeth. Emma suddenly felt less awkward.

'I'm okay, thanks,' she almost whispered.

'No, you're not, or you wouldn't be here.' Dr Chakrabarti smiled but was then completely wrong-footed as Emma burst into tears. He picked up the box of tissues from his desk and, propelling himself forward in his swivel chair across the few feet between them, offered her the box.

Emma was embarrassed and apologised between sobs, but the doctor waved his hand, dismissing any apology as unnecessary as he patiently waited for her to become composed enough to speak.

'That's better,' he said as she finished blowing her nose and mopping her face. 'Do you think you can tell me what's troubling you?' His voice was gentle and reassuring. Perhaps his fatherly tone had prompted her tears; she'd always liked this man who seemed to sense his patients' problems before they even told him.

'My friend suggested I come to see you as I've been feeling a little down recently...' She faltered in her prepared speech and the doctor stepped in.

'Okay, Emma, can you tell me exactly how you've been feeling, or if there's any particular reason for it, and then we'll decide what the best course of action is.' He smiled again, and she felt able to continue.

'I got married in the summer and don't seem to be coping well with all the changes – I keep making silly mistakes and seem to have become somewhat forgetful. I don't know what's happening and things are getting on top of me. If I'm honest – I'm just not happy anymore.'

This final revelation triggered more tears. Dr Chakrabarti

waited quietly. This was his last patient of the morning, there was no need to hurry, and it was evident something was seriously troubling her.

Emma pulled her emotions back into check while searching for the words to explain her feelings. 'There've been times lately when I've even thought I'm going mad, losing it mentally, you know?'

'I'd have to say that medically it is improbable you're going mad, and if it were the case then you'd probably be the last one to notice, so I'm pretty sure we can rule that out. Now tell me what's making you feel like this?'

'It sounds pathetic but I've done things I can't remember doing, like putting my purse in the fridge and not making the bed when I could have sworn I had. Simon, my husband, gets a bit cross at times although generally he's good to me. I can see why I'm annoying him but he says he'll always be there to look after me.'

'And is that what you want?'

'What do you mean?'

'Do you want your husband always to look after you?'

'I suppose so. We were very happy – yet since we married – I don't know, it's not like I thought it would be.'

'What about your parents, Emma? Have they noticed any change in you?'

'No. I haven't seen Mum and Dad for ages. Simon says we shouldn't set precedents by always seeing them. I'm married now and things have to be different.'

Dr Chakrabarti slowly nodded. He tapped a few keys on his computer and then turned to face his patient again.

'It sounds to me as if you're a little depressed. I have a few questions I'd like you to answer and then we can decide the best course of action.'

Fifteen minutes later, Emma was walking through the surgery gates heading back to work and taking in huge gulps of fresh air.

Fiona looked up from the desk as Emma opened the door, her eyebrows raised. Emma shrugged off her coat and settled down in the empty reception area to tell Fiona of her visit.

'Some of Dr. Chakrabarti's questions were difficult to answer. He even asked if I'd ever had thoughts of suicide! The worst thing is I couldn't honestly say the thought hadn't crossed my mind – not particularly killing myself – but I've felt so bad at times that I didn't want to wake up in the morning.'

'So, what did he suggest?'

'He's given me a prescription for some antidepressants, although I'm not sure I want to take them. He advised me to fill the prescription and keep them as a last resort if I'm not coping. He also asked if I'd consider seeing a counsellor, yet Simon would never agree.'

'Oh come on, surely it's what's best for *you*, not Simon.'

'I'll think about it. Thanks for listening, Fi, and for encouraging me to see the doctor. Maybe I'll get those antidepressants and give them a try.'

Fiona sighed and reminded Emma she could talk to her any time. 'By the way, a lady was here earlier looking for you. She didn't want to leave a message.'

'Oh? Did you get her name?'

'No, she seemed in a hurry to get off.'

'It wasn't my mum, was it?'

'Not unless she gave birth to you in infant school! This lady wasn't much older than you.'

'What did she look like?'

'She was wearing a long green raincoat, about your height, a little heavier maybe with short dark hair cut in a feathered style

– quite pretty but very serious – she seemed anxious about something. When I offered to take a message she said no and dashed off.' Fiona's attention switched to a patient who'd just arrived and Emma was left baffled as to who her mystery visitor could be. If it were a friend, perhaps she'd call again or give her a ring.

By the end of what turned out to be a hectic afternoon, Emma had forgotten all about the anonymous visitor, too worried about what kind of mood Simon would be in when he collected her.

CHAPTER TEN

Emma's weekend started badly. When she awoke, Simon was already up. Glancing at the clock she discovered it was only 7am, much too early to get up on a Saturday, so Emma turned over for another hour's sleep. That was when the banging began downstairs. Nothing specific or easily identified yet Simon must be responsible for the noise, which made her uneasy. Emma ignored the din, closed her eyes and tried to drift off for a little longer.

The noise increased, almost as if Simon was trying to wake her. The vacuum cleaner suddenly burst into life, making Emma jump up in a sudden panic. Grabbing her dressing gown she rushed downstairs to where her husband, in an apparent rage, was vacuuming the hall carpet.

Sensing Simon's dark mood, Emma explained. 'I was going to do the cleaning when I got up.'

He switched off the cleaner and looked at his wife, his face contorted with anger. 'And when would that be?'

'It's Saturday. Weekends are for pleasure as well as cleaning,' Emma ventured. For a minute she thought Simon might explode.

'If you think I can relax when the house is in such a state, you're bloody mad. Perhaps you can lie in bed till all hours – I certainly can't!'

'But it's only seven.'

'It's well after eight. You'll be expecting me to bring you breakfast in bed next!'

Emma was close to tears and trembling, unsure what to say. 'I must have misread the clock.' Her voice was barely a whisper as she turned to go back upstairs and into the bathroom. Then, locking the door and sitting on the toilet seat, she put her head in her hands and cried.

'Why? Why is he treating me like this?' she whispered.

After a few minutes, Emma took off her nightshirt and stepped into the shower, letting the warm water run over her puffy face and massaging life into her still-tired limbs. As she washed her hair and scrubbed vigorously at her body, a mixture of sorrow and fear rose within her.

'This isn't like me,' she whispered as the tears came again, angry frustrated tears this time and Emma sat in the shower hugging her wet legs and sobbing like a child.

Towelling herself dry, she went back into the bedroom to dress and her eyes went automatically to the clock – 8.45am. Pulling on a pair of jeans and a T-shirt, Emma told herself it was a simple mistake and even if she had slept until eight or even nine it wouldn't be the end of the world; it was the weekend. Why did Simon always have to make an issue of every little thing? The tears were replaced by a measure of anger, simmering below the surface. Dare she talk to Simon and attempt to explain how she was feeling?

Why not? she thought. The rising anger was furnishing her with strength. *It's about time I stood up for myself. I can't go on like this for much longer.*

Heading for the kitchen, Emma's determination to confront

her husband grew. First, she would sit down in case her legs gave way and ask him why his attitude towards her had changed since their wedding.

Simon smiled lovingly at her as she entered the kitchen. 'Hi. I've made your breakfast, darling. There's just the toast to do.'

Emma was completely wrong-footed. Was this the same man who'd scowled so darkly at her less than an hour ago?

'Simon.' Her voice came out rather wobbly. 'Can we talk?' Emma remained at the kitchen table.

'Of course, sweetheart. What's on your mind?'

Now she was nervous. 'Why were you so angry with me before?'

'Was I? When?'

'You know when. You were angry with me when I got up.'

'I wasn't angry, darling. I was teasing, sleepyhead.'

'No, you weren't, and it's not the first time either.' Emma felt somewhat bolder. It was time to address this with her husband, and as he appeared to be in a better mood, perhaps he'd be open to listening to her point of view. 'I can't seem to do anything right these days. You get angry with me and I don't know why or what to do about it.' Tears were threatening to spill but Emma sniffed them back, determined to say her piece.

'Hey, where's all this coming from? I don't get angry with you – you must be imagining things. You know how much I love you. I wouldn't hurt you for the world.' Simon moved to Emma's side, wrapping his arms around her. The tears fell as he stroked her hair, whispering loving words. It was so utterly confusing. Was she imagining it all? Emma couldn't trust Simon and his moods anymore, but could he be right? Was she losing it? Was it really all in her mind?

Emboldened by her husband's apparent good mood, Emma decided to attempt a more serious discussion. Maybe he was in a receptive mood. If she explained her feelings, perhaps even told him she'd been to the doctor, he'd understand. 'I went to visit the doctor yesterday.'

Simon's head turned in her direction, his eyes wide. 'I hope you're not going to tell me you're pregnant – you're supposed to be on the pill!' His anger took her by surprise. His moods changed like flicking a light switch. Shouldn't he be concerned that she was perhaps unwell?

'No, I'm not pregnant. I've been feeling under the weather lately and the doctor's given me some antidepressants to help me get over it.'

'What the hell have you got to be depressed about – and what have you been telling him? I hope you don't discuss our marriage outside these four walls!' Simon's face grew darker with each word. Emma flushed at the memory of what she'd told the doctor and the details she'd confided to Fiona.

'Simon, this is half the trouble. You seem to want to tell me what to do all the time, who I can and can't see – it's no wonder I'm depressed.'

'Oh, so it's all my fault, is it? After all I've done for you!'

'It's a two-way street, isn't it? I do plenty for you too. But it's not only that – there are other things.' Emma took a deep breath, uncomfortable at having this conversation. 'I'd like to have more money to spend, only having a few pounds in my purse at work is embarrassing.'

'Why do you need money? I pay all the bills, don't I? Is this about those silly magazines because I thought by now you'd have grown out of reading such rubbish.' Simon was becoming increasingly angry and Emma's nerve was beginning to dissolve, yet she was determined to put across her side of things. It wasn't as if she was asking for much. Simon needed to know how she felt in order to understand.

'It's not about the magazines. There are other times I might need money.'

'Such as what? I pick you up from work so you don't need bus fares.' His face was growing darker. Was he trying to intimidate her? Although trembling, Emma was intent on continuing.

'My birthday's coming up in a few weeks and at work we always treat the team to cream cakes on birthdays. I don't want to be considered mean and can hardly tell them I haven't enough money, can I?' It wasn't perhaps the best illustration and it seemed to annoy Simon.

'So buying the staff cream cakes is more important than saving up for a proper home, is it?'

'Of course not, that's not what I mean but I've got to live and enjoy life as well as saving.'

'Oh, yes, it's all about you isn't it. Do you expect me to be the only one to go without so you can gorge yourself on cream cakes?' He appeared to be deliberately misunderstanding Emma's words, twisting them and lobbing them back to make her feel bad.

'No, but we can afford to relax our spending at times. There's enough money coming in to pay the bills and save up. Anyway, it's not just about the money. Not seeing Mum, Dad, and my old friends also gets me down. I still don't understand why we can't–'

'That's the trouble, Emma. You don't understand!' He glowered at her, his eyes bright and hard. 'You think you know better than me in everything but you don't! Your parents are a bad influence although you can't seem to see it. Your mother makes a hobby of going shopping for things she doesn't need and she'd drag you along with her if I let you go – and as for your friends, well, they just waste time and money on frivolities – expensive coffees and meals out, they're not true friends!'

'But it makes me happy to see them. What's wrong with that? And now you're bringing it back to money. It's not only money – it's about quality of life, enjoying those little things I've lost, can't you understand?' Tears of frustration trickled down Emma's face while Simon remained hardened to her pleas, anger burning in his eyes.

'You're my wife and you'll do as I say – and that's the end of this conversation!' Simon stepped closer to her. For one awful moment, Emma thought he was going to strike her. She raised her arm to cover her face but he appeared to think better of it and turned sharply to walk out of the house, slamming the front door behind him.

Emma spent the rest of the day simultaneously regretting her attempt to reason with him and wondering where he could have gone. There were no friends she could ring to see if he was with them, but that would be the sort of action which would undoubtedly annoy him even more. Emma was tempted to ring her parents, just for a chat, yet if she heard her mother's voice she would surely break down and it would all come tumbling out, making the situation much worse.

Simon didn't return until 9pm. He walked into the house and glowered at his wife.

'Have you got over your little tantrum?' His eyes bored into Emma.

She felt defeated, all strength and hope knocked out of her and lacking the energy to contradict him over his use of the word 'tantrum'. So instead, she nodded and went to put the kettle on.

CHAPTER ELEVEN

After a most confusing weekend, Emma was eager to return to work, silently acknowledging it had become her escape from Simon. At least there was Fiona to talk to, a woman who spoke good old-fashioned common sense, a rare commodity, her mother would have said.

Fiona was the first in the surgery on Monday and looked up from her computer as Emma arrived. 'That friend of yours is over the road,' Fiona said. 'You know, the one who came in the other day asking for you.'

Emma turned back towards the door, keen to see who it was. Fiona joined her, and they looked across the road, up and down the street but saw no one except the postman and an elderly gentleman walking his dog.

'How funny,' Fiona said, 'I'm sure it was her, wearing that same green raincoat. She was there when I arrived and I assumed she was waiting for you.'

'Not to worry, if she wants to see me, she knows where I am.' Emma wondered if Fiona was mistaken – if it were the same person who'd enquired after her last week, surely she'd have come in again by now.

'So, what kind of weekend have you had?' Fiona asked.

Emma wrinkled her nose, searching for the right words to reply. 'I'm struggling. Simon's mood swings are so unpredictable, it's a relief to get to work and some days I just don't want to go home. Silly, I know, but that's how I feel.'

'Not silly at all. He sounds like a right pig and certainly doesn't deserve you.'

'Don't mince your words, will you?' Emma was a little surprised at her friend's opinion. 'You know, I do think Simon's unreasonable but perhaps I'm not being fair to him. Maybe it's me who's a bit crazy.'

'Nonsense, you're as level-headed as the rest of us and always have been. From some of the things you've told me, Simon's the crazy one. Doesn't he know slavery was abolished years ago?'

'Now look, I've coloured your judgement and you don't even know him, which isn't fair. Sometimes I *do* mess things up – like on Saturday morning – I didn't get up until after eight even though I'd looked at the clock and could have sworn it was only seven, so I know I'm doing some rather stupid things lately, enough to try Simon's patience.'

'Really?' Fiona's eyes widened with mischief. 'Even eight's too early to get up at the weekend! Kevin and I – well, perhaps I'd better not go there!'

'And there's another thing,' Emma lowered her voice even though they were alone, 'I'm getting to the point where I don't want him to touch me. Surely that's not normal for someone my age? Sex with Simon feels like a duty, something I must do to keep him sweet.' She looked down at her computer, embarrassed yet relieved to have admitted what was troubling her.

Fiona's mood changed to one of solemn concern. 'Oh, Emma, that's not how things should be. You should never feel obliged to have sex or agree to it because you're afraid of him. Tell me to butt out if you like but he seems to be controlling you. I'm not an expert in this stuff, yet even I can sense that your husband has some very odd ideas about marriage.'

'I've done it again, haven't I? Sorry. It wasn't my intention to pour out my troubles. Let's talk about something more cheerful, shall we? Tell me about your weekend.'

Fiona had only a few minutes to reply before the first patient of the day arrived and the surgery started to buzz, but Emma remained troubled.

Over the weekend, Simon had vacillated between his usual fusion of moods, one minute angry over some trivial incident, the next all sweetness and light, and Emma didn't know which was preferable. One thing was becoming apparent. She couldn't carry on living under such pressure for much longer. If she was in this state after only a few months of marriage, what would become of her after a lifetime with Simon? Talking to Fiona helped, yet her colleague couldn't understand how difficult it was to speak to Simon, to put her point of view across.

In many ways, Emma struggled to understand her feelings. It was the twenty-first century and theoretically it was within her power to change her circumstances, yet she couldn't. Maybe it was something to do with her upbringing. Emma's parents instilled their own moral values in their daughter, not only by what they said but by example. Therefore her idea of marriage was one of total commitment, underpinned by selfless love and respect. Perhaps this view was immature and too simplistic but she believed marriage was for life and her promises to Simon were not to be taken lightly.

With everything going on, at the back of Emma's mind was still the nagging fear of insanity. Doctor Chakrabarti had offered reassurance that this was not the case. Still, there were so many inexplicable instances which only Simon witnessed, and it crossed Emma's mind that he could be right, maybe she did need looking after. It was all too confusing and the more she dwelt on it, the more muddled she became.

At least there was her job. Perhaps not the most exciting career in the world but she felt safe and confident there. Emma knew she was good at her job and the banter with colleagues and clients provided a welcome refuge. Life was comfortingly predictable at work, which certainly couldn't be said about life at home with Simon.

By lunchtime, Emma's mood had lightened. Fi seemed to be trying to keep things cheery and Emma's soul searching was put aside for the time being.

Just after Fiona left for lunch, the woman in the green raincoat came in. Emma was alone in reception.

'Hi, can I help you?' Emma smiled. The lady looked familiar, yet most patients did. The woman looked as if deciding whether to speak or not, which wasn't unusual – many patients were nervous – no one enjoyed visiting the dentist.

'Do you have an appointment?' she tried again.

'Are you Emma?'

'Yes.'

'Emma Beecham?

'Er... yes, I'm sorry, should I know you?'

'No, but I think we should get to know one another.'

The stranger was unnerving Emma. What could she want?

Before there was time to ask, the woman leaned closer and, speaking in a low, almost threatening voice, said, 'Meet me in half an hour at the coffee shop on Main Street.' Abruptly, she then spun round and left.

Emma didn't know what to make of the brief, unsettling encounter. Half an hour would be the start of her lunch break and the café she mentioned was nearby. How did this woman know her name and other things, such as where she worked and perhaps even when she took her lunch break?

A sudden cold shiver ran through Emma's body, one of fear but also of curiosity. And she had only half an hour to decide whether or not to go.

CHAPTER TWELVE

'You don't have to go, you know,' Fiona said when she came back from lunch and heard of Emma's visitor.

'Yes but if I don't she might come back, or if she doesn't, I'll probably drive myself crazy wondering what it's all about.'

'True enough. Look, why don't you go? It's a public place and probably quite busy, so you'll be safe.'

'Do you think so? Yes, I'm going. What can she do anyway?' Emma gave a nervous half-smile while pulling on her coat.

Pushing open the door of the café ten minutes later, Emma immediately saw the woman in the green coat sitting by the window, nursing a cup of coffee with a second one on the table. As Emma sat, the woman pushed the extra cup across the table.

'Here, this is for you – you're going to need it.'

Emma felt cold even though the temperature outside was relatively mild for October. Sitting opposite the stranger, she wrapped her hands around the coffee cup, drawing warmth from it.

'Who are you?' was the first and most obvious question, followed immediately by 'and what do you want?'

The stranger smiled, a rather sad smile as if she was utterly exhausted or coming to the end of a difficult time. 'Diane, Di, if you like.'

'Well, Diane, what's all this about?' Strangely, the woman's demeanour made Emma feel less intimidated and more in control. She sat upright in her chair, looking directly into a pair of grey-green eyes which gave nothing away as to why she'd been summoned. Diane stirred her coffee with the plastic teaspoon, unhurried and thoughtful as if debating what to say next.

'Diane Beecham, if you want my full name.'

Emma felt a sudden jolt like an electric shock had passed through her body. 'Beecham... are you a relative of my husband's?'

'Not exactly – I'm his wife.' The smile was gone. She looked at Emma with an expression of concern and possibly even pity. Emma's face turned pale – her head was spinning. This couldn't be true. Surely it was a sick joke.

'That's ridiculous. I'm Simon's wife.' Her words sounded bold but any previous confidence she'd mustered now deserted her.

Diane slowly shook her head. 'I'm sorry, Emma. I know how much of a shock this must be and there's no easy way of telling you. I married Simon Beecham six years ago and we have never divorced.' An uneasy silence followed as her words sank in – the noise of the busy café faded into the background. Emma's head throbbed as she focused on the woman in front of her – the woman who claimed to be Simon's wife. As Diane continued, it was all Emma could do to concentrate on breathing.

'It was only by accident that I discovered he was in a relationship again,' Diane explained. 'A mutual friend noticed him sitting in a car outside the dentist's surgery where you work.

He told me he'd seen Simon picking you up. I thought you might be a girlfriend or perhaps living together, and then when I went into the surgery the first time to find you, I saw the staff photographs displayed on the wall in the lobby with your name as Emma Beecham. I've been looking for Simon for the last six months, not because I wanted to see him but to discuss a divorce. I've met someone else, you see. After Simon, I swore I'd never marry again but my new boyfriend has changed my mind.'

'So why come after me and not Simon?' Emma asked, still shell-shocked by the news.

'Initially, I was curious. When we split up, Simon left the firm where he worked and didn't tell me where he lived. I didn't care at the time. I was in a mess, a breakdown of sorts I suppose. By the time I got my life back on track there was no sign of him anywhere. He'd never had friends of his own and most of our mutual friends were glad to see the back of him after witnessing what he'd done to me.

'When I heard he'd been seen and given the address of where you work, I couldn't help but wonder what kind of relationship you have and how he treats you. I also wanted to warn you about him but it appears I'm too late, although I never dreamt he'd marry again, especially as we hadn't divorced.' Diane glanced at Emma as if waiting for a reaction. Pain was etched on Emma's face.

'Is it a happy marriage?' Diane ventured.

Emma shook her head as a slow trickle of tears rolled down her cheeks.

'I thought as much.' Diane pushed a tissue into Emma's hand – she appeared to take no pleasure in the situation. 'Look on the bright side, Emma, you're not legally married to Mr Simon Beecham. He's a bigamist so you can walk away any time you choose. I'm the one who needs a divorce.'

'And he's the one who wants locking up!' Emma added

bitterly, beginning to think coherently again. 'I don't think I can return to work after this. I'll make a quick call to my colleague and then we can talk some more.'

'No problem,' Diane answered, 'I'll get a couple more coffees and some of those tempting doughnuts – you've had a shock. You need the sugar.'

When alone, Emma made the call to Fiona, assuring her she was okay but unable to go back to work that afternoon and promising to explain later, before ending the call.

Emma was experiencing a strangely distant feeling, as if she was an outsider looking down on the surreal events of someone else's life from some high vantage point. Her emotions were in total confusion but somewhere amongst them was relief – *she wasn't legally married to Simon* – the realisation sent a small thrill darting through her body.

The first, and technically the real Mrs Beecham, returned with coffee and doughnuts and they both ate hungrily, needing the sugar boost.

'So, what has Simon been like as a husband?' Diane asked.

'Moody, unpredictable, sullen at times... my friend thinks he's controlling.'

'Tell me about it! Emma, does Simon play mind tricks with you?'

'What do you mean by "mind tricks"?'

'Oh, silly things really, has he done the shopping thing with you?'

'The shopping thing?'

'We'd done the shopping one evening and I'd put it away and gone to watch telly. Then, half an hour later, Simon came through shouting about my laziness and why I hadn't put the shopping away.' Diane chuckled as Emma's mouth dropped open.

'Yes, he did! At first, I thought it was me – that I was going mad or something. But then I put it down to him playing some silly practical joke.'

'And was Simon the one who planted the *going mad* seed? You know, the *I'll look after you* bit.'

'Yes... he did it with you as well?'

'Oh yes, classic Simon, turn every situation around to his advantage. Of course, it's all your fault – but caring Simon will be there to look after you. Bloody hypocrite! And did you ever lose your purse?'

'Yes, but I thought it was my fault. I can get a little distracted.'

'Where did you find it, in the ironing pile?' Diane grinned.

'No, in the fridge.' They both smiled, though rather glumly.

'And did you ever lose the contacts from your phone?' Emma asked.

'Ah yes, more than once.'

'The pig! And all this time, I thought it was me!'

Diane sighed deeply. 'The question now is what are we going to do about him?'

'He's committed bigamy. We'll have to go to the police,' Emma said solemnly.

Diane's eyes widened. 'I think we should do this together.'

'Fine with me, I could do with the support... let's go.'

To most people, news like this would be devastating. It was undoubtedly a massive shock to Emma, yet her feelings quickly changed from horror to a sense of reprieve as reality sank in. Anger was bubbling inside, but it was channelled into a feeling of confidence, even hope. She wasn't going mad after all; Simon had been manipulating her for his own selfish purposes. Sudden energy infused Emma's body, a release perhaps. Yes, she felt violated and disgusted towards Simon whilst berating herself for her stupidity in being drawn into his sick ways. She'd given herself wholly to him in every possible way and he'd used her shamefully. However, Emma knew for sure that she would overcome this and keep whatever dignity she had left intact. Emma was the victim, but one who was about to fight back.

CHAPTER THIRTEEN

DI Samantha Freeman was tossing pieces of her torn-up polystyrene cup at a waste paper bin in the corner of her office, her aim improving with each attempt. If anyone challenged her on this childish activity, she would claim it aided her concentration. The truth was that Samantha presently had nothing to concentrate on which captured her imagination, no new case sufficiently engrossing to excite or maintain her interest. Yes, there was always paperwork to do and endless reports to catch up with, but being a good DI, she delegated much of the mundane work to junior detectives – to help them improve their skills, naturally.

Since her promotion to detective inspector, Sam had worked on several absorbing cases, including two murders, challenges on which she thrived. Solving serious crimes was her lifeblood. Currently she was working on a couple of cold cases, a twenty-year-old missing person case and a kidnapping from the same year for which the child was never found. It wasn't as if the work was uninteresting or unimportant and Samantha's desire to solve these cases was strong, but she relished the physicality of police work and getting out of the confines of the station. She was a woman who needed the pressure of deadlines to stretch her mind into lateral thinking.

Samantha was a petite five foot two, with a perfectly proportioned, honed body, a cap of dark hair above a pleasant face, devoid, as always, of make-up, and she was dressed as sharp as a blade in a fitted indigo trouser suit, with a pale-blue cotton blouse clutched at her throat. Her mind was as taut as her body, intelligence shining from bright green eyes.

Samantha stretched like a cat. Procrastination over, she turned back to her computer to again bring up the twenty-year-old witness statements regarding the missing person. Reading them for about the fourth time, DS Jenny Newcombe's interruption was more than welcome as the sergeant appeared at her side.

'Want a break from history?' the DS asked.

'Do I ever?'

'I've got an interesting case in interview room 3. Two women have just come in to report a bigamist. I'll happily run with it myself but I thought you might like to sit in with me?' Jenny looked hopefully at her boss, correctly guessing the novelty would be irresistible. Neither detective had worked a case of bigamy before and undoubtedly two heads would be better than one. Sam jumped at the chance to interview the women.

Jenny led the way – she was four inches taller than Samantha and carried more weight but it was mostly muscle and suited her frame. Her blonde hair was swept up into a knot on top of her head and she favoured fitted trousers and loose tops for work. The detectives strode down the corridor in silent anticipation.

———

It was 2.30pm, only an hour since Emma Beecham's world had been turned on its head. She was sitting next to Diane Beecham, Simon's legal wife, in a police interview room, shivering more from shock than cold. Weird to say the least. Diane appeared relatively calm but then she'd had more time to anticipate this event and as the detectives entered the room to ask their questions, Diane supplied most of the answers.

'Mrs Beecham...' Jenny began and both women looked at her. 'Er, perhaps it would be better if I used your Christian names. Will that be okay?' Two nods permitted her to continue. 'Diane, how did you find out your husband had married again?'

'Through a friend who saw him with Emma by chance. He knew I'd been trying to trace Simon to get a divorce. I want to marry again, you see. This friend spotted Simon picking Emma up from the surgery where she works on more than one occasion and told me about it. I eventually plucked up the courage to approach her, initially to warn her about Simon. I didn't know they were married until I saw her name in the surgery. We only met earlier today but now we've had time to talk and compare notes we thought we should come to report Simon together.'

Emma entered the conversation. 'Will he be arrested? I don't think I can go back home to face him and I can't pretend I don't know about Diane.'

Jenny picked up on the fear in the younger woman's eyes. 'Is Simon violent towards you, Emma?'

'Not physically, no, but he likes things to be just so and if his routine's disturbed he can become angry.' Emma couldn't express how she felt about living with Simon, not in a concise way in this bland interview room. It was all so confusing and there'd been much to take in in such a short time. The one thing she was sure of was that she was afraid to see him again.

Diane took over. 'Simon Beecham is a controlling bully. He plays mind games to make you think you're at fault – he enjoys seeing people squirm – he's a bastard.' She didn't sugar-coat her words. 'Emma's afraid to go back to living with him, and rightly so. I think he's dangerous. Will you arrest him today?'

'It's usual procedure to investigate a claim like this. I'm sure you understand we can't simply go out and arrest people on someone's word. We'll need to see your marriage certificates for a start,' Jenny explained.

Diane was already rummaging in her bag. 'Here's mine. I brought it to show Emma in case she didn't believe me, and I wouldn't be trying to find him if I had the divorce papers to cancel this.' Diane slapped the certificate on the table for Jenny and Samantha to see.

Samantha picked it up and examined it.

'My marriage certificate is at home. I can get it later and let you have it,' Emma offered.

'We'll certainly need to see it at some point. If you're afraid to go back home, Emma, is there somewhere else you could go?'

'I could go to stay with my parents, although Simon will be expecting me to be at work now, he'll pick me up at 5.30. I don't know what he'll do if I'm not there.'

The detectives continued their questions for a while longer, with Jenny Newcombe taking notes. Finally, they asked where Simon worked and his present and past addresses. Then they left the pair alone for a few minutes while they stepped out of the room to discuss the issue.

Jenny looked at her boss. 'What do you think?'

'I think we should go and arrest him. It's not as if we're doing anything which won't keep. My current cases have waited twenty years already. So let's get the process started, I'm rather keen to meet this Simon Beecham and it'll put Emma out of her misery.'

'Johnson & Co Insurance is only a couple of miles away. We

can pick him up, bring him in to charge him and still finish the day in reasonable time.' Jenny looked hopeful.

'Let's do it,' Samantha agreed, so they went back into the interview room to make their decision known to a solemn-looking Emma and a delighted Diane.

'We're going to pick him up at his place of work and bring him here to question him. He'll be advised to secure the services of a solicitor who will arrange bail if we arrest him, so he'll probably be home sometime this evening,' Sam explained.

Emma's face paled as the detective continued. 'Perhaps it would be better to go and stay with your parents anyway, to avoid any fallout. Unless you want to take out a restraining order against him so he can't come back to your present home?'

'But where would he go? It seems mean.'

Diane blurted out her frustrations. 'After all he's done you're still bloody concerned for him!'

Emma blushed. 'I think I'd rather go to my parents anyway.' She turned to address Samantha. 'Will you ring me to let me know what happens?'

'Yes, of course, and we'll have a word with him about not approaching you if you like?'

'Please, I don't think I ever want to see him again after this. Will you be going now because he'll be leaving work at about 5.15 to pick me up?'

'We'll be there before then, don't worry,' Jenny assured her confidently.

Emma and Diane left the police station, followed shortly by Sam and Jenny who made their way to Johnson & Co Insurance, curious to meet Simon Beecham.

CHAPTER FOURTEEN

The drive was short, allowing Jenny and Samantha little time to speculate on the details they'd gleaned from Simon's two *wives*.

'Why would anyone get married again without getting divorced? It's such a simple process these days and most couples would live together while waiting for the decree anyway?' Jenny wondered aloud.

'Emma seems old-fashioned to me; maybe she refused to live with him until after the wedding, or he might have thought she'd not want to marry a divorced man. But, of course, it's just speculation. No one knows the intricacies of other people's relationships, although it sounds like both Diane and Emma have had a rough ride.'

Johnson & Co Insurance was housed in a large, modern, glass-fronted building over three floors, and the detectives entered the lobby just before 4.30pm, in good time to catch Beecham before he left for the day. Several employees were already heading home but a woman still staffed the reception desk as Sam approached the long, sleek structure and showed her ID badge to an equally sleek receptionist.

'I'd like to speak to Mr Simon Beecham, please. I believe he's in claims management.' She smiled at the woman on the other side of the desk.

'Just a moment, I'll try to locate him.' After a few taps on her keypad, a frown appeared on her well-made-up face. 'I'm sorry, we don't seem to have an employee of that name. Perhaps you could spell it for me?'

Jenny obliged and the receptionist tried again.

'No, there's no Simon Beecham on our staff.' She looked blankly at the visitors as they exchanged puzzled looks.

'Are you sure?' Samantha persisted.

'Yes. We have nearly two hundred people working here, and each is logged into the system. There's no one by the name of Simon Beecham.'

'Perhaps he's a consultant, not regular staff?' Jenny suggested.

'Everyone who works here is in the system. If Mr Beecham were a visitor, even for the day, his name would appear on the visitors list and it doesn't.' The receptionist sighed, clearly bored with the conversation and the persistence of the officers.

'Do you have another location where he might work?' Sam was thinking on her feet, not knowing where to go next.

'Our sister office is in Scotland. I can ring them for you if you like, to ask if they know Mr Beecham? He should still be on our system though.'

'No, that won't be necessary. Thank you for your time,' Samantha said and the detectives left.

'Do you think Emma gave us the wrong place of work?' Jenny asked once they were back in the car.

'I shouldn't think so. Give her a ring to check. There's

plenty of time to get to the surgery where Emma works and intercept him when he arrives. Ask what make of car he drives.'

While Jenny made the call, Samantha started the engine and listened to the one-sided conversation while trying to think of a plausible explanation for the mix-up.

'Emma's as puzzled as we are. She says Simon's worked at Johnsons since she met him over a year ago. Or at least that's what he told her. He drives a green Nissan Micra.' Jenny recited the registration number as they pulled outside the dentist's surgery. Rain was beginning to fall and the heavy clouds made for a dark evening. The detectives sat watching the rain splashing into puddles, the rhythmic pounding on the car almost mesmerising.

Samantha sighed. 'So much for a reasonable finish. I wonder what this man's like – and if there's more to this situation than we thought?' She was thinking aloud again, surprised at how much she relished the complication – at times, Sam felt she possessed an almost morbid desire for an interesting juicy case and despised herself for hoping this might turn out to be more than a simple matter of bigamy.

Samantha noticed the car first after a wait of over thirty minutes. 'Here's our boy! Did Emma say if he went in to get her or will he wait in the car?'

'He waits outside.' They watched Beecham park opposite the surgery and switch off his engine. The Nissan interior darkened and there was no movement, so the two women exited their car and walked over to their unsuspecting quarry.

Samantha tapped on the window, ID at the ready. A startled Simon looked up, then wound down the window.

'Mr Simon Beecham?' she asked. Initially, Simon hesitated and she thought he might be considering his options but he'd seen her badge; there were few options to choose from.

'Yes... has something happened to Emma?' His eyes

widened and his demeanour changed. Sam thought that was the moment when Simon Beecham slipped into a role he was playing – a concerned husband – a model citizen. She couldn't pin it down, yet already she disliked the man.

'You mean your wife, sir? No, she's fine. We'd like you to come to the station to answer a few questions.'

His expression was the picture of innocence, seemingly perplexed to be summoned to the police station. 'What about?'

'It's concerning your wife, sir.' Samantha was thinking this time about Diane Beecham. Was he? she wondered.

Simon asked if he could drive in his car and meet them there. He tried to be polite about Samantha's insistence on travelling with them, yet even in the half-light his eyes betrayed the man's anger.

At New Middridge station, the detectives left Simon in interview room 2, the smallest and coldest room in the building, offering him coffee which he declined, before getting some for themselves. Not wanting the evening to drag out, they left him for only ten minutes, enough time to make him sweat.

After switching on the tape recorder and introducing those present, Samantha began the interview.

'Mr Beecham. How long have you been married?' she asked.

His hesitation and the look in his eyes confirmed to Sam that he knew why he was there. 'Five months, a little over, I think.'

'No, I mean to Diane Beecham, your legal wife.' She smiled sweetly at him, enjoying the flash of anger that his eyes betrayed.

Simon shuffled in his seat, his mouth set into a thin tight line. 'I want a solicitor.'

'Certainly. Do you want your own, or should we call a duty solicitor for you?'

'A duty solicitor will be fine and I don't wish to say any more until he's here.'

'Okay, we'll get straight onto that and let you know when he arrives.' Samantha and Jenny stood to leave the room.

'Make the call, please, Jenny, and try to get a woman solicitor if one's available, then grab a couple of sandwiches and coffees. I'll ring Emma to update her.'

Jenny smiled, understanding her boss's thinking. A woman would probably infuriate Beecham. Hopefully, there'd be one on call.

Sam rang Emma. 'Hi, it's Samantha Freeman. Just to let you know we have Simon here at the station. He's asked for a solicitor so he should be here for a while longer. Are you at your parents' house now?' The detective's initial concern was for Emma's safety and peace of mind, yet she also wanted her take on the fiasco at Johnson Insurance.

'I'm at home, just packing a few things. My dad's with me, and he'll take me to their house. Has Simon admitted bigamy?'

'Not yet. He's waiting for a solicitor before we have that particular conversation. Have you had any more thoughts about his place of work?'

'No. I don't know what to think. Simon drops me off at work and then goes there every day until he picks me up. Or so he tells me. Are you sure they didn't make a mistake?'

'They seemed pretty certain. But, look, don't worry about it now. We'll be asking him about it in due course. You just get off to your parents' home. I'll speak to you tomorrow to bring you up to speed.'

'I've got my marriage certificate here. Dad said we can drop it at the station on the way home if you need it,' Emma offered.

'That would be great. Leave it at the front desk and ask

them to bring it straight to me. Goodnight, Emma.' Sam rang off, wondering what kind of relationship this couple must have had. Her thoughts then turned to her boyfriend, Ravi Patel, a detective in the fraud squad. They'd recently moved in together and Samantha gave him a quick ring to let him know she'd be late.

Sighing heavily, she smiled. Hadn't she been longing for an interesting case?

CHAPTER FIFTEEN

George Porter held Emma while she cried on his shoulder, huge sobs she'd kept at bay since meeting Diane Beecham that lunchtime. As Emma knew he would, he'd set off immediately after her call, and she'd been grateful he didn't press her for details. When she took Samantha's call, Emma knew it was time to explain that Simon was legally married to someone else.

She could tell her father was furious but more detailed explanations could wait until they were home. Emma finished packing, grabbing only the minimum of items to get out of the house as quickly as possible. On leaving that dark, forbidding place, she knew with certainty that she never wanted to step inside its walls again. It was her first home as an adult away from the nest of her childhood and her parents' protection, yet it had turned into a prison – the childhood dream of a wonderful life as a married woman was tainted. Her *husband* had abused and humiliated her and she must face the world alone, a victim of the ultimate betrayal.

Walking away from the house, Emma's face was wet with tears. This day was undoubtedly the worst one of her life.

Weary and unable to think straight, the thing she most wanted to do now was to be enfolded in her parents' love and protection as she'd been in childhood.

Grasping her marriage certificate in her hand, the paper seemed to burn Emma's skin like acid and she felt a strong desire to rip it into tiny pieces, yet she knew it was evidence. George took the document from her and tucked it in his pocket – he would drop it at the police station.

Emma struggled to hold herself together during the journey. She felt tired, angry and humiliated, plus a dozen or more other emotions yet to be identified. This was not how her fairy tale marriage was supposed to end.

As her mother ran out to greet them, concern etched on her face, Emma allowed her warm embrace to enfold her and lead her into their home as if she were a little girl. George Porter hung back as his wife steered their daughter into the lounge but couldn't escape hearing Emma's wounded sobs. Instead of following the women, he headed for the kitchen where he set the kettle to boil.

Ten minutes later George ventured into the lounge with a tray of tea precariously balanced in his hands. Emma knew it was time to explain the situation more fully. Her parents deserved as much. So, drawing a deep breath and taking the hot tea her father offered, she attempted to tell them everything Diane had revealed about Simon. It seemed a lifetime ago yet it was only a few hours earlier that she'd discovered he was not legally her husband. It was a huge shock and devastating for her parents to learn how he'd manipulated her throughout their short 'marriage'. Emma was embarrassed to admit the kind of life she'd been living with Simon – realising how gullible and naive she'd been only added shame to an already complicated state of affairs.

George and Margaret listened quietly, which was difficult, especially for George who clearly grew angrier by the minute.

Emma struggled to verbalise her thoughts. 'With hindsight, we were all duped. Simon played the situation cleverly, gaining our trust and even love. I only wish I'd known the difference between love and infatuation. He had me fooled – big time!'

Margaret shook her head sadly. 'Simon appears to be very adept at deceit; we were taken in too. But what about this other wife, his real wife I suppose she is?'

'Diane? I was afraid initially. She'd been watching me to find out as much as possible. Now I actually quite like her. We have a lot in common and will have to keep in touch to see what happens... legally.'

'Will the police keep Simon in custody?' Margaret asked.

'I doubt it unless they think he's a flight risk which I'm sure they won't. I shouldn't think bigamy falls into the category of a serious crime. So that's why I came here. If they release him, I don't want to be around if he comes home.'

Her father was quick to speak. 'Of course not. You did the right thing, love. This will always be your home.'

Emma's shoulders relaxed – how she'd missed spending time with her parents. They were such wonderful people who she loved so much. They'd also been taken in by Simon, but they would work through this together.

'DI Freeman promised to ring me tomorrow to let me know what's happening,' she said, thinking for the first time about the next day and the following one – how could she possibly face everyone?

'You stay in bed in the morning, love. I'll ring the surgery to let them know you won't be in tomorrow. I'll just say you're unwell and then we can plan where we go from there.' Margaret smiled reassuringly at her daughter. Emma knew she'd do anything for her only child, as would George.

It was getting late. The evening outside was black, cold and gloomy, matching Emma's mood precisely, and aching tiredness was taking over her body – it had been a gruelling day. Margaret insisted on a milky drink and a couple of paracetamols to which Emma meekly complied before climbing the stairs to the familiar and comforting bedroom of her childhood.

After their daughter went to bed, Margaret and George sat up for another hour. Self-recriminations were expressed and then dismissed. Simon was believable, ingratiating himself into their family, gaining their trust and affection, and so obviously skilled at deception. Initially, they'd had no reason to doubt him until he requested a loan which surprised them and should have rung alarm bells.

When Simon didn't pursue the issue, they assumed he'd thought better of his business idea and put the matter down to his immaturity. But this was something else entirely, something they couldn't possibly have anticipated. As George pointed out, when someone asks for your daughter's hand in marriage, you don't think to ask if they already have a wife, especially when the couple seems so happy and in love.

Admittedly, they'd missed regular contact with their daughter but tried to be unselfish, thinking the young couple needed time alone to settle into married life. They ran the gamut of emotions, primarily a feeling of having let their daughter down and regret that they'd not insisted on keeping in touch on a more regular basis. How wrong they had been about Simon, but how could they have foreseen such a devastating outcome?

Upstairs, Emma found it impossible to sleep. The day's events played through her mind on a loop, dredging up the numerous emotions she couldn't seem to banish from her thoughts. When Diane had first approached her, curiosity overcame her fear. The woman had been following her, which was a bit scary, although Emma couldn't have anticipated the reason.

The news Diane imparted was a shock yet also a relief, and as Emma lay in bed with her tears spent, an inappropriate desire to laugh bubbled up inside her. Yes, she was sad, mortified, embarrassed even, but the truth was that she was also free. She was still ashamed and humiliated at the stupidity of being taken in by Simon, but he was not her husband!

She was not legally married to him and never had been. The reality prompted a smile. Released from suffering any more of his nasty little ways, Emma wanted to celebrate. Was she verging on hysteria? Before she could delve deeper into such soul searching, she fell into a deep and surprisingly dreamless sleep.

CHAPTER SIXTEEN

'So, what do you think of our bigamist then?' DI Freeman asked her DS.

'He's got a certain attraction if you like the pretty boy look, but his ears are too small. I don't like a man with small ears. The rugged sort's more my type,' Jenny replied distractedly.

'I didn't mean his looks!' Samantha laughed as Jenny blushed.

'Oh, well, it's too early to tell what he's like, a bit arrogant perhaps – certainly cagey and cautious in what he says, which you'd expect wouldn't you?' Jenny pushed the last bite of the sandwich into her mouth as Sam slowly nodded in agreement. The duty solicitor had finally arrived and was getting to know her new client. As Sam had Emma's invalid marriage certificate as well as Diane's original one in her possession, they were ready to go.

'Come on, they'll be waiting for us. Let's get this sorted and then we can go home. With a bit of luck Ravi should have a nice hot curry waiting for me by then.'

'Ooh, lucky you. I'll be going home to a cold house and cheese on toast if the bread hasn't gone mouldy.'

Samantha stood to go with Jenny tagging on behind, each in their own way relishing the interview.

Simon Beecham was sitting silently, his face grimacing, hands clasped on the table. Turning his head as the women entered, he was obviously struggling to control his infuriation. His solicitor, Ms Irene Marshall, was jotting down a few notes and smiled weakly at Samantha and Jenny. They'd met before on several occasions.

Ms Marshall opened the dialogue. 'My client would like to make a statement.'

Jenny turned towards the tape, switching it on before anything else was said. Stating the names of those present and the reason for the interview she then cautioned Simon before Samantha took over.

'Okay, Mr Beecham, what would you like to say?' Sam asked.

The man looked at her with such contempt in his eyes. 'I realise now how stupid I've been and am truly sorry for causing so much pain.'

Sam thought Simon didn't look sorry, except perhaps at being caught.

'I know I shouldn't have married Emma without a divorce but I suppose I simply got carried away in the emotion of it all and I'm prepared to do whatever it takes to put things right.'

Beecham's face certainly didn't reflect his words – his mouth remained tight, his eyes narrow – he was a man going through the motions – damage limitation, Sam thought.

Samantha continued the lead. 'Bigamy is a criminal offence, Mr Beecham, and we will be charging you. For now you will be released on bail with conditions. You'll be able to return to your present address. Emma is no longer there but please do not attempt to contact her in any way; she does not wish to see you.

We also require you to report to this police station each week until your court hearing.'

Sam studied the man as he attempted to look penitent. The anger simmering beneath the surface was clearly hard for him to disguise. 'There are, however, a few other questions we'd like to ask before we charge you. Firstly, could you tell me where you're currently employed?'

Simon hesitated a moment too long. Samantha assumed he was wondering exactly how much they knew.

'I'm a claims manager at Johnson & Co Insurance company.' His voice held a slight catch.

'At their New Middridge branch, sir?'

'Yes.' He wasn't going to elaborate.

'That seems rather odd as when we called there earlier this afternoon they'd never heard of you and there was no record of your name on their computer files.'

Now Simon knew that they knew, his expression changed.

'Ah.' He paused, studying the riveting wood grain pattern on the table. 'I assume Emma told you where I worked. Actually, I left their employment about a month ago. I decided to move on and have been looking for a new position. I didn't tell Emma because I didn't want her to worry. She can become rather depressed at any little bumps in the road of life.'

'So, you've allowed Emma to think you're still employed at Johnsons and left the house each day to support this fantasy?' Samantha confirmed.

'It's hardly a fantasy, detective. As I said, it was to protect Emma; she's quite highly strung, and I knew she'd only worry. I'm confident of securing another position very soon. Will you charge me with protecting my wife now, DI Freeman?' Simon's tone held more than a bit of sarcasm, his confidence and arrogance returning.

'Emma is not your wife, Mr Beecham,' Sam countered.

'Jenny, please read Mr Beecham his rights and formally charge him.'

The DS proceeded to do so, after which Samantha wrapped up the interview.

'I think we're done here for this evening. Ms Marshall will go through the details of your bail conditions and see to the paperwork with the duty sergeant. We'll be in touch, Mr Beecham. Thank you for your time.'

Jenny spoke first as soon as they were clear of the interview room. 'What a bloody pig!'

'Of the first order. Emma's lucky to have him out of her life, although I shouldn't think she'll feel lucky for some time yet. We can begin the process tomorrow. Mainly paperwork on this one, and then off to the CPS for a court date. It should be fairly straightforward. It's getting late, Jenny. You're welcome to come home with me and share that curry if you like?'

'Oh, thanks, but I wouldn't want to intrude and Charlie will be waiting for me.'

Sam raised an eyebrow and her sergeant laughed.

'My cat! You'll be the first to know if there's any news on the romance front, but to be honest, Stuart's put me off men for quite a while. A cat's so much more understanding and far less demanding, and he can keep a confidence.' Jenny's ex-boyfriend had recently landed her in hot water at work. He'd anonymously leaked sensitive information to the press about a case they were working on which had ground to a standstill. Stuart claimed it was to help move the case forward but it almost lost Jenny her job and landed a severe blow to her self-confidence. The couple split shortly afterwards and she adopted a rescue cat for company, a move she would highly recommend.

Samantha smiled at her colleague. 'Okay, enjoy what's left of your evening with Charlie.'

They went their separate ways. Sam's first job the following morning would be to ring Emma and Diane to update them on the arrest and what would happen next. It had been an interesting day and a brief respite from the historic cold cases on her computer.

CHAPTER SEVENTEEN

Emma woke to the sound of the radio playing softly in the kitchen and her mother pottering with breakfast dishes, the familiar and comforting backing track to her childhood. As the previous day's events flooded her mind, the temptation was strong to pull the duvet over her head and close her eyes again, but she knew sleep would be impossible and was surprised at having slept at all. Climbing from the warm bed she pulled on a dressing gown and went downstairs. Her father's voice could be heard from his study as Emma passed the door, a telephone conversation in which he sounded unusually animated. In the kitchen her mother smiled a rather too bright greeting.

'Morning, love. Did you manage to sleep?'

'Yes, thanks. Isn't Dad going to work today?' She glanced at the wall clock ticking away the minutes of their lives as it had done for as long as she could remember. 'It's half past eight.' George Porter was always busy with a long list of patients, yet his family came first.

'He's taking the day off. We need to form some kind of plan but first, breakfast. What would you like? I've some nice lean bacon in the fridge.'

'Thanks, Mum, but a slice of toast will be fine.'

Margaret frowned as she popped two slices of bread into the toaster while Emma sat at the table and launched into an apology. 'I'm sorry to have brought all this to your d–'

'Enough.' Margaret held up her hand. 'There's no need for apologies, we're in this together and we'll get it sorted out. Don't you go fretting about it.'

George Porter appeared in the kitchen doorway and smiled at Emma. She felt the last few months roll away and wished she'd never set eyes on Simon Beecham. Then her life could have remained one of contentment here with these two people who loved her unconditionally.

'Jack McArthur's agreed to take on our case,' George announced. 'He's a solicitor and a good man, Emma. We're lucky to get him.' George sat beside her at the table and covered her hand with his own. 'We've got an appointment to see him tomorrow, but he suggests we go to the bank today and get your finances on track – we need to close the joint account, open one of your own and arrange to have your salary paid into it.'

'I haven't a clue how much is in the account.' Emma felt stupid having to rely on her father; she was a grown woman.

'We'll sort it out at the bank and Jack says it needs doing today.'

'Okay, I'll get ready.'

Margaret frowned. 'Finish your breakfast first, love; you need to eat. I'd not thought about the legal and financial implications. Will you be able to draw on the account if you're not Simon's legal wife?'

Before they could discuss the matter further, Emma's phone rang. It was DI Freeman.

'Hello, Emma. I just wanted to let you know we charged Simon with bigamy last night. He admitted the charge, so it was pretty straightforward and he's out on bail. We made one of the conditions that he has no contact with you, so if you do hear from him let me know immediately, or if you feel threatened ring 999.'

'Thank you. I appreciate how quickly you've acted. I'll be staying with my parents for the foreseeable future. I'm certain Simon won't want to face them so I should be okay.'

'Great, well, it's simply a waiting game now. We'll get the paperwork in place and sent off to the CPS but I'm afraid the justice system moves at a snail's pace. It'll be some time before it comes to court. I'd advise you to get a solicitor as soon as possible. He'll be able to help you sort out the practicalities.'

'My dad's already found one. The solicitor advised going to the bank today and that's what we'll do next. Things keep coming to mind and I haven't a clue what I should be doing. It's a good job Dad's taken charge of sorting out this mess. Can you tell me what Simon said about not being at Johnsons?'

'He said he'd left there a few weeks ago but didn't want to tell you until he found something else.' Samantha didn't elaborate further.

'And did you believe him?'

'Sadly, deceiving you isn't a crime – you know him better than me – do you believe his story?'

'No, I don't think I do.'

'I'll be speaking to Diane soon but I'm here if I can do anything to help.' Samantha finished the call leaving Emma with more unanswered questions than before. Where was Simon going to every day if he didn't work at Johnsons? And how long had he been deceiving her about it? She didn't know what to think anymore. It appeared that life with Simon had been a complete sham. Could she believe any of what he'd told her? Emma climbed wearily upstairs to get ready for her trip to the bank.

It was a dark wet day, the late October drizzle reminding Emma that winter was settling in and things would become worse before they improved, in more ways than one. She was grateful for the solid and dependable presence of her father beside her as they drove to the bank. To Emma's relief, George had automatically assumed the role of protector, chauffeur and comforter.

Emma thought about her last visit to the bank. It was before her wedding when, with Simon, they'd opened the joint account. Since then she'd only used her debit card occasionally to withdraw small amounts from the cash machine and had not seen a statement. Emma turned to her father as a thought crossed her mind.

'If I'm not legally called Beecham they might not let me withdraw any money or close the account.'

George manoeuvred the car into the last available parking spot in the town centre car park. 'Jack said you can use the name to access the account as it's the name you opened it in.'

Together they entered the bank – a beautiful Victorian building – a bank since being built in 1860. However, the inside was much more modern with several tills staffed by smiling, uniformed employees. George and Emma chose the till with the shortest queue and were soon greeted by a dark-haired young woman with a pleasant face.

'Could you give me a balance on this account, please?' Emma asked. George had suggested checking the balance first and then transferring the funds into a new account in Emma's name only. The woman took the card Emma offered and entered the details into the computer.

'I'm sorry, but this account has been closed.' Emma was stunned.

George stepped forward. He looked anxious. 'Can you tell us when it was closed?'

'Yes, certainly.' The teller continued tapping, unaware of the panic her words were causing. 'It was only this morning. The balance of three thousand and sixty-two pounds was withdrawn as a cheque, made payable to your husband, Mrs Beecham.' The teller gave a tight smile and returned the card.

'Can the cheque be stopped? There are extenuating circumstances.' George frowned while Emma looked around the bank to see if Simon might still be there. It was only 10am. He must have made the withdrawal within the last hour. She swallowed hard and barely heard the conversation between the teller and her father.

'Perhaps you should speak to one of our supervisors. If you'd like to take a seat, I'll see who's available.' The teller left her seat to find a supervisor while Emma and George moved to the side of the hall and waited on a rather plush bench seat.

'Is three thousand the amount you expected to be in the account, Emma?' George asked.

'No! I thought there'd be much more. My savings were in there and my salary goes in each month – I assumed Simon's did too. We also put in the cheque for ten thousand pounds which you and Mum gave us for a wedding present – we were supposed to be saving up for a deposit and hardly spent anything. We never went out...' It was another shock for her to absorb and there were no other savings accounts she knew of, certainly none in her name. George nodded silently. It appeared Simon was guilty of much more than bigamy.

After ten minutes, they were greeted by a supervisor, a middle-aged capable-looking woman who led them into a cubicle away from the main lobby.

'Mrs Beecham, is it?' the woman asked.

'That's what I thought too.' Emma offered a rather sad smile and explained her situation as briefly as she could.

George smiled at his daughter. Emma had summed the situation up accurately and concisely but now there were tears in her eyes. He took over the conversation.

'Can this cheque be stopped so at least my daughter can have access to some of the funds?'

'I'm afraid we can't stop the cheque without the proper authority. As far as we're concerned, Mr Beecham has done nothing illegal. When the account was opened, both parties agreed that only one signature was needed to withdraw funds. Perhaps this is a matter for your solicitor or the police, but quite honestly, even if we did get authorisation to stop the cheque, by the time it happens, Mr Beecham will probably have cashed it elsewhere.' The woman looked sympathetic yet her hands were tied by protocol.

'What about monies paid into this account?' George was moving on. 'My daughter's salary went in each month. What happens to that?'

'You'll need to open a new account for future payments and inform your employers of the details otherwise they'll be unable to make the payment. I can do it now for you if you like?'

'Yes, please.' Emma took in a deep breath and smiled at the supervisor.

Emma remained quiet and unsurprisingly pensive in the car on the way home. George broke the silence.

'Don't worry about it now. We'll let Jack McArthur know what's happened and he can take it up with the police. You still have a home, Emma, and a family who love you.'

Emma squeezed her father's arm, absorbing his words and feeling comfort in their truth.

CHAPTER EIGHTEEN

Emma felt decidedly weary when they arrived home and asked George to tell her mother what had transpired at the bank. Margaret listened with concern and curiosity as her husband related the full extent of Simon's wrongdoings, shaking her head at what she heard.

Margaret then turned to face Emma. 'Diane's been on the phone. I hope you don't mind but she wanted to come round to talk to you. So I invited her to come after lunch.'

'That's okay. I suppose we still have plenty to discuss.' Emma didn't relish another session with Diane, yet they were curiously linked now and so many thoughts were flooding her mind, things she regretted not asking the day before. Finishing the coffee her mother had thrust into her hands, Emma said she'd like to go upstairs for a rest before Diane came.

'I'll wake you when lunch is ready,' Margaret offered.

'No, don't. I'm not hungry, Mum, just tired – I'd rather sleep. Wake me when Diane comes if I'm not already up.' Emma kissed her parents before escaping to her room, where she lay on the bed and sobbed bitterly until finally falling asleep.

Emma didn't hear the doorbell when Diane arrived. Margaret let their visitor in, leading her through the house into the conservatory overlooking the garden where she thought the two could talk in privacy.

'Wow, what an amazing house you have here, Mrs Porter.' Diane gazed at the sizeable elegant hallway and wide staircase leading to the upstairs.

'Thank you. We like it here.' Margaret smiled. 'And please call me Margaret.'

'I love these paintings. Are they originals?' Diane paused by a row of four watercolours, different landscapes in matching frames.

'Oh, they're all Emma's work – she's quite a talented artist. We have a little studio in the attic where she used to work.' Margaret sighed and added, 'I don't think she's done much painting since she married.'

'She's certainly gifted. They're stunning views.'

'If you'd like to sit down I'll go and fetch Emma. She's been sleeping.' Margaret left their visitor and went to wake her daughter.

Popping her head around the bedroom door, Margaret spoke softly. 'Diane's here. I showed her into the conservatory.'

Emma woke suddenly, somewhat disorientated. When reality dawned, she swung her legs off the bed and dutifully followed her mother downstairs.

'Hi, how are you doing?' Diane's expression held concern and it struck Emma that she, above anyone, knew something of what she was suffering.

'I'm coping – just.' Emma offered a weak smile and sat opposite her visitor. Talking to this woman who was Simon's legal wife felt strange, yet being a *wife* was a status she was by no means sorry to relinquish. Diane was keen to launch into conversation.

'There are dozens of things I wanted to tell you and ask about when we first met; most of them just flew out of my head. I imagine now you've had time to think there are things you want to ask me too?'

'Yes! So many questions keep occurring to me but isn't it rather macabre to want to know about your marriage to Simon? I'm curious to compare notes and it's probably best to present a unified front on the legal side of things too.'

'Talking about legalities, have you found a solicitor yet?' Diane asked.

'Yes, my dad's taken over that side of things – he and Mum have been brilliant about everything. I'd buckle under without their support.'

'My parents were great too.' Diane's mood grew suddenly pensive. 'Emma, are you an only child?'

'Yes, why do you ask?'

'I've been reading up on psychological abuse. It's amazing how much my experience with Simon fits into the classic example. I'm also an only child, and he picked his target well with me. We met soon after the breakup of another relationship when I was so low in confidence that it was easy for him to have me eating out of his hand in a short time. I feel foolish now, but we're all much wiser with hindsight.'

Diane shook her head sadly and continued. 'Psychological abuse often follows a pattern and is well thought out by the perpetrator. The victim is often young, sometimes vulnerable and nearly always an only child. From the perpetrator's point of view, an only child is an easy target because there's less extended family to deal with – he wouldn't want you to have a sister to whom you were close – that would scupper his plans so isolating an only child is much easier. And Simon can be charming; my parents took to him readily and we were engaged and planning the wedding in a very short timeframe. He has a knack for knowing how to make a girl's fantasies about romantic love come true, but it's all a sham. He's a bastard at heart!'

'It sounds so calculated and cunning.' Emma was horrified by the reality of what Simon had done. There were indeed echoes of her own story in Diane's tale.

'It is! Did he discourage you from maintaining any friendships?'

'Oh yes, and deleting the contacts on my mobile phone was presumably part of it?'

'Yep! You're getting the picture, Emma. Tell me, did he suggest taking power of attorney for your parents?'

Emma raised an eyebrow in surprise. 'No, never, but as you're asking, I suppose he did with you?'

'Right again. Another reason an only child is the best target – power of attorney and then all of the inheritance will eventually come to him, through you. And if you don't mind me saying so, your parents have a beautiful home. I would assume they're quite comfortably off?'

'Yes, Dad works for the NHS as a surgeon and has a thriving private practice. I suppose that's part of the attraction?' It was heartbreaking to realise she'd been taken for a fool. Was she really so gullible?

'I'm afraid so.' Diane continued, 'And did Simon handle all your finances?'

'From the very beginning – he convinced me I was no good with money even though I'd managed for years without him.'

'Exactly the same here.' Diane smiled sadly. 'And perhaps if you'd been together longer he might have tried the power of attorney thing. I ended up feeling so inept about everything that in only two years Simon had me exactly where he wanted me, convinced all I could do was hold down my part-time job and look after him. He frequently piled on the guilt about me not being very good at work. I even believe he changed all the clocks in the house at times to confuse me and make me think I was going mad. I became a gibbering wreck. He's nothing short of a monster, a selfish pig of a monster who only left when my parents intervened and he was about to be found out.'

Diane's eyes sparkled with tears as she spoke, from sadness or anger Emma couldn't tell. 'Mum and Dad were increasingly unhappy about not seeing me regularly, so when he suggested power of attorney, they became suspicious and stepped in, asking awkward questions and spoiling all his plans. My parents may be elderly but they're more than capable of taking care of their own affairs; he'd gone too far. I've wondered what his next step would have been if he'd been successful with a power of attorney – to have me declared insane, perhaps? When Mum and Dad insisted on speaking to me, Simon couldn't take the challenge and simply disappeared one day, no goodbyes, no divorce! He even left his workplace without notice or a forwarding address.'

'It must have been so hard for you, Diane.'

'No more than it's been for you. I'm sorry if my approach scared you; I'd tried to summon up the courage to see you before and chickened out.'

'Don't worry about it. I'm grateful, honestly. I was getting to breaking point and don't know how much longer I could have coped. In retrospect, Simon's plan seems almost obvious. He had me just about believing I was going insane, and as I was growing increasingly afraid of him, it became simpler to go along with what he wanted – in every aspect of our life. I'm ashamed to say I even pushed my parents away to please Simon, but his moods could be terrifying – it became easier to give in to him. Anyway,' Emma felt the need to lighten the conversation, 'you have a new man in your life now?'

'Ah, yes, and he's everything Simon isn't. It took some persuasion before I even agreed to go out with him yet I'm so glad I did. He's gorgeous and wants to marry me.' Diane's expression spoke volumes.

'You're so brave to be trying again. I'll probably be off men for a long time after this.'

'That will change in time. If you let Simon sour any future relationships, he's won another victory over you. Don't give him the satisfaction, Emma. Live your life as you want to and to hell with Simon bloody Beecham!'

It was time for Diane to leave and she stood to make her way through the house, pausing again to look at the display of landscapes in the hall.

'Your paintings are amazing, Emma. You're very talented.'

'Thanks.' Emma gave a weak smile. Painting had been her joy but that was her old life when the world was a happy, carefree place. She could no longer imagine mixing her colours and raving over the landscapes she'd once loved so much – Emma felt different, only half the person she'd been before Simon.

Diane left with promises to keep in touch and Emma went back to sit alone in the conservatory for a while, quietly reflecting on their conversation. Hopefully, like Diane, she would also get over this terrible experience enough to trust another man, although that time was surely a long way in the future. Emma first needed to face other people – people who would learn how she'd been deceived. It would prove difficult and embarrassing.

The next hurdle for Emma to face was the appointment with the solicitor, Jack McArthur, and she was grateful her father was on hand to help. She would concentrate on the positives. Emma wasn't destitute and had a home with her parents, a safe, happy home with their love to support her.

CHAPTER NINETEEN

Despite Margaret's protestations of it being too soon, Emma chose to return to work after only three days off.

'The longer I leave it the harder it'll be, Mum,' she insisted, and Margaret couldn't argue with such reasoning. Emma wasn't relishing the prospect of telling her colleagues why she'd been absent, but she couldn't hide away forever and needed to earn a living.

Emma allowed George to take her to work the following Monday morning, a compromise to keep him happy although she insisted she'd make her own way home. She would enjoy the bus journey alone like so many times before Simon. It would be a statement that Emma Porter was reclaiming control of her life.

Taking a deep breath and pulling her shoulders back, Emma entered the dentist's surgery with a smile.

Fiona smiled back. 'Hi, how are you? We've missed you.'

Emma took the question as rhetorical and offered only a vague reply. 'I'm fine, thanks, Fi, and I've missed you too. You'll have to fill me in on all the gossip later.' Undoubtedly more detailed questions would follow, which Emma would feel obliged to answer. The first patient of the day was arriving and the opportunity for a more private conversation would have to wait.

When the chance did present itself at lunchtime, Emma related recent events to Fiona and her friend's genuine concern soon had her spilling out her problems, holding nothing back. Her colleague responded with a spontaneous bear-hug, expressing empathy with genuine warmth. Such kindness brought tears to Emma's eyes and she struggled to keep control.

'I know people say this glibly sometimes, but if there is anything I can do, please ask.' Fiona was sincere, dissolving some of Emma's apprehension about returning to work and making her feel much better. Her friend was proving to be a very wise and empathic confidante.

Emma groaned. 'I feel like a complete idiot to have been taken in so completely.'

'Deception is cruel; it's bound to take time to get over this. It must be difficult to accept that he specifically targeted you – there are people out there who are very skilled at deception and Simon appears to be one of them.'

'But I was so gullible, utterly stupid. How could I have not known?'

'You weren't expecting it, Emma. That's the point about deception; our natural inclination is to trust people, which is generally good. Remember, most people you meet are genuine and hopefully, you'll find someone you can trust one day.'

'I don't know. I'm not sure I'll ever be able to trust a man again.'

'You're bound to feel like that after what you've been through. To get things into perspective, look at the men you do know. There's your father. Can you trust him?'

'Yes, although that's different. He's my dad.'

'He's also your mother's husband. Can *she* trust him?'

'Hmm, I see what you mean.'

'Just because you've been hurt and badly betrayed doesn't mean you won't recover and be a happy woman again.' Fiona's comments made Emma feel much better and encouraged her to share more of her feelings.

'Dad hasn't said as much but I know he's pretty angry about the whole thing. Simon deceived them as well as me. They thought he was the perfect son-in-law, kind and caring before we were married. I feel guilty about the money they spent on the wedding too. They were so good and encouraged me to have everything I wanted. I suppose as their only child they thought it would be a once-in-a-lifetime event. Now we know it was a sham and I'm not legally married. Dad went with me to the bank the day after it all blew up but we were too late. Simon had already been, closed the joint account and taken everything.'

'The bloody bastard! But what will you do? Don't you have funds in your own name?' Fiona stared, incredulous.

Emma shook her head bitterly. 'Simon insisted on handling all our finances. I must seem an idiot, but I didn't expect it to work out like this. I trusted him.'

'Of course you did. Anyone would – don't beat yourself up about it.'

'Anyway, I know Mum and Dad will support me. They've made it clear we're in this together and have made everything so much easier for me to handle. At least I won't have to go through a divorce which Diane has to face, yet there will be other legal problems. Dad's employed a good solicitor to advise us and we'll work through it in time. I was beginning to feel trapped in my relationship with Simon and now I'm suddenly free, although it presents a whole pile of practical problems. I never want to return to that house, yet I suppose I'll have to if only to collect my things.'

Fiona tilted her head to one side. 'Do you know if Simon's gone back there?'

'No, I haven't a clue where he is, but if I do go, it'll be when we're sure he's not there. I can't imagine what would happen if I saw him again.'

'You can ask your solicitor to apply for a restraining order if you're worried he might try to see you.'

'Yes, the police suggested that but I don't think he'll want to see me now he's been found out, especially as he'll have my dad to face. Apparently, when Diane's parents stepped in and asked questions, he disappeared.'

Fiona nodded thoughtfully. 'Bullies are often exposed as the cowards they are when they're eventually confronted.'

'It could take months for it all to come to court. At least I still have a roof over my head. And I've no idea what sentence he'll get – hopefully a long custodial one.' Emma hadn't thought to ask Samantha about jail time. 'Regrettably, I'll probably not get any money back – I don't know what Simon's done with it all – there should have been much more in our joint account. We deposited the money Mum and Dad gave us as a wedding present in there, and I had more than that in savings. I'll be glad to put all this behind me, although it seems I'll have to be patient. It's incredible, isn't it – how he got away with it.'

Having talked it all out, Emma felt much better for sharing, and Fiona promised to explain the bones of the situation to their colleagues so Emma didn't have to repeat her story. They were a close-knit supportive group and would undoubtedly be understanding.

With Fiona's sympathetic reaction, Emma felt a little ashamed of her worries about returning to work. Perhaps it was another effect of Simon's undermining of her confidence. It was slowly dawning on her just how much her *husband* had, over time, chipped away at her self-assurance, altering her previous outgoing personality and making her an introverted dependent wife. Emma knew rebuilding her life wouldn't be easy yet her resolve to do so was growing by the hour. At least going to work wasn't the trial she'd anticipated. Her first day back couldn't have gone any better – so far.

CHAPTER TWENTY

Samantha Freeman yawned. She was on a late shift and wouldn't finish until 10pm. Moreover, her back ached after hours spent bending over her computer screen – she longed for fresh air and decent coffee. Perhaps a quick walk over the road to the deli could provide both, and then another hour and she'd finish for the day. The telephone ringing changed her plans.

'DI Freeman? This is George Porter, Emma's father.' The man was breathless. Sam could hear the panic in his voice. 'Emma hasn't come home from work and we're getting worried. She's not answering her phone either. It's not like her!'

'What time were you expecting her?' Sam spoke slowly, attempting to instil a degree of calm in George Porter.

'She should have been home just after six – I wanted to pick her up but she refused – Emma wanted to get the bus as she did before Simon.'

'And are you at home now, Mr Porter?'

'Yes. Do you think I should go out looking for her?' His voice cracked, heavy with emotion.

'No, stay there and try not to worry. There could be an innocent explanation but I'm coming round anyway.' Samantha didn't believe her own words. Adrenaline was pumping through her veins as she thought of Simon Beecham's smug face, convinced he had something to do with Emma's sudden disappearance.

It was nearly 10pm when Samantha pulled up in front of the Porters' large detached house and the rain was drumming on the little Mini giving the familiar feeling of being in a sardine tin. The house was well lit and she could see the couple peering anxiously from the window, awaiting her arrival.

After almost dragging Samantha into the hallway, a red-eyed Margaret gripped the detective's arm. 'Do you think Simon's got her?'

'It's something we must consider although Emma could still turn up. Have you tried to ring any of her friends?' Sam asked the routine questions, going through the process before searching for Simon Beecham.

George answered. 'She doesn't see any of her old friends – we did ring Fiona, the girl she works with, Emma gave us her mobile number once, but she told us Emma left the surgery at 5.30 as usual.'

'Did Fiona say how Emma was feeling, what her mood was?'

George cast Samantha a knowing glance, suspecting the reason for these questions; his daughter had been through a traumatic experience yet surely wouldn't harm herself.

Margaret answered. 'Only that her first day had gone well. Emma was apparently quite upbeat and glad to be back.' Sam had a mental picture of the Porters huddled around the telephone, on speaker, eagerly hoping for a simple explanation for their daughter's disappearance.

'What about Diane Beecham? Do you think Emma could be with her?'

'I know they've been keeping in touch and Diane's been here to visit. We never thought of her.'

Samantha took out her phone and located Diane's number. The woman answered immediately but claimed not to have seen or heard from Emma. Her voice betrayed her concern. If anyone knew what Simon Beecham was capable of, it was Diane.

'Right, I'm going to Beecham's house – do you have a key? If he's not there, I'd like to look around. And also could I take that photo of Emma and Simon on their wedding day? I'll make sure you get it back.' Sam was decisive. She worked best under pressure.

'Do you want me to come?' George asked.

'No. I need you both to stay here and if Emma comes home ring me immediately. Keep trying her phone. She could have simply forgotten it was switched off.' None of them believed this – with everything which had happened over the last few days, they knew Emma would never be so irresponsible or thoughtless as to be so late home without letting her parents know. George retrieved Emma's house key from her bedroom and gave it to DI Freeman while Margaret took the photograph from the frame.

'Keep it,' she said. 'We don't want to be reminded of that particular day anymore.'

As Sam left the Porters' home, she glanced admiringly at the colourful landscapes on the wall.

'They're Emma's work. She loves painting.' Margaret sniffed, dabbing her eyes with a tissue.

Samantha smiled. 'They're beautiful. Emma's very talented.'

'Yes, she is...' Margaret's voice was breaking.

As she left, Samantha squeezed the older woman's arm. 'I'll do my best to find her, Mrs Porter.' Then she was on her phone, calling for backup to meet her at the address of the rented house where Emma and Simon had lived.

The rain poured steadily, huge puddles forming in the potholes of the narrow roads in the part of town where Samantha was heading. The place was in darkness as she pulled up on the little terraced street. It was a complete contrast to the house she'd just left, drab and uncared for and needing more than a little TLC. Somehow Sam couldn't imagine Emma living in a place like this – a girl who'd grown up with loving parents – who wanted for nothing. Yet Emma had been led to believe it was only temporary and better times would come.

Sam tapped her fingers on the steering wheel, anxious to get inside. It looked as if Beecham wasn't there unless he'd gone to bed early, but she wanted to search the place anyway and with Emma being missing and at risk, Sam was confident she could waive a warrant in the circumstances. She quickly rang Jenny Newcombe to bring her up to speed with what was happening. Jenny offered to join her at the house, but Sam declined.

'Backup should be here any time now and I need you to be in early tomorrow. It looks like we could have a full-scale search on our hands.' Sam shivered at the thought, wondering where Emma was and more pertinently how she was.

A squad car pulled up behind Samantha's Mini and she jumped out, keen to get moving. A lanky PC unfolded himself from the driving seat apologising for taking so long. Samantha waved his apology away. She'd only been there five minutes, although it seemed longer. The officer was well over six feet tall, making Sam feel like a little girl beside him. However, built like a shed, his bulk was reassuring as he took up position beside her on the doorstep, both soaked from the pouring rain. There was no answer to the bell and Samantha didn't hesitate to use Emma's key.

Once inside and with the light on, the constable, Gary Cox, asked what they were looking for.

'Primarily a missing young woman.' Seeing surprise cross his face, the DI expounded. 'I'm not looking for a body at this time, although we can't rule it out so search every nook and cranny however unlikely. I'm looking for evidence of another property owned by this perp, or something out of the ordinary. Anything of interest, give me a shout.'

PC Cox ran upstairs while Sam moved into the kitchen. The fridge was almost empty and as she sniffed a milk carton, the sharp sour odour suggested Beecham wasn't living there – unless he was an absolute slob, which the general cleanliness of the place didn't suggest.

Moving into the lounge Sam first checked the understairs cupboard – holding her breath without realising it – just the usual glory hole – ironing board, vacuum cleaner and assorted household items. Breathing a sigh of relief, she rummaged through the sideboard drawers.

Strangely there were no copies of bills, utility or otherwise and no bank statements. Beecham must keep them elsewhere. There were also no clues as to another address where she might find him and this was the only one he'd given at his arrest. He wasn't due to report to the station until the next day, a week since this case had landed in Sam's lap. Now she had doubts about whether or not he would appear and regretted not taking his passport.

PC Cox thundered down the stairs, answering Samantha's expectant look with a shake of his head. 'Nothing you wouldn't expect. It looks rather sparse, with more women's clothes than men's. Is that what you'd expect?'

'No, it should be the other way round.' Sam ran up the stairs two at a time to see for herself. It appeared Simon had removed most of his clothes and toiletry items from the bathroom – done a runner – her instincts screamed at her, but did he have Emma with him? There were still several of Emma's clothes in the wardrobe yet Sam knew the woman had left in a hurry taking only a few essentials and probably hadn't wanted to return for fear of bumping into Beecham.

From the bottom of the wardrobe, Sam pulled out a wooden box and a sketch pad, curious why Emma would leave them. Opening the box gave her an explanation as very little was useable – maybe she'd taken most of her art equipment back to her parents' place. Thumbing through the sketch pad, Samantha came across the charcoal picture of a dark, depressingly ugly house. It wasn't this house, it was much larger, yet it wasn't the Porters' either.

Remembering her training in basic psychology, Sam imagined this to be an image of how Emma saw herself as Simon's wife – this dismal house was the young woman's life – unwelcoming, cold and fearsome, without animation, breath or colour. It was the complete antithesis of those beautiful colourful landscapes hanging in pride of place in the Porters' hallway. Is this what Emma's life had become, what Beecham had cruelly moulded her into in only a few short months?

Samantha discovered nothing of further use or interest in the house and sent PC Cox home before locking the front door and climbing back into her Mini. Making the necessary phone call to the Porters was heartbreaking. They needed to know she hadn't found Emma, but there was nothing good she could offer them as consolation except a promise to rigorously search for Simon Beecham and do her best to find their daughter.

The DI doubted George and Margaret Porter would get much sleep that night and Sam would also struggle to rest. One last thing she could do was contact the station and put an APB out on Beecham's car. Yet the man proved a clever adversary; it was doubtful he'd still be using the same vehicle.

Cold, wet and tired, Samantha finally went home to rest. She would be back at the station organising a massive hunt for Emma Porter in just seven hours.

CHAPTER TWENTY-ONE

It was reminiscent of setting up a murder incident room, a notion which sat heavily on Samantha's mind. Could she have foreseen Beecham would be this dangerous? Perhaps not but doubts always niggle with a bit of encouragement from retrospection.

'Of course, we can't be sure that Beecham is involved in her disappearance,' Jenny reminded her boss, a sentiment she didn't subscribe to either.

'Okay, so where are we now?' Standing in front of a large whiteboard with blown-up photographs of Emma Porter and Simon Beecham, Sam called her team to attention. The irony that the images had been cut apart from the wedding photograph wasn't lost on the small assembled group.

'We know there's been no one of Emma's description admitted to any local hospitals so what have we got?' Sam looked hopefully to her colleagues, marker pen in hand, ready to go.

'We have Beecham's car registration number logged into ANPR, so if he's on any major roads nationwide, we'll find him,' DC Paul Roper offered. 'And I've been onto his mobile phone provider. If he uses it we'll get a ping and be able to triangulate the call, unless he's ditched the phone he told us about.'

Roper was confident. He was a good detective who should have made sergeant by now but had recently failed his first attempt at the exam. Samantha wasn't surprised. Paul was a valuable team member, intelligent and intuitive but laziness let him down. If he came across a corner, Paul Roper would cut it and his boss was pretty sure he'd not prepared sufficiently for the exam, assuming his natural ability would see him through. Still, she was grateful to have him working with her and his skills on the computer were an asset.

'I've started the full disclosure and found several gaps from his early years with some of the details sketchy to say the least. Employment history has gaps in it too,' Jenny chipped in.

ANPR – Sam wrote on the board, then *Triangulation* and *Disclosure* underneath. A dash after each one with a space seemed to emphasise the lack of information but she mentally scolded herself – it wasn't even 9am – they were up and running, the hunt was only beginning.

'Keep at it, everyone,' Samantha said to the little group. 'Jenny, you come with me, first to the Porters and then we're going to visit Diane Beecham.'

In the car, Jenny rang Diane to ensure she'd be available after they'd seen the Porters. The woman was about to leave for work but agreed to stay until they'd been. Diane sounded incredibly concerned and expressed regret at being the catalyst for all this trouble. Unfortunately, Jenny could say nothing positive to assuage her fears, nothing which didn't sound patronising anyway.

The Porters' house was quiet with a single light in the kitchen, the room where the two detectives were shown into. George and Margaret looked pale and tired and admitted they'd not slept. Margaret offered coffee which the visitors accepted if only to give the woman something to do.

Samantha gave a brief outline of the wheels they'd set in motion.

'So you do think Simon's taken her?' George looked a decade older than the day before, worry lines defining his face, his voice small and weak.

'It's a fairly logical assumption, I'm afraid, and the present line of enquiry we're taking.' Sam felt they deserved honesty. It was how she worked.

'Have you had any more thoughts on where she could be?' Jenny asked. 'Did they have access to a friend's holiday home, for instance, or did Simon have any other property he mentioned?' She knew it was a long shot but the man had to be somewhere and if Emma wasn't with him, Beecham would surely know where she was.

As she passed around mugs of steaming coffee with trembling hands, Margaret looked exhausted. 'No, we've wracked our brains all night and come up with nothing. Simon didn't appear to have many friends if any. He claimed it was because he'd moved around a lot as a child – he grew up in care – foster homes and the like.'

'Do you know if he had contact with any of these foster families? Perhaps some of them came to the wedding,' Jenny persisted.

Margaret groaned at the mention of the wedding and shook her head. 'It was only our side of the family. Simon said there was no one he wanted to invite. We should have suspected something was wrong then, shouldn't we?'

The tears fell again as George slid a protective arm around her shoulder. Samantha knew the Porters were thinking the worst yet she could offer nothing concrete to alter their thought processes.

'What about a best man? Surely he had someone there to support him?' Jenny continued.

'There was an old friend, Alex, I think his name was – he lives in Edinburgh and was to be the best man, but a few days before the wedding his mother died quite suddenly and he backed out. Simon was devastated but it was too late to ask anyone else – he did without.'

'And do you have an address for this *Alex*?' Sam asked.

'No. Maybe there's one at Emma's?' George suggested. But Sam hadn't seen anything resembling an address book during her search the previous night.

'Did Emma ever meet Alex, do you know?'

'Again, no. Simon never mentioned him again. We wondered if they'd fallen out – if he'd felt let down.'

'Where was Simon living before he and Emma married, Mr Porter?'

'He had a flat on the north side of town, the one near North Park, I think.'

'Do you have an address?'

'No, sorry. We never actually visited Simon there. He always came here – said it was a pokey bachelor flat which he didn't want us to see. It was a bit of a standing joke with him and Emma. I think he was embarrassed about it so we didn't make an issue of it.'

Jenny and Samantha exchanged looks, both feeling rather uncomfortable.

'It seems stupid now, doesn't it?' Margaret said. 'We knew so little about him, although we did spend plenty of time with him – he was always here with Emma or they were out at some nice restaurant or the theatre, and he had a secure job, a responsible position, or so we thought.'

'Can we look at Emma's room, please?' Jenny asked, moving off the subject.

'Yes, but I don't know if you'll find anything to help you.' George stood to lead the way, his steps heavy and slow.

The room was neat as a pin, bright and airy, with one of Emma's paintings on the wall above the bed. Jenny stared at it.

'That's Alnwick, isn't it?' she asked George.

'Yes, Emma painted it from photographs she'd taken on one of our visits. We love Northumberland.'

'Emma painted it? It's lovely.' Sam moved into the little en suite attached to the room. Only a few items were on display, the essentials Emma had grabbed in her hurry to leave her 'marital' home. A quick poke around by the detectives revealed nothing of significance.

'Do you know if Emma has an address book?' Jenny asked.

'She didn't bring one here if she has but I think she keeps most details on her phone. It's the modern way, isn't it?' George shrugged his shoulders, looking helpless, lost.

The trio returned to the kitchen with nothing new learned.

'We're going to interview Diane next. She might know of a place Simon would run to and a team back at the station is looking into his past life – work history and such. Naturally, we'll keep you informed and if you think of anything, no matter how trivial it might seem, please ring.' The couple nodded and thanked Samantha and Jenny as they left the house and hurried off to their next destination.

Both women felt a sense of relief in leaving the house, which seemed to have had all the life sucked out of its walls, a place which appeared to be waiting for something to happen, its occupants anticipating the worst.

'He's quite a mystery man, our Mr Beecham. Do you think he's been spinning them a yarn about this Alex character – the best man? I don't think he exists,' Jenny said.

'You could be right. Simon's certainly a charmer and had

them all taken in. We need to find an address for Beecham in the north end of town. Give Paul a ring. This is his forte.'

'The Porters are such a lovely couple. I do hope things work out for them. Emma seems to be their whole world.' Jenny spoke quietly.

'I've not given up hope yet. We'll find Beecham, no matter what,' Samantha replied, her mouth set into a firm line.

CHAPTER TWENTY-TWO

Diane Beecham lived with her boyfriend in a neat semi-detached house on an estate at the edge of New Middridge, a pleasant area which would be lovely in the summer, albeit rather muddy now. Her car was in the drive and she was watching from the window, keen to learn if there was any news. Unfortunately, Samantha and Jenny had none.

'How are Emma's parents holding up?' Diane asked, leading them into the house.

'Not good, as you'd expect.' The three sat in the lounge and having declined coffee the detectives commenced their questions.

'Can you think of anywhere Simon might run to if he was in a fix?' Sam asked.

Diane shook her head slowly and sighed.

'Not really. I've been trying to think of somewhere since you rang but with no luck. When we were married we didn't do holidays, or even friends come to think of it. It was pretty much as it's been for Emma, almost complete isolation with only each other for company. Simon even shunned my family, trying to separate me from them.'

'Where did he work during your marriage?' Jenny asked, taking notes.

'He worked for an estate agent, not a partner or anything, just showing clients around properties and brokering sales, that kind of thing.'

On hearing this Sam's mind went off at a tangent imagining Simon with a huge bunch of keys and access to all kinds of empty properties – endless possibilities to hide someone, hours of work to search for them.

Diane continued. 'It was Moore and King, who've sadly closed down since then. I think Mr Moore died and his partner took the opportunity to retire about three years ago.'

The words dashed Sam's hope. It was quite a stretch anyway and too far back in the past.

'When we split up, and it was quite a fiery split in the end, Simon left work without notice and disappeared hence not getting a divorce which didn't bother me until recently. I was glad to be rid of him at the time, my life had become a misery and I was on the point of a breakdown. I feel rather guilty for starting all this now. Do you think Emma's really in danger?'

Samantha wasn't prepared to speculate. 'We're making her safety a priority.'

'How did you and Simon meet?' Jenny asked. Building up a complete picture sometimes shook loose information which could be relevant.

'In a coffee shop in 2015. Simon was behind me in rather a long queue and we started chatting. He seemed such a lovely man and I fell for him almost immediately. Although, in my defence, he behaved entirely differently before we were married. It was only afterwards that the Jekyll and Hyde personality came out. He's very manipulative and controlling but seems to possess a knack for making you think he's always in the right – after the first year of our marriage I was a nervous wreck.' Diane's eyes dulled as she spoke about that time.

Jenny felt guilty for having asked but wanted to know more. 'So, how did you manage to extricate yourself from the relationship?'

'Controlling me wasn't enough for Simon. He wanted to make decisions for my parents too – ironic as he'd tried to push them out of my life. My dad was in a wheelchair with MS, and Simon seemed to equate this with mental deficiency. Not so! Dad knew his own mind, and when Simon began pushing to take control of my parents' finances, Dad put his foot down. They were far from needing anyone to have power of attorney over them and still don't. The mere suggestion prompted Dad to ask questions.' Diane paused and took a breath.

'Dad pushed his way back into my life for which I will be eternally grateful and I confided in him exactly how unhappy I was. Stupidly, I maintained it was all my fault and that I'd failed as a wife. Dad saw things differently and confronted my husband. Things became pretty ugly then and I think Simon simply decided to cut his losses and run – only it wasn't him left with the losses – he emptied our bank account and left me with debts on the house and several bills. I'd have gone under without my parents' help.

'I think it's been pretty much the same for Emma, the poor girl, and in an even shorter timeframe. When I pulled myself together enough to want a divorce, Simon wasn't anywhere to be found. He'd left his job without notice and no one knew where he lived. I let it ride for a while until I met Jim, my new boyfriend. We've been living together for a year, but he wants me to marry him before we start a family, so I decided to look for Simon.'

'Did Simon have any friends when you married, Diane,

maybe someone he invited to the wedding, a best man maybe?' Samantha asked.

Diane shook her head sadly. 'I wish I could say yes but no, there's no one. When we met, Simon was an introvert which I put down to his unhappy upbringing in care and I felt quite sorry for him. I suppose the desire to rescue him became confused with love. He was a damaged human being from the start. It was only looking back on some of the things he did which made me realise how sick he is. I should have questioned him more about why his first marriage didn't work out...'

'His first marriage?' Sam gasped, stunned. 'But I thought you were his first wife?'

'Er, no, didn't I say at the interview? When I met Simon, he was divorced. His first marriage ended after only a few months.'

Sam's eyes were bright with new enthusiasm. Finally, here was another lead, a badly needed lead and one she wanted to pursue immediately. 'Can you give me any details, Diane?' She wanted to know everything this woman knew and begin searching for Simon's first wife as soon as possible. 'Her name and an address?'

'Sorry, he rarely spoke about her. They lived in Newcastle upon Tyne and she was called Angela but that's all I can tell you, I'm afraid.'

Equally as fired up as Samantha, Jenny jumped up from her seat and stepped out of the room to ring Paul Roper, asking him to find out the whereabouts of Angela Beecham, if she was still using the name, and giving him Newcastle as the only clue. It was a big ask yet if anyone could locate the woman, Paul could.

Jenny nodded to her boss as she entered the room again and Samantha knew the wheels were in motion. 'Diane, is there anything else you think might help us?'

The woman looked sheepish. 'I'm sorry, I should have told

you about his first marriage before. I didn't think it mattered. Do you think it's important?'

'I honestly don't know but it gives us another line of enquiry and we're looking into every possibility at the moment. Please ring me if anything else occurs to you and thanks for being so candid with us. It helps us to build a bigger picture of Simon and hopefully lead us to the man himself.'

CHAPTER TWENTY-THREE

'Got anything for us, Paul?' Samantha asked as she struggled out of her coat.

'It's only been twenty minutes since Jenny called, boss.' He rolled his eyes. 'Why do you all expect instant results from computers? It's a matter of knowing where to look, the right keywords to type in and a dozen other factors. I need time, even to work a miracle.' Paul's search list was growing with the addition of another wife and the mystery flat near North Park.

'Well, as soon as – shout me.' Sam was wired and moved to another team member, DC Layla Gupta, who was working on the disclosure into Beecham's past. 'Anything of interest, Layla?' Samantha was almost prowling, anxious for a break.

'I've got a list of schools he attended, some locally and one in Newcastle, the Felling district. It appears our man was a poor attender for some reason, perhaps a rough childhood?' Sam raised an eyebrow at Layla's sympathetic tone. But schools were a long shot. Sam didn't want to go as far back until other avenues were exhausted, it would be time-consuming with possibly very little by way of results, and with Emma missing, they didn't have the luxury of time to spare.

'What about a record, anything interesting?'

'A speeding ticket for which he paid the fine – didn't fancy the course.'

That figures, Samantha thought, Beecham didn't seem to like being told what to do. He needed to be in charge. She went back to Jenny's desk.

'What if the first wife has changed her name, gone back to her maiden name? I know I would,' Jenny considered.

'Paul – have you searched the marriage records yet?' Samantha shouted over to the detective constable.

'Not yet. I'm doing the electoral role and DVLA – marriage records are next on my list.' He ran his fingers through his mop of dark curly hair.

'Let Layla do the marriage records – Layla, leave the disclosure. We've got all that's going to be useful for now. Take over the marriage records. You're looking for Simon Beecham, a marriage before 2015 when he met his second wife. I need to know the maiden name of wife number one.'

It was 11am. Emma Porter had been missing for less than eighteen hours. Usually the police wouldn't become involved until an adult was missing for forty-eight hours but this was different. There were extenuating circumstances and Sam was becoming antsy; a lot could happen in eighteen hours and she was finding it difficult to rein in her imagination. The DI needed coffee and a break from the buzz of the office.

'I'm going across the street, Jenny. Want a coffee?' she asked.

Jenny kept her eyes focussed on her computer where she typed the notes from the morning's interviews. 'Please.'

It was raining again. Sam dashed into the deli and put in an order for coffee for the whole team. It said something about their relationship that they each knew how the others liked their coffee, how many sugars Paul liked, and skinny milk for Layla.

Sam asked for a bag of assorted pastries too. They needed the energy as goodness only knew when they'd have time for a proper meal.

She took a minute to sit in the window seat, waiting for her order to be filled. The rain drizzled down the glass and Samantha traced it with her finger. Where would she go if she wanted to hide someone? No answer came, but she wasn't Simon Beecham, a charlatan, a bully but hopefully not a murderer – although she couldn't rule out the possibility even if the idea had not yet been verbalised.

The coffee and pastries were welcomed by all in the little office as they worked under pressure. Paul and Layla remained in their seats, concentration etched on their faces knowing that moving on the investigation rested primarily on their shoulders.

Jenny passed the pastries around and then sat beside Samantha. 'Do you really think this Angela holds the key to where Simon is?' Samantha sighed.

'I know it looks as if I'm pinning all my hopes on a rank outsider yet what else have we got? And at least this gives us a new location. Beecham will find it much easier to disappear in Newcastle than in New Middridge. Jenny, will you call the Porters and tell them we're still going flat out on this? I know we haven't anything concrete to tell them...'

'Got her!' Layla's voice rang out and Jenny and Sam scooted over to her desk.

'Angela Elizabeth Maddison married Simon Beecham on September 5th 2011.' The young DC grinned, clearly proud to be the one to make the discovery.

'Well done, Layla, have another pastry!' Sam could have hugged her but instead peered over her shoulder to read the details in the register.

'The address will presumably be Angela's parents. Jenny,

take a note of this and find a phone number for the Maddisons.' Samantha's energy levels were rising and it wasn't just the sugar rush. It was tempting to jump in the car and set off to Newcastle, less than an hour's drive away but Angela Maddison would probably not be living with her parents now or nearby. There was more digging to do before meeting Simon's first wife.

'Do you want to make the call?' Jenny waved a slip of paper in her hand.

'Good stuff, give!' Samantha grabbed the number and punched it in on her phone. Jenny listened to her boss speaking to someone and a sigh of relief escaped her lips; unfortunately, finding people at home when they rang wasn't always easy and getting mobile numbers for people was even more problematic. But Sam's expression changed to one of disappointment as she listened to the voice on the other end of the line – then suddenly her smile returned.

'That's really helpful, Mrs Howard, thank you.' She ended the call and waved her phone around. 'The Howard family bought the house from Mrs Maddison in 2011, around the time of Simon and Angela's wedding. She doesn't know where Angela is but is reasonably sure her mother's in a local nursing home, Fairweather Court. Find the contact details will you, Layla?' The young DC was already working her keyboard and, within a minute, recited a number which Sam tapped into her phone.

Introducing herself, the DI was transferred to the matron and a rather frustrating conversation ensued. After speaking sharply to the woman, Sam ended the call and looked up at Jenny.

'Matron won't give me the address of Mrs Maddison's next of kin. She won't even reveal if the woman is still a resident – data protection – she says I could be anybody.'

'She has a point; do you want me to arrange for a local PC to visit her for the information?'

'No. Grab your coat, Jenny, we're off to Felling.'

CHAPTER TWENTY-FOUR

Emma could hardly move. Her limbs ached and a sharp pain shot through her head when she tried to move her neck.

Where the hell was she?

There was something over her face, a bag of some description which smelled of sackcloth and her mouth was gagged so tightly she couldn't shout out. Darkness enveloped her, but whether it was due to the bag or because it was night-time, there was no way of telling.

After an initial panic shuffling, Emma disciplined herself to breathe – in and out – not too deeply or she'd be dizzy. Questions crowded her mind. Where was she? Why was she trussed up like this and who could have done it? The answer to the last question came first – Simon!

Think, Emma, think!

Moving her arms proved impossible. They were tied behind her back hence the aching shoulders and the pain when she tried to wriggle free. Her legs were stiff but unbound so she attempted to stand. Nausea washed over her – she fell back, fearing being sick and choking with the gag in her mouth.

Remaining still seemed to be the best option, at least until she formed some sort of plan.

Ha! A plan, what is this, a bad film, a nightmare?

Listening seemed to be the only thing Emma could do without feeling ill or dizzy, so she took another deep breath and listened. Nothing except the distant sound of rain drumming on a roof or window somewhere, steady rain, nothing unusual for the end of October. Was it night-time? She'd obviously been out cold and could remember nothing after leaving the surgery after work – so – how did she get here, wherever *here* was?

The aching limbs, nausea and dizziness suggested she'd been drugged. Would Simon have the brains to do it? His darker side was becoming increasingly evident, an insight helped by Diane, who'd suffered many of the same awful experiences as she had. The man appeared to thrive on cruelty, a sobering thought which led to another more fearful one – why had he kidnapped her and brought her here?

Revenge, punishment, retribution? All of the above and more?

As Emma shuffled about and thought about her predicament, the more information she gleaned from her surroundings. She was sitting on a hard floor, wooden but smooth with no carpet. The space she was in felt large and empty, yet the hollowness Emma experienced could be from within her body, an after-effect of whatever drug Simon had used to knock her out. It was cool but not cold, suggesting a house or partially heated building. Someone had removed Emma's coat and her shoes. Fortunately, her clothes were still on her body. Although she'd been married to the man and intimate with him the thought of being undressed in his presence sickened her.

Emma breathed in the darkness through her nose. There were no tell-tale odours other than the bag. The silence also didn't enlighten her. She could have been anywhere if it was the middle of the night. Her thoughts turned away from her own dilemma as an image of her parents flitted across her mind. Her eyes stung with tears. What would they be going through and how long had she been missing? Emma was confident her Dad would have rung the police immediately – unless instructed otherwise.

Kidnap, ransom, money. Simon wants more money!

It was a plausible idea. Emma had learned the hard way what a greedy man he was. He'd taken her money and her parents', although it was beyond her comprehension what he'd done with it. Possibilities sped through her mind, including drugs, and an image of Simon shooting heroin flashed through her head, but wouldn't she have known if he had a drug habit?

Simon liked to dress well, better than Emma, and she didn't know when or where he bought his clothes. Yet the house they lived in was shabby and far from luxurious. The man was inconsistent, an enigma, impossible to fathom. Could he have a gambling problem? But again they spent so much time together – except he wasn't going to work when he pretended he was.

So where the hell had he been going?

Emma tried to stand for a second time, slowly, without moving her head – onto her knees first and then a halting push upwards until she managed to plant one foot on the floor. Then, after a short break and an effort to push up onto both feet, she experienced a sense of triumph at this simple success. But what next?

She could explore her surroundings but in the dark and with her hands tied there was the real fear that she'd trip or fall off an unseen height, an open staircase, perhaps? Yet it was only by moving around that she'd learn more about her situation. So, placing one foot in front of the other, pinhead steps, Emma tentatively explored the room with her feet.

Ten steps before she hit the first obstacle. Her shin collided first – something low and solid, a coffee table? Emma rubbed her leg along the edge of the object, exploring. It was hard and about three feet long with a sharp corner, yes, definitely a coffee table – she was most likely in a room in a house.

Moving slowly and keeping her body stiff made her ache. It was like walking on ice when you were afraid to bend your knees for fear of falling. She needed a rest but didn't want to sit down again so kept going. Eight more baby steps and she struck a wall, stubbing her toe but it was solid enough for her to turn round and lean on for respite. Emma took deep breaths and tried to relax her body. If she could free her hands maybe she'd be able to remove the sack from her head and work on the gag. Perhaps that was where she should expend her energies.

With her shoulders pressed on the wall for support, Emma wriggled her hands. Her fingers were long and slim, and her wrists narrow, but the binding was tight. Being behind her back made the task difficult and her skin felt sore after only a few minutes. Frustration bubbled inside and tears filled her eyes.

Pull yourself together, Emma. You have to do this!

It was no good; the binding was too tight, her wrists were raw, and her skin was bruised if not broken. Emma slid slowly down the wall to a sitting position, allowing the tears to fall. For ten minutes or more, she held her own little pity party, feeling sorry for herself, being what Fiona would label a PLOM – Poor Little Old Me.

The tears dried up and Emma sniffed hard. She raised her head and thought she detected a change in the light. Turning her head one way and then the other, she decided yes, to her right it was definitely getting lighter; dawn must be breaking. Did it mean there was a window there? Could she make her way towards it and bang her head on the glass to gain attention?

Emma struggled to stand again, her legs aching and her

shoulders painful but when she managed to get to her feet she was stopped by the sound of a door opening nearby. It wasn't in the room where she stood – she figured it must be the front door to the house or whatever place this was.

Silently Emma listened – the heavy tread of someone getting closer, the flick of a light switch. Emma could see a bar of light to her right through the sack on her head, a gap under a door perhaps? She shuffled back to the wall, pressing her spine against the robust structure, furious at its solidity and inability to allow her to melt into its fabric and disappear.

Emma had never felt so alone and exposed. Her head throbbed.

Is this the end? Am I going to die?

CHAPTER TWENTY-FIVE

On the way to Felling, Jenny called the Porters while Samantha drove. It was a difficult call. Apart from the stock phrase of 'following new lines of inquiry', they could disclose little. Jenny did share the surprising discovery of Simon Beecham having been married before Diane and listened to Margaret Porter's gasp. The news that they were currently trying to find this first wife was met with the question, 'Do you think she'll know where Simon is?' A hope they all harboured yet realistically doubted.

'It's a matter of gathering as much information as possible, Mrs Porter, shaking the tree to see what falls.' It was of little comfort except to reassure the couple that the police were working hard to find their daughter.

Fairweather Court was a long low building, sixties built and needing a complete overhaul or, Sam thought, pulling down. However, the inside was at least warm with cheerful if dated décor and a buzz of happy busyness. The buxom matron, Mrs Palmer, was as fearful in the flesh as she'd been on the phone and took the detectives' ID cards to scrutinise closely before leading them to her office.

'You can't be too careful,' she said. 'We adhere to all the new data protection procedures. So how can I help you?' Her smile was polite yet her manner suggested she had better things to do.

'Mrs Maddison,' Samantha reminded her, 'is she a resident here and if so can we see her?'

'Ah, Elsie Maddison, she's been here nearly ten years now – follow me. She'll be in her room as usual.' Mrs Palmer set off at pace, turning corners and weaving through a rabbit warren of corridors until she stopped at room 53. The door was ajar and a woman lay motionless in a high-sided bed, rails on one side and the wall on the other.

'A stroke,' the matron explained. 'Which is why she came to us initially and there's been very little change ever since. Elsie can't communicate but is aware of her surroundings.'

The woman's plight touched Sam yet she was growing increasingly frustrated. Time was moving on and their investigation seemed to lag behind.

'Can you give us details of Mrs Maddison's next of kin? We must speak to her daughter.'

'Angela, yes of course – you should have said.' Matron set off back through the labyrinth to her office where she tapped on the computer then wrote an address and phone number on a medical pad, tore off the paper with a flourish and gave it to Jenny. 'Keir Hardy Avenue isn't far from here and she'll probably be at home as she has little ones. Can you tell me what this is all about, Inspector?'

Sam smiled her sweetest smile and headed towards the front door. 'Sorry, no. Data protection prevents it. But thanks for your help.'

———

'Time-waster,' Sam muttered as she started the engine. 'She could have told us the poor woman couldn't speak before leading us to her.'

Jenny was busy ringing Angela's number. Her surname was Knight; presumably she'd re-married. The woman was at home and surprised to hear from the police, although mentioning Simon's name seemed to answer her unspoken questions.

Keir Hardy Avenue was opposite a school where infants played noisily in the yard; it was just after 2pm, playtime. A kettle was singing in the kitchen as Angela Knight invited the two women inside and they readily accepted her offer of tea. Angela balanced a baby on her hip and deftly made the tea as if used to the appendage. A little boy of about three played on the floor with toy cars, making engine noises louder than the original would be.

'I was surprised to get your call. To be perfectly honest I'd hoped never to hear the name Simon Beecham ever again. So, what's he done now?'

'Have you seen your ex-husband recently, Mrs Knight?' Jenny asked.

A pained look crossed her face at the memory. 'Not since the divorce – no, before that even – 2012 would be the last time I laid eyes on him. The solicitors sorted out the divorce. I wasn't up to seeing anyone then, and please call me Angela.'

'You asked what he's done. We think he may be holding a young woman against her will. Have you any idea of a place he might go to hide?'

'Oh, poor sod. A girlfriend is it?' Angela pushed a plate of biscuits toward her visitors.

'It's a woman Simon married yet failed to mention he was already married to someone else. Your ex-husband is a bigamist; our fear now is that he's abducted this woman. Is there anywhere at all you can think of where he might go to hide?'

Samantha's voice was almost pleading. They needed a break. Could this woman provide it?

'I'm sorry – nothing comes to mind. We were very young when we married, too young. It was a disaster from day one. We lived in Felling in a rented house. Simon had nothing except ideas of grandeur and a desire for money – there's nowhere I can think of. He had no family, so I'm sure there's no one he'd go to around here.'

'What about friends? Was there someone from school, an old pal he was close to or knocked around with?' Jenny asked.

'No, no friends. Simon was a bit of a loner. He had an air about him, always felt he was a cut above the rest of us – as I said, ideas of grandeur.'

'Do you mind me asking what went wrong with your marriage?' Sam asked softly.

Angela shifted the baby to her other hip and gave him a biscuit to suck on. 'Wow, where to begin? We were far too young. I met him at the hospital when I was visiting Mum. She'd had a stroke and the doctor didn't think she'd pull through. There was only Mum and me. Dad died when I was a little girl; I don't remember much about him. I suppose I was vulnerable at the time. Simon was in the hospital café and asked if I was okay. He worked at the hospital as a clerk in the finance office.

'Stupid me burst into tears and ended up sobbing on his shoulder. Initially, he was wonderful, he gave me a lift home in his car and kept in touch, always concerned about Mum, and our relationship blossomed from there. I leaned on him and mistook gratitude for love so when Simon eventually asked me to marry him, I agreed. He seemed like the answer to all my problems.' Angela paused and wiped her eyes with the back of her sleeve.

Samantha apologised. 'I'm sorry to make you relive this – there may be something you can tell us which will help.'

'I don't know what and it's history now. I shouldn't let it get to me. Anyway, Mum didn't get any better and soon after we were married she had to go into care. Simon wasn't happy; he'd expected her to die and quite honestly so had I. We lived in Mum's house then but were forced to sell it to pay the care fees and find somewhere to live.

'When Mum improved slightly it seemed likely she'd be in long-term care and the money would be eaten up in fees. Simon was furious – he'd proved himself to be a mean-spirited bastard by then and his frustration turned to violence.' Angela pulled her hair back and tucked it behind her ear, revealing a three-inch scar from her cheekbone to her chin. The detectives noted it with solemn expressions. Their case had just moved up a notch on the scary scale. If Beecham was capable of physical violence, something Diane and Emma hadn't experienced, the danger to Emma was more significant than they'd assumed.

'Was it the only instance of violence?' Jenny asked.

'Not the only one but certainly the most serious. I needed stitches but made up a story about falling in the kitchen. I was too afraid to go to the police. Strangely I think the incident shocked Simon as much as me. He pushed me around a bit after that but nothing too serious. It was the end of our marriage though, and when Mum didn't oblige him and die, he decided to walk out. I was relieved. It was only afterwards it dawned on me that he'd never loved me. It was the house which was the attraction and Mum's money, she wasn't badly off but long-term care's changed all that.'

Concerned by Angela's story, Sam was running every possible scenario through her mind, the best one being that Beecham wasn't perhaps violent by nature. He was a man who liked to be in control which probably included being in control of his own emotions too; hence the physical violence would have shocked him as much as Angela. She hoped this was the case. This visit had served to heighten Sam's fears for Emma's safety. She tuned back into the conversation just in time to hear another more exciting revelation from Angela.

'I don't know if this is relevant, but I'm almost certain Simon used another name. After he left and I wasn't sure where he was living, letters arrived at Mum's house for Mr Christopher Simpson. The house was up for sale by then and I was alone in the little rented place we'd taken on. I returned the first few marked, *unknown at this address,* but I opened them when they continued to arrive. They were mostly bills for unpaid goods, credit cards and such, which I thought strange as Mum and Dad had lived at the house forever and I'd never heard of Christopher Simpson. It took a while for me to twig that they could be for Simon and as I wasn't in any kind of emotional state to investigate myself, I passed them on to my solicitor who said he'd take it up with Simon's solicitor.'

'Thank you, Angela, that could be very helpful.' Samantha handed her a card with her details and said, 'If you think of anything else which might help, please get in touch, and thanks for the tea.' She smiled as they stood to leave.

'I hope you find the poor girl and that bastard, Simon. I'll have to dash now...' Angela nodded towards the school over the road. 'I've another one in reception over there and they'll be finished for the day soon.' Her smile had returned and Jenny was pleased that Angela seemed to have found contentment in her children. They wished her well and left.

CHAPTER TWENTY-SIX

'Get Paul on speaker, Jenny.' The engine of Sam's little Mini roared into life as she performed a U-turn in Keir Hardy Avenue and pointed the car toward New Middridge.

'Paul? I want you to get round to Johnson & Co Insurance and ask them if they have, or ever have had, an employee named Christopher Simpson. Our Mr Beecham's not averse to using an alias. An address would be brilliant too – oh and take a photo of Beecham – if he can use one alias he might use another. We're heading back now – we'll meet you at the station in an hour for a brainstorming session.' Sam was fully motivated once more, a light at the end of the tunnel, albeit very faint.

'Using another name would certainly explain the lack of any kind of trail on Beecham. It's incredible how he's got away with so much,' Jenny observed.

'He chooses his women carefully and uses fear as his weapon of choice.'

Sam remained silent for the rest of the journey, mulling over everything they knew about Beecham and disliking him more with each new piece of information they uncovered.

DC Paul Roper proffered his card at the reception desk of Johnson & Co Insurance. It was nearly 3.30pm, plenty of time to find out what the boss wanted to know and get back for the briefing.

'I had your colleagues here looking for a different man last time.' The receptionist typed the name Christopher Simpson into her computer. 'You seem to be losing quite a few people, detective.'

'It's the same man actually... and I'm in rather a hurry,' he replied with a tight smile matching her own.

'Sorry, we have no record of this man either.' The receptionist seemed almost pleased she couldn't help.

'How about this one?' Paul pulled out the photo of Simon Beecham, smiling and dressed for his wedding. The woman paled instantly.

'I think you'd better see the manager.' She lifted her phone and moved out of earshot to speak confidentially. Paul tried to lip-read – he was rubbish at it.

'Would you like to come with me, sir?' Her attitude had changed completely. Paul was now made to feel welcome as she led him to the lift and up to the top floor. She stopped outside a door with a shiny plate which read, Michael Johnson, MD.

Mr Johnson was out of his seat and heading to shake hands as Paul entered the room. 'DC Roper. Are you with the fraud squad?' he asked.

'No, sir, my enquiries concern a man we're looking for whom we believe could have worked for you recently. We know him as Simon Beecham.' Paul placed the photograph on the desk.

'I know him as William Clinton.' Johnson appeared unhappy to know him at all.

'William Clinton? Is that a joke?' Paul wondered if his friends called him Bill.

'Far from it. Clinton was employed by us for over two years but disappeared a couple of months ago, along with around £300,000 in fraudulent claims settlements.'

Paul resisted the urge to whistle. 'And presumably you've been working with the fraud office to find him?'

'Yes, and to recover the money, although, like yourself, they've not had any success locating his whereabouts. May I ask why you want to find him if it has nothing to do with our fraud?'

'We need to speak to him urgently concerning a missing person.' Paul wasn't going to elaborate but wanted the man to know how serious the situation was.

'This is the address he gave us when he worked here although your colleagues in fraud have failed to locate him there or anywhere else. Perhaps you need to liaise with them?'

'We'll certainly be doing so, sir. Could you outline how this employee managed to get away with such a large amount?' Paul watched the managing director blush from his neck up as he briefly summarised Beecham's nefarious activities.

Paul allowed himself that whistle as he drove back to the station for the briefing.

DI Freeman and DS Newcombe were already at the station and about to start reviewing the case. Paul had rung in his findings en route and now the team were anxious to hear the full details. Layla sniggered when Paul told them the insurance company knew Beecham as William Clinton but straightened her face when she heard precisely how much the man had stolen.

'Over the two years he worked there, Beecham regularly made bogus claims for anything from house fires to stolen jewellery. The genius of it was that he didn't sign all the claims off in his own name. He managed a team of twenty-two and spread the claims around, forging his colleagues' signatures to authorise the payouts. By the time the auditors suspected something was amiss, their list of suspects included the full team, necessitating careful and painstaking investigation so as not to let the real perpetrator know they were onto the scheme.' Paul looked a little too impressed by Beecham's cunning when Samantha felt he should be more disgusted. He continued. 'When they called in the fraud squad he got wind they were onto him and did a runner. No wonder when we asked for Simon Beecham, they had no record of him.'

'Good work, Paul. First thing tomorrow get onto fraud and tell them of our interest in "William Clinton". Jenny, can you summarise our meeting with Angela Knight please?' Sam was keen to move things along and Jenny gave a brief account of everything they'd learned, emphasising the violence against Angela, a sinister new development to the case.

Sam took over again. 'Needless to say this is concerning. Now we know he has a history of violence the risk increases and it's even more imperative to find Emma Porter and find her quickly. Right, a brief summary before we call it a day. What are the common denominators here? What have we got so far?' Sam pulled the top off her marker pen, poised to note her team's ideas.

'He seeks out vulnerable women with no siblings,' Layla offered. Samantha scribbled it down.

'He likes to be in control, he's manipulative and it's clear that he can be aggressive too,' Jenny added.

'He likes money but doesn't seem generous with it,' Paul chipped in. 'I know how I'd spend £300,000.'

'Yes,' Sam said, 'I think money is the key element with our man, especially now we know about William Clinton.' They all smiled. 'It's not the women who are Beecham's focus but the parents – not filthy rich parents who'd probably be overcautious and have suitors checked out, but comfortably off families. Parents who would give their children anything. He tried to get POA from Diane's parents and we know the Porters gave them money to set them up and would probably have done so again. Angela's mother was comfortably off until the care home fees came into play, and she didn't die when Beecham expected her too. He cut his losses with the first two wives, so why take Emma, why not disappear again like before?'

Paul attempted an answer. 'Perhaps he's fed up with disappearing? He's apparently made a killing – sorry, bad choice of words – from Johnsons. It could be that he wants to enjoy it.'

'Or he could want a ransom from the Porters?' Layla suggested.

Jenny spoke up. 'Boss, you don't think he could have approached the Porters for money and they're keeping quiet about it – playing his game to get her back safely?'

'I don't think so. They're a couple who play straight and I'm sure they'd have told us if that was the case.' However, Sam wasn't entirely convinced by her own words and decided to call in at the Porters' house on her way home from work.

There was little more the team could do except sleep on it and be back in early the following day to pick up the threads of the investigation.

CHAPTER TWENTY-SEVEN

Emma heard footsteps on what sounded like a wooden staircase. She must be in an upstairs room. A door handle turned slowly and she sensed another presence enter the room, but the silence continued. Holding her breath, an uncomfortable feeling of being observed washed over her. She could almost feel eyes upon her but was powerless to speak or even move, rigid with fear.

Tightness gripped her chest, panic squeezing her ribs so forcefully that her breathing became constricted. Fear was probably the exact reaction her captor desired, a captor who could surely only be Simon, a fact confirmed as he moved closer to her and the scent of his distinctive aftershave reached her nostrils.

Suddenly the sack covering her head was ripped from her and she blinked into the semi-darkness, her eyes adjusting to the gloom.

'Hello, *wife!*' Simon almost spat the words. His face was close to hers, too close. 'I see you've woken up to greet me. Have you missed me?'

Emma was glad she couldn't reply, glad to be gagged so

nothing was expected of her but then Simon untied the gag and stroked her cheek with his fingers, moving them down to her shoulders and on to her breast where he caressed her almost lovingly. Emma thought she was going to vomit.

'I need the bathroom.' Her voice sounded strange, hoarse and unfamiliar, although her words were true. Emma's bladder was so full that she was in pain yet she refused to lose her dignity.

Simon laughed. 'How do I know you won't do anything stupid?'

'I won't. Untie me, please.' Her voice trembled and only determination kept her terror from showing. Emma did not want to give him the satisfaction of seeing her becoming a gibbering wreck. Simon moved back towards the door where a large brown paper bag sat on the coffee table she'd found earlier. Slowly he reached inside and withdrew a gun.

Emma gasped.

'My insurance policy.' His face was still in shadow. The grey metal of the gun glinted in the light from the doorway. Unexpectedly the room then flooded with light. Emma screwed up her eyes, pained by the bright artificial beam.

When she managed to focus she noticed he looked different. His sandy-coloured hair was now dark, almost black, making his skin look pale and sickly – he wore a heavy pair of spectacles which seemed to alter the shape of his face. He grinned.

'Do you like the new look? I think it rather suits me.' There was that laugh again – the sound of madness. Emma had seen Simon in some strange moods before but this was utterly terrifying with the effect of keeping her still.

Simon jiggled the gun in his hand, swapping it from one palm to the other as if it were a toy. 'Okay, if I let you pee you have to promise to be a good girl and not to try anything stupid...

or you'll regret it.' He pointed the gun at Emma's head and moved towards her.

Panic constricted her breathing again so she couldn't speak.

Still holding the gun, Simon reached behind her and tugged roughly at the binding around her wrists. Pain shot through her hands, her skin was raw, yet suddenly, miraculously, she was free.

Her shoulders screamed at the sudden release but Emma could only move her arms back to their natural position very slowly. Simon nudged her in the ribs with the gun, edging her towards another door at the far side of the room and through a lobby where a bathroom became visible. Emma almost fell through the doorway.

Simon studied her for a moment. 'Don't bother trying. The window's locked.' She thought he intended to stay and felt suddenly sick, then he laughed and turned back into the other room.

After using the toilet, Emma tried the window, hoping he'd been bluffing. He wasn't. Even if it had opened she probably wouldn't have been able to squeeze through the tiny top pane and there was the gun to consider.

Looking around her, Emma realised what a beautiful bathroom she was in, modern with expensive fittings, a roll-top bath at one end and a double shower at the other. It was spacious too, and as she turned on the taps, instant hot water gushed out, filling the deep bowl. Looking in the mirror, her tear-streaked swollen face shocked her.

Cupping her hands, Emma filled them with water and splashed it over her sore and dirty face, a small comfort in an unimaginable situation. Although reluctant to touch anything of Simon's she couldn't resist the large tablet of soap and proceeded to wash her face more thoroughly. Her wrists were bleeding and painful – the water stung – she bit her tongue and soaked them in the warmth before dabbing them dry on the fluffy towel hung over the heated radiator.

A rap at the door made her jump.

'Don't take all day. We have things to discuss!' Simon growled but didn't open the door as she expected – there was no bolt. Afraid to annoy her captor further and with an image of the gun etched in her mind, Emma made her way from the bathroom back to where Simon waited.

Even with her thoughts in such turmoil it was impossible not to be aware of the room in which she found herself. It was spacious with polished natural wooden flooring, the hues of red and gold catching the light. A large picture window filled one wall from which she glimpsed treetops and sky with scudding white clouds. The other walls were painted brilliant white and hung with large colourful prints. The furniture was of exceptional quality, Scandinavian design, not the mass-produced items most people settle for but superior pieces, possibly even custom-made. The main ceiling lights had been switched off and soft lighting enhanced the space, picking out the russet colours of the scatter cushions and woollen rugs on the floor. The ceiling beams looked original, suggesting a split-level barn conversion.

Whose house was this? Emma wondered. Simon had no friends she knew of and no family. Could he have rented it, a holiday let perhaps? Outside was eerily silent – no traffic noises, only the birds singing in the trees, their exquisite song of freedom – how Emma envied those birds.

'Come, sit,' Simon ordered, so she moved towards him keeping her eye on the gun in his hand. Emma had never seen a gun in real life before, only on the television and it scared her, especially the casual way he handled it, as if he took delight in being reckless.

'Like the place?' He swept his free hand around the room

and she nodded dutifully, not daring to speak. 'It's mine, my little bolthole, a place of refuge where no one can find me. You're the only person who's ever been here, Emma, a rare privilege but one which presents me with a problem. What do I do with you now?' His eyes travelled over her body, causing her skin to crawl. 'I have to say you're not looking your best, then you have been through something of an ordeal haven't you?' He laughed, a miserable, cruel laugh mocking her vulnerability.

Emma decided on silence. Answering him risked saying the wrong thing.

Part of Emma's brain didn't believe this beautiful house could be Simon's. Yes, he'd stolen money from her, her parents and Diane but a place like this must cost a fortune and it was all presented so tastefully. Where would he get so much money? And if this was the real Simon, how had he managed to suffer living in that poky rented house they'd shared for the last few months? She only stomached it in the hope it was temporary.

If he liked such extravagant furnishings why did he make a fuss if she as much as bought a glossy magazine? It didn't fit. Nothing was right. Which one was the real Simon? Emma had not known the man she'd thought to be her husband, the man she'd given herself to in love. Who was he, this stranger before her?

'Why did you have to disappoint me, Emma?' Simon sat forward in his seat, too close for her comfort. She tried not to recoil. 'You know, you could have been the "one" – third time lucky – but no, you had to spoil it all.'

What did he mean, third time lucky? She was his second "wife", wasn't she?

'So now you leave me at an impasse – Hobson's choice. It will have to be plan B – and I don't think you're going to like it.'

CHAPTER TWENTY-EIGHT

DI Samantha Freeman was nothing if she wasn't single-minded and this case was undoubtedly delivering focus. The pace of the investigation was picking up and with it the detective's motivation. Calling at the Porters' home after an already long day would mean another late night yet Ravi was understanding when she rang to let him know.

Light flooded from the lounge as she pulled into the Porters' drive. Samantha knew her presence on their doorstep would bring mixed emotions; hope and dread.

'Just a few more questions,' she said almost too quickly, wanting them to know there was nothing new to report about Emma. Silently George led her into the lounge where Margaret offered coffee. Sam declined, not wishing to prolong the visit.

'So, there was another wife as well as Diane?' George asked, bitterness lacing his words. 'Had he divorced her or is the man a double bigamist?'

'They were legally divorced but finding her has been a breakthrough. She suggested Simon may have used another name on occasions, a line of enquiry we immediately looked into and found to be the case. So now we have two pseudonyms to work with.' Sam longed to offer positive news, barely able to imagine what the Porters were going through. They both looked exhausted as if they hadn't slept for days. Margaret remained silent and even George couldn't get excited about this development.

'So, what questions do you have?' he asked.

'Have you heard from Simon since we last spoke?'

'No, of course not. If we had, you'd be the first person to know.' The immediacy of George's answer confirmed its truth in Samantha's mind, and she nodded her thanks.

'If he does make contact and asks you not to involve the police, will you go along with his request?' Again, she watched closely for his response. This time there was a slight hesitation. It could be that George hadn't considered this possibility, yet it also suggested he might waver if such a dilemma presented itself.

'Do you think it's likely?' Margaret asked.

'Not likely but certainly a possibility and one we have to consider. If Simon took Emma on a whim without any real plan, he might decide to use her as a bargaining tool to get money. From the picture we're putting together of his character, money appears to be a motivating factor.'

George was suddenly a little more animated. 'Simon came to us to ask for money almost as soon as they were home from their honeymoon. Do you think he might approach us with a ransom demand?'

'It's a scenario we should consider. Could you tell me about this request for money, Mr Porter? It might help to complete the picture we're building to understand him better.'

'He had some ill-conceived business idea and wanted us to invest £80,000 and use our house as collateral for a bank loan.' George shook his head at the memory while Samantha's eyes widened – it was a big ask. 'Needless to say we didn't go along with the idea. I tried to humour him for Emma's sake by saying I'd consider reviewing a business plan but it was never forthcoming and he didn't mention the idea again. I've come to realise the man's a complete charlatan.'

'He did stop Emma from seeing us as well,' Margaret chipped in. 'Said he'd allow her one visit a month – the nerve of him! That's when we knew things weren't right and Simon wasn't the man we thought he was. We should have done something then, insisted on seeing Emma or having it out with him.' Regret dulled her eyes.

'What did Emma say about this request for money and not seeing you so much?' Sam asked.

Margaret had tears running down her cheeks, tears of remorse perhaps that they hadn't handled things better. 'He didn't tell her about the loan, said she didn't understand finance and would we keep it quiet and as it was all a bit embarrassing, we agreed. As for not seeing us more regularly, I know she wasn't happy about it but argued it was probably best to go along with what Simon wanted. As it seemed to make her life easier, we let it pass and just enjoyed the little time we did have with her.'

'Thank you for telling me. I understand how difficult this is but if Simon does contact you the best thing you could do for Emma is to call us immediately. With this in mind I'd like to send a team around first thing tomorrow to put a tap on your landline – and if I could have the details of your mobile phones we can trace any incoming calls from them too.'

Sam was still unsure she'd persuaded them to keep her in the loop. If Beecham did decide on extortion, he would use threats to convince them to go along with his plans and exclude the police. Would they take the risk of trusting him or do the right thing?

Samantha left the house to finally return home.

A delicious smell greeted Samantha as she walked through her front door, and a bottle of wine stood on the table. She smiled, hearing Ravi upstairs and the sound of running water, how she loved him. Having rung him when she left the Porters, a coffee and a ready meal would have sufficed but to her delight, he'd gone a step further.

'Hi!' Sam shouted upstairs, rewarded a moment later by her boyfriend's lofty figure skipping down towards her with a massive smile on his face.

'Perfect timing.' He beamed. 'Dinner will be ready in twenty minutes so there's just time for a quick soak.' He leaned down to kiss her forehead. At six feet tall, Ravi was ten inches taller than she was.

'Smells divine.' Sam willingly obeyed his instructions, shrugged off her coat and shoes and tramped upstairs to soak away the cares of the day.

An hour later, glowing in the aftermath of a good meal and two glasses of wine, Sam sat on the sofa and snuggled up to the love of her life.

'Have you encountered an insurance fraud with Johnson & Co in New Middridge?' she asked. Ravi hesitated, as if searching the files of his meticulously ordered mind. 'The perp goes by the name of William Clinton?' Samantha offered helpfully.

'Ah, yes – the presidential file.' He laughed. 'It's not one of mine but the nickname's sort of stuck – apt, eh?'

'Mr William Clinton's real name is Simon Beecham and I'm currently looking for him in connection with the disappearance of a young woman he married, bigamously. He's gone to ground and is proving hard to find.'

'D'you think this girl's in danger?'

'Absolutely. We've tracked down a third "wife". Beecham displayed violent tendencies while with her, which somewhat upped the risk level. He uses another name too, apparently, Christopher Simpson. Do you know much about the progress in the fraud case?'

'I know they're struggling to locate the guy. He's been clever, covering his tracks by using other employees' names at Johnsons. But he must have known such huge losses would be discovered sometime. Casting suspicion on his colleagues wasted valuable time for our guys, and by the time they were closing in, Clinton had got wind of the enquiry and disappeared into the ether. Those other two names will certainly help. I'll pass them on tomorrow and needless to say if you find him first give us the wink, won't you?'

'Naturally and I'll expect the same in return. Enough shop talk for now. Is there any wine left in that bottle?' Sam reached up and pulled Ravi's face down to hers.

CHAPTER TWENTY-NINE

Simon stared at his captive, his eyes willing her to speak, to enquire exactly what his 'plan B' was, to beg him to release her. But Emma refused to give him the satisfaction. Her heart rate had finally slowed unless she looked at the gun he still held rather too casually in his hand, so she determinedly averted her eyes from it to concentrate on the positives.

Being free from her bindings was definitely a positive, although her body still ached from being bound so tightly. Pains were shooting through her shoulders at the slightest movement. Her head throbbed, making her wonder what he'd given her to knock her out so soundly. Would chloroform have such an effect? And where would Simon access such drugs?

Although she'd tried, Emma had no memory of anything after leaving the surgery. Simon must have been waiting in the shadows. There were plenty of dark streets on the way to the bus stop, with poor lighting being on his side and the bad weather keeping people off the streets.

She wondered what time it was – judging from the dim light outside, probably early morning, which meant she'd been out cold for hours and where had her captor been during that time? The house he was holding her in also posed questions. Where was it? Would anyone hear her if she screamed? So many questions rattled around her brain, yet she didn't want to give him the pleasure of admitting her curiosity.

Simon suddenly grew restless, jumping up from the seat and declaring, 'I'm hungry. There's bacon and eggs in the fridge over there.' He waved his free hand toward a large American-style fridge which dominated the open-plan kitchen, his intent obvious. She was to cook for them. Emma remained in her seat.

'Get up and cook, bitch!' He poked the gun in her face, hard into the hollow of her cheek. Emma flinched. It was an act she couldn't ignore, so she did as he commanded. Making him angry was undoubtedly dangerous, yet it was a tiny victory for her – the balance of power shifted slightly, imperceptibly, and his reaction proved the point. Simon dropped back into the chair with a smirk, in control again.

Emma scrabbled through the cupboards searching for a frying pan and then proceeded to cook breakfast. She would need to tread carefully. Crossing such an unstable man was a hazardous path to take, especially one holding a gun, but strangely her fear was morphing into something else, a feeling she didn't quite understand. It wasn't outright bravery, she was still terrified and Simon had the upper hand. She was still alive, wasn't she – did that mean he didn't intend to kill her? Emma knew she needed to discover his purpose, the plan B he'd hinted at, but how? Her head was filled with questions that she couldn't ask outright, so hopefully, Simon would be unable to resist boasting about his plans. He seemed inordinately proud of this house and smug that Emma was his prisoner. Perhaps she should play to his arrogance and his need to always be in control.

Emma put two plates of eggs and bacon on the table.

'About time too.' Simon sat to eat, the gun, incongruous on the table, almost touching his plate. The idea of refusing food crossed Emma's mind, yet she was hungry. It must have been twenty hours or more since she'd eaten and common sense told her she must preserve her strength if a way out of this situation was to be found. Being faint from lack of food would give Simon another advantage. Reluctantly, she sat opposite him and without appetite or enthusiasm started to eat.

Pushing away his empty plate, Simon looked at Emma. Then, picking up the gun, he caressed it almost lovingly in his right hand. He appeared to be waiting for a reaction. Still refusing to look at the gun, Emma removed the plates and ran water into the sink.

'Good girl, you're beginning to learn your place!' he sneered.

Emma kept her back to him and continued clearing the detritus of their meal, hoping he couldn't see the tremor in her legs. Then, when the kitchen was tidy, Simon ordered her to sit. Emma obeyed, remaining silent.

'You should have tried being this compliant when we were married,' he observed.

'We were never married!' Emma instantly regretted breaking her silence, but her temper got the better of her. He laughed, chalking up another minor triumph.

It was fully daylight outside and Emma's thoughts turned to her parents. They would be frantic – and the police – would they be searching for her – where would they begin? Even she had no idea where this house was or who Simon Beecham was either. Maybe talking to him would work, asking him why he was holding her. Perhaps it would be playing into his hands, doing what he wanted, but something needed to give. The not knowing was a form of torture in itself.

Finally, Emma plucked up the courage to speak. 'Are you

going to ask my parents for a ransom?' Surely there was no other reason for all this. A bitter laugh escaped Simon's mouth, yet he remained silent with a mocking look, as if asking, *What do you think?*

'Why, Simon? They've been so generous to you, accepted you into the family – what have they ever done? What have I done to deserve this?'

'Ha! You think your parents are generous? You haven't a clue, Emma. You grew up with all the advantages of rich parents, everything you ever wanted. Do you know what it's like to have nothing? To be passed around to so-called "carers" all your life with no one who actually did care? People like you make me sick. Everything comes easily and you take it all for granted – and those precious parents who you think are generous are just selfish pigs!'

Emma was confused. 'But they gave us £10,000 to put towards a deposit.'

'A drop in the damned ocean for them – don't even try to defend them!'

Stunned, Emma lapsed into silence. Simon appeared agitated, the gun waving in his hand as he spoke. Finally, he stood and prowled around the room.

'I'm planning something special for your parents, a late Halloween trick, nothing more or less than they deserve!' Speaking seemed to calm him and he soon sat again. Emma fought back her tears. She would much prefer Simon to take his anger out on her rather than her parents – what could he be planning?

'This is ridiculous, Simon. You'll never get away with it, the police will already–' She didn't get to finish her sentence as he lurched towards her and slapped her hard across the face. She gasped at the sudden pain, tasting blood inside her mouth and confronted with the feral look in his eyes. The sudden violence confirmed his desperation. Simon was volatile, out of control and Emma was terrified.

CHAPTER THIRTY

Once again, Emma was tied up. This time bound to a chair in the lounge area of the open-plan space, arms behind her, ankles splayed and tied separately to the chair's front legs. Simon wasn't taking any chances. The rough twine cut into her already-sore wrists, and she could feel a warm trickle of blood dripping down her fingers.

'I'll not bother with the gag, shout and scream all you like, little lady. No one's going to hear you.' Simon stepped back to view his handiwork, apparently pleased with the bindings and the humiliation he'd inflicted. 'Be a good girl!' He took her chin in his hand, looked into her eyes, then laughed, turned around and went out of the door.

The sound of receding footsteps was a welcome relief, followed quickly by the noise of an engine starting up, not his little Nissan Micra, something more powerful, larger. She didn't remember hearing the same engine when Simon arrived that morning. By Emma's reckoning, it was somewhere around mid-afternoon and from what she could see from the window, the sky was darkening, a grey early November day. Halloween had come and gone, a more terrifying one she couldn't remember.

With no idea where Simon was going or when he'd return, Emma decided to structure her thoughts, to plan rather than panic. Feeling sorry for herself wouldn't help – it would weaken her mindset and hinder any constructive thinking. She sniffed and drew in a deep breath.

Think, Emma, think!

If she could work out why Simon was doing this then maybe she stood a chance of talking him out of his plan, whatever it might be. Her thoughts kept returning to money. He appeared to be obsessed with money. Emma was puzzled as to why he couldn't accept how generous her parents had been with them. £10,000 is a significant gift, especially as they would have spent much more on the wedding itself.

Was there something she didn't know? Did Simon want to control her parents' finances as he'd tried with Diane? But if money was his goal, why hadn't he already approached her parents with a ransom demand, something she felt sure he couldn't have done. If this was the case, Emma had no doubt her dad would have raised the money. He would mortgage his own soul for her, she was certain.

The light was fading quickly and after a couple of hours, Emma was sitting helplessly in the dark – it must have been later than she thought – there were no clocks around to keep track of time. The darkness amplified her vulnerability. It seemed to clothe her with fear. Strange and unwelcome thoughts crowded her mind, weaving themselves around her aching body, suffocatingly tangible. Emma remembered nightmares from her childhood, scary dreams of monsters and bad people, which one or both of her parents would banish with a hug and a night light. The memories were choking, wrapping themselves fiercely around her ribs, crushing any hope out of her.

Stop it – positive thinking – remember!

But it was difficult with very little to concentrate on and no information to form a feasible plan.

I should have asked him to leave on a light.

Asking Simon for anything was an anathema, something she didn't want to do yet the reality was that he was her only hope of escape – her captor and her means of escape – an impossible mockery.

It was almost a relief when Emma's thoughts were interrupted by the sound of the vehicle returning and within a minute Simon burst into the room. The idea that he might be being chased flashed through her mind. But, no. There was no saviour behind him, no rescuer to untie her and take her home to the warm embrace of her parents.

Emma winced as Simon switched the light on and it flooded the room. She swallowed hard as Simon approached and screamed with pain as he yanked at the twine on her wrists. Without appearing to notice or care, he was equally rough with her ankles, but at least she was free.

The gun was tucked into his waistband – for an instant Emma thought about grabbing it, then, as if he'd read her mind, Simon pulled it free and held it close to her temple. Then, laughing at how she jumped, he flopped onto the sofa.

'Can I use the bathroom?' She hated asking anything of him but needed to go. He flicked his head in agreement prompting her to scurry away, glad to stretch her limbs. The warm water stung her wrists as she held them under the tap. Dabbing them with a towel, Emma looked around hoping for something to soothe them. In a wall cabinet she found a tube of Savlon which she spread liberally over her broken sore skin, doing her best to ignore the pain.

After taking as long as she dared, Emma returned to the lounge where Simon sat at the table drumming his fingers impatiently.

'Sit down,' he barked.

There was no choice except to obey; the gun was still in his hand. He was a big man with it so close. A writing pad and a pen were on the table. 'Write what I tell you.'

Emma picked up the pen as Simon dictated.

'Simon is treating me well. I think you know why he had to take me, and now it's time to make amends.'

Emma glanced at him. She hadn't a clue what he meant and was sure her parents wouldn't either. He nudged her hand with the gun and continued.

'Two hundred thousand pounds is all he wants to release me. It's not much. He's being very reasonable, considering what you'll be getting in return. I'm sure you'll have contacted the police by now, so somehow, you'll have to shake them off. Keep the phone with you at all times. Please do as he asks, and I'll be fine. If not...'

Simon grabbed Emma's wrist and smeared it across the bottom of the paper, leaving a trail of blood from the raw grazes. She yelled in pain, pulling free as he laughed loudly, clearly enjoying the drama of his own making. Emma was suddenly angry. Without thinking she sprang at him, fists flailing with no consideration of the consequences.

The noise of the gun was deafening and as Emma fell to the floor, hands over her ears to block out the resounding blast, she was momentarily stunned, uncertain of what had just occurred.

'You idiot. You stupid bloody fool!' Simon's face was contorted in anger as he grabbed Emma's arm and pulled her to her feet. 'Look what you've done!'

A bullet-shaped hole was in the wall, plaster dust settling where it had penetrated. Still trembling with shock, Emma tried to wriggle free. He held her even tighter, pushing her back to the chair and winding the rope around her again. Tears welled in Emma's eyes as her captor's anger appeared to reach new heights. Sniffing back her sobs she wondered what he would do next.

Emma didn't struggle. Silence was probably the best policy for the moment. She was hungry and thirsty but doubted Simon cared. Only the knowledge that Simon wanted money brought a small degree of comfort – he'd have to keep her alive. Isn't that how it worked? Her parents would ask to speak to her to establish she was well.

Look for the positives! You're still alive.

CHAPTER THIRTY-ONE

DI Samantha Freeman studied the whiteboard in the office at New Middridge police station. Underneath Simon Beecham's image were three names – his real one, Beecham (they assumed it to be his real name but nothing would surprise them about this man), Christopher Simpson and William Clinton. Although it was a long shot, she'd asked Ravi to let her know if these names helped his colleagues locate Beecham. What more could the fraud squad find than the sketchy details her team had turned up?

Beside Beecham's image was Emma's – the other half of the photograph they'd copied and torn in two, symbolic of the couple's fractured relationship. Emma looked so happy and beautiful as a bride, smiling and trusting, her head tilted towards her husband, a long figure-hugging dress sweeping the grass upon which they posed. Sunshine mirrored the young woman's happiness and innocence, a soft yellow glow giving no hint of the darkness waiting for her over the next few months.

Sam wondered what was going through Beecham's mind on their wedding day. The man knew he was committing bigamy – a crime which could earn him up to seven years imprisonment.

Simon must also have known he was ruining a young woman's life and causing immeasurable grief to her family, so what was his aim?

Had he a plan on their wedding day? Did he really think he could get away with bigamy and bleed Emma's parents for money? Had their home been in his sights from the very beginning? It may be that she would never find the answer to these questions, yet answers weren't their priority. What Beecham would do next mattered more. It was the question she needed to concentrate on – what he would do and where he was – and time was not on her side.

Jenny appeared at her elbow, two decent coffees from the deli across the road in her hands. 'Coffee, boss?' They were the first two in the office – it was only 7.45am.

Sam accepted the coffee gratefully. 'Thanks. Any ideas?'

'Perhaps another search of the house where they lived?' It was something concrete to do and Sam still had the key the Porters had given her. Jenny hadn't been inside before and a fresh pair of eyes was always welcome.

'Okay, as soon as Paul and Layla arrive we'll get off. Ravi's familiar with the fraud case although he's not working on it. He's going to pass on Beecham's aliases to his colleagues. They haven't any leads on his whereabouts either but at least someone else is looking too.'

They drank their coffee while waiting for their colleagues. The pair arrived together, early and keen to continue the search for Beecham and the four detectives quickly caught up on where they were in the case. Then, after updating them on her evening visit to the Porters, the DI asked if anyone had fresh ideas.

'I thought trawling the car-hire companies might give us a break – the ANPR hasn't picked up Beecham's Nissan. He's probably ditched it and is using another vehicle,' Layla suggested.

Samantha was delighted with Layla's idea. 'Good, and extend it to car dealerships. The man's got money so he may have bought a new car. If you work from the date we first arrested him it should narrow the search and we now have three possible names.'

Paul turned to fire up his computer. 'Talking of those new names, I suppose I should do the land registry searches again in his other two aliases. As you say, he has money and he must be holed up somewhere.'

'You could try estate agents too, Paul. And find out when Beecham got his first big payout from his fraudulent claims at Johnsons. That should give you a starting date, then get onto the land registry and estate agents. Five-mile radius to begin with, then widen it if there's no joy.'

DC Roper smiled. It was well known that he preferred desk work to being out in the field and he was good at it.

With the work divvied up, Sam and Jenny set off for the rented house where Emma Porter had begun what she thought would be her married life.

A cloying smell of damp greeted them on opening the front door.

Jenny frowned. 'This must have been a comedown for Emma after her parents' place.'

A handful of letters were sprawled on the doormat. Sam glanced through them, ever hopeful of a new lead.

'We'll take these with us to open; you never know.'

Jenny wrinkled her nose as she gazed around. 'Ugh, surely Beecham could have afforded better?'

'Yes, but for some reason he chose not to, and Emma went along with him. He must have had money; he'd conned £300,000 from Johnsons, and the Porters gave them a generous gift. Emma had savings too. I'm not hopeful of finding anything here, Jenny, but we'll give it a good going over anyway.

An hour later, every drawer, cupboard and piece of furniture had been searched with little to show for their effort.

Samantha sighed. 'Perhaps what we haven't found tells us more than what's still here.'

'What d'you mean?'

'Beecham's passport isn't here. I suppose it was too much to hope to find three passports for his aliases?'

'Do you think he intends to flee the country?'

'It's likely, but I'm more concerned with what he can do before then – Emma's safety's still the priority. Ring the station, will you, and get Paul to contact ports and airports to flag up his details. Let's hope he's not already left the country.'

Jenny made the call before they headed back to the police station.

Paul greeted them. 'An all-ports alert is out, boss. We'll catch him if he attempts to leave unless he's already gone.'

'Any luck with the searches?' Jenny asked.

'*Needle* and *haystack* come to mind, especially with the Christopher Simpson alias. Do you know how many Christopher Simpsons are in this area alone?'

'It's a good job there are plenty of hours left in the day then.' Sam grimaced. 'We need to track this man down before it's too late.' The unspoken meaning of her words hit home, emphasising the urgency of their task.

CHAPTER THIRTY-TWO

Emma woke and for one blissful moment was unaware of where she was, but the pain throughout her body served as a cruel reminder. Still bound to the chair, her whole body ached. Panic again flooded through her as recent horrendous events came to mind – the letter Simon forced her to write, which would crush her parents, the sound of the gun going off. Had she really been so stupid as to lunge at a man holding a gun?

It certainly wasn't bravery, nothing more than a knee-jerk and thoughtless reaction. Her ears still felt strange, the noise of the gun reverberating in her head, an unwelcome echo. Simon had appeared more upset about the ugly hole in the wall than that one of them could have been killed, and her punishment was to be again trussed up and left alone in the darkening house for how long she couldn't tell. Emma's instinct was to give up and cry, to feel sorry for herself and her bizarre predicament. But what good would it do? She needed to keep her wits about her.

On Simon's return his eyes rested initially on the offending bullet hole before turning to Emma. He unbound her in silence and dragged her to the far side of the room, to a door she'd not been through before. She was shoved along a small passageway into a bedroom and then pushed roughly onto the bed before Simon turned to leave.

'I need the bathroom,' she begged and was thankful when he stood aside and allowed her to walk back to the bathroom she'd used before. Once inside, Emma used the toilet and then drank a long, much-needed drink straight from the tap. She stayed there for as long as she dared, drank again, and then returned to face her tormentor.

Simon shoved her into the bedroom and locked the door as he left. There was no clock in the room and it wasn't yet fully light outside but when Emma tried to switch on the light she discovered there was no bulb in the fitting, only a bare wire hanging from the ceiling. After trying the window and confirming it was impossible to open, she finally collapsed on the bed, worn out mentally and physically.

Don't give up; don't let him win.

Exhausted, Emma fell into a fitful sleep. Simon's face drifted in and out of her mind, leering at her, angry and full of hate.

Daylight slowly banished the night. No sounds were forthcoming from inside the house. Could she be alone again? A visual search of the room revealed how stark it was; a wardrobe which on inspection proved to be empty, a small table and the bed on which she'd slept. At least it was more comfortable than the previous night when she'd slept on the floor, bound and gagged. Emma supposed she was fortunate to have been left without being tied. Her muscles felt easier for that one little concession.

If she hoped to find something in the room to use as a weapon, Emma was disappointed; a vase to smash into sharp shards would have been great, or a mirror perhaps, but no,

Simon had clearly anticipated her occupation of the room and made sure there was no way to escape or anything to be used against him.

Her stomach growled, reminding Emma she hadn't eaten since the eggs and bacon the morning before. Had Simon been eating when he was out? Almost certainly. He wouldn't mind her going without but not himself.

Frustrated and afraid, all Emma could do was wait. At least there was a window and a view to remind her there was still a world outside. Yet the sight which met her eyes was rather bleak. It was an upstairs room and the window looked down over woodland, winter-bare trees, their leaves recently shed and branches like gnarled hands reaching out to grab at her – muddy paths below and grey cloudy skies above. There was nothing to give hope or comfort.

Usually, Emma would have seen beauty even in such a wintry landscape. She loved all seasons and felt each one offered its own unique splendour but never before had she viewed a scene from captivity. It inevitably coloured her judgement. It was difficult to find beauty in the cruelty of her confinement.

A road with traffic would have been a welcome sight, cars with commuters travelling to and from work, pavements with people going about their business, anything to bring hope that the world still turned as usual – yet there was nothing. Simon hadn't lied about the isolation of the place. At any other time, in another scenario, the isolation might have been regarded as peaceful or tranquil. Now she would love nothing more than to see a crowd of people marching through the trees, drawing closer to the house, near enough to see her plight and offer the help she so desperately needed.

Don't get maudlin! Be strong.

It was hard to find positives when there simply weren't any.

It seemed an age until signs confirming Simon was in the house reached her ears. A slamming door, footsteps in the passage – what mood would he be in? Yet the more fearsome question was what his plans were and how this day would pan out. A key turned in the lock and the door was thrown open.

'Out!' he barked and Emma did as he said, or rather obeyed the gun clenched in his hand. Simon shoved her before him into the lounge. Surprisingly there was food on the table, a large bread roll and a mug of something hot; steam was curling from it – the sight almost made her cry.

'Eat,' Simon commanded, which she did greedily, pushing the dry bread into her mouth and then raising the mug to her lips. For an instant, Emma thought he might snatch the bread and tea away from her as part of a cruel sick joke – but no, he watched her, expressionless, until she finished. Perhaps he'd been reflecting on alternative outcomes of the gun episode. Emma certainly had. Did he intend to kill her, she wondered, and a shudder passed through her body at the thought. Eventually Simon spoke.

'I hope you're not going to do anything stupid today.'

'No.' Agreeing seemed prudent.

'Good, because today could be the day your parents decide your fate.' His face relaxed into what she supposed was a smile. She remained silent, hoping he'd elaborate. When he didn't she ventured a question.

'If they give you the money will you let me go?' It was the most direct she'd dared to be so far and she was unsure if she actually wanted to know the answer.

'Now there's my dilemma. That's how it would normally proceed. Yet if I do, will you help the police find me? And don't answer. I know you'll only lie.' Simon's cold green eyes were searching her face again, unnerving her.

'Your parents don't deserve to get you back. Then again,

taking their money is too simple, too easy on them. They're going to pay with more than money, Emma, and there's nothing you can do about it. They have your letter now.' His icy stare was searching her face for a reaction, wanting to see her fear. Emma turned her head so he wouldn't notice the tears welling in her eyes and finished the food.

CHAPTER THIRTY-THREE

George Porter was on indefinite compassionate leave from work. Although regretting the patients whose surgeries would be cancelled, he was in no state to perform delicate operations. The last two nights had been torture, with hardly any sleep and an active imagination playing the most frightening scenarios on a loop through his mind. George was exhausted, his eyes gritty and restless, needing activity but unable to settle to anything constructive. Reading was impossible, his concentration zilch.

Listening to music strangely annoyed him. How could he enjoy anything when his daughter was missing, most likely in mortal danger? Getting out of the house wasn't an option either. It worried him. What if the detectives called with news, or Emma arrived home? Physical activity would have been welcome. Digging the garden might have expended some of the nervous tension that gripped his body, but the recent rain had left the garden little more than a plot of mud.

George envied Margaret her kitchen – at least she had something to do – the endless cups of coffee and the meals neither could eat. She had routine, yet he knew it was cold comfort. He'd heard her quiet sobs through the night when she thought he was sleeping, seen her heavy eyes and the lines which seemed to have sprung upon her face since they'd last seen Emma. Common sense told him they needed to eat, to sleep and build up their strength for whatever lay ahead, but he readily abandoned common sense. What good could it do?

The couple had talked endlessly on the first day, initially trying to convince themselves there would be a reasonable explanation for Emma's absence – her phone needed recharging, she'd lost track of time or was with a friend. Still, they didn't fool themselves or each other. Then the 'what ifs' dominated their conversation until their imaginations drifted into such dark places which they dismissed as speculation, verbally at least.

George vacillated between anger and despair, wanting to get hold of Simon bloody Beecham and make him pay for all he'd put their family through, but the despair was probably more frightening than the anger, leaving him feeling impotent, powerless and a complete failure.

Waiting was the hardest thing to do. If George could climb Everest to get Emma back he'd happily do so, but DI Freeman said there was nothing to do except try to think of places Beecham might be. She might as well have asked him to climb Everest – it was a more feasible option.

The police technicians had arrived early in the morning to 'tap' their phones, completing the job in only minutes and now the couple were alone again with only their thoughts to torment them.

'Coffee, love?' George hadn't heard Margaret enter the room.

'Thanks.' He took the mug and set it down next to the last one she'd made which stood untouched on the side table.

Margaret sat opposite her husband, eyes searching his for a solution he couldn't offer. She sighed but said nothing, words were distressing, a useless waste of time, yet they had nothing else.

After a few moments Margaret remembered something.

'There was a package addressed to you on the mat this morning. You were in the shower so I put it on the hall table. Have you ordered something?' Margaret appeared not in the least interested if he had, but the news seemed to interest George who went straight to pick it up, bringing it back to the lounge and holding it between his thumb and forefinger as if it might be a bomb.

'I haven't ordered anything.' He opened the package with trembling fingers and slowly pulled out a cheap mobile phone and a letter. Margaret watched, horrified. She'd not considered the delivery could have something to do with Emma's disappearance and now felt rather stupid.

George's face paled as he read the one-sided letter – he sank into a chair as if he'd been physically pushed. His wife grabbed the page from him and read it, groaning as the words sank in.

'Is that blood?' Margaret barely whispered yet her words echoed in her husband's thoughts at the sight of the reddish-brown smear at the bottom of the letter. Margaret stood, suddenly needing to be active. 'We'll have to call the police!'

'No! Read what he says. We need to shake them off and do this alone.' George was back on his feet, prowling the room, attempting to think of a response.

'But DI Freeman said this could happen. You promised you'd let her know.'

'I didn't promise anything. We have to do what's right for Emma here, not what's right for the police.'

Margaret shook her head, her arms wrapped around her body, swaying as if to some inner music, as a child would do in an attempt at seeking comfort. 'But he doesn't say what to do... only how much he wants. Can you get such an amount together?'

'Not quickly, but he's not stupid, he'll know that.'

'Then what shall we do? How can we persuade him to give us time?'

As if in response to the question, the mobile phone rang, and the pair turned to look at it, horrified as if it would explode.

George moved first, picking up the phone and answering the intrusive call with a simple 'Yes?' He knew who would be on the other end.

'Good morning, George. I see you've received my little package. Sorry about the bloodstains. Emma's had one or two little accidents.' The scorn in his voice angered George, yet he remained calm, realising the importance of playing along with Beecham.

The first thing to address was the need to know his daughter was still alive. 'Where is she? I want to talk to her.'

'All in good time, money first, you know the routine, surely?'

'You won't get a penny until I know she's okay.' George sounded braver than he felt, and Margaret's mouth literally dropped open as she listened.

'You don't think I'm serious, do you, *father-in-law*? Well, you'd better listen carefully. I want the money in cash, in a nice combination of tens, twenties and fifties. Friday should allow you enough time to get it all together. I'll ring at noon to let you know where to bring it. If you do anything silly, like letting the police in on our little arrangement, Emma will be the one to suffer. If you behave and do as you're told, I'll let you speak to her next time I ring.'

'I need longer to get the cash together – two days isn't

enough time. You know how things work, Simon. The bank needs notice for large withdrawals.'

'Then you'll have to use your influence to persuade them you're a special case, won't you? Oh, and just to let you know I'm serious, there's a little surprise for you in your garage.' Simon ended the call abruptly.

Margaret had caught only one side of the conversation. 'What did he say? Is Emma all right?'

'I think so. He said we could speak to her before we give him the money and we need to check the garage...' George was already heading for the door, afraid of what he might find waiting for him.

The Porters' garage stood a good twenty yards from the house, a double detached structure large enough for both their cars yet Margaret chose to park hers at the side of the house unless it was icy. George drove a two-year-old Hyundai Tucson, his wife a silver Ford Focus, purchased only a couple of months before.

Hurrying after George, Margaret wondered why going to the garage was so imperative but she soon found out. All appeared well outside, but the single side door had been forced and stood ajar. George pushed it open and gasped at the sight before him. All four car doors were jemmied open, and bright-red paint covered the vehicle inside and out.

'No!' Margaret followed George into the garage, stepping carefully to avoid the puddles of paint. 'Did Simon do this?'

'Who else? I think this is supposed to convince us he's serious.'

'More likely that he's mad! Why would he do such a thing? Why does he hate us so much?' Upon further inspection they discovered Beecham had slashed the leather seats inside the car and all four tyres. It was a frenzied attack. The man must have been near hysterical.

'We have to phone the police, please,' Margaret pleaded, trembling with shock.

George steered her from the garage and back towards the house. Once inside he ran his fingers through his hair, his face a study of pain and confusion as he paced the length of the room.

He eventually spoke. 'If we involve the police, he might do something worse.'

'We have no assurance he'll return Emma whatever we do. Maybe we could do both, inform the police but still go along with his demands?' Margaret looked hopefully at her husband.

'His demands include no police.'

'But we can't do this alone. The man's insane. He won't act reasonably whichever way we jump. I'm scared, George. We need help.'

George Porter sighed heavily, took out his phone and dialled DI Freeman's number.

CHAPTER THIRTY-FOUR

'Any luck?' Sam Freeman hovered behind Paul Roper, wanting instant results even though it was barely an hour since he began searching.

Paul sighed and stretched his arms above his head. 'Nothing so far, but the Land Registry only updates its data every month or so; if our man bought within the last four weeks it wouldn't show up. I've located six Christopher Simpsons who own property in the Durham and Northumberland area, and that doesn't include Christopher Andrew Simpsons or Christopher David Simpsons. They're all long-time owners – I know we can't rule them out, but they're probably not Beecham. It's going to take time, boss.'

Samantha nodded and moved away to let him continue. She knew Paul didn't like pressure and worked as quickly and meticulously as possible, aware, as they all were, that time was paramount. Sam then approached Layla Gupta, who answered her question before it was even asked.

'Nothing here yet either, boss, but I've a long way to go too.'

'Jenny, ring Beecham's first two wives will you and see if

they've thought of anything else?' The DI was itching to be active. Her phone rang and she answered it rather brusquely. 'Yes.'

'DI Freeman? It's George Porter here. We've heard from Simon.'

Half an hour later, Samantha and Jenny stood in the doorway of the Porters' garage looking at the senseless destruction Beecham had inflicted.

Margaret shook her head in disbelief. 'Why would he do this?'

'Let's go into the house, shall we?' Jenny suggested. 'We can talk better there.'

Once inside, Sam looked at the letter from Simon. The phone he'd sent was in a plastic evidence bag, although she knew it would tell them very little.

'He's sending you a message, showing you what a big man he is and that he's in charge. Are you sure you didn't hear anything through the night?' Sam asked.

'Nothing. It's double glazed and our bedroom's on the other side of the house from the garage. I'm not sleeping well and for some time was listening to the radio with earphones to avoid disturbing Margaret. She'd taken a sleeping pill last night and was out cold.' George seemed frustrated and angry at having missed Beecham.

'You've done the right thing by contacting us. I know what a difficult decision it must have been but we have the resources to get through this and get Emma safely home. Can you tell me again exactly what he said?' Sam asked. George tried to repeat Beecham's words verbatim while Jenny wrote them down.

'Good, you've done well. This demand for money is a game changer. Previously, although we suspected Simon had Emma, it was still a missing person case. The demand means we can throw extra resources into our investigation. Jenny will stay with you during the day and take up the role of Family Liaison Officer, an FLO. She'll be able to answer any questions you might have and keep you up to date with any progress we make. You couldn't have a better officer for this – she's the best.' Samantha smiled. 'We'll also have someone watching your house at night. Now that Beecham's been here, he could do so again.'

Margaret shuddered at the prospect. Sam noticed and tried to reassure her. 'It's a possibility yet improbable. Simon took you unawares with this action but coming again won't have the same element of surprise. He'll probably not risk it a second time. Now, George, we have to discuss the money. Can you raise £200,000 before Friday?'

'I'll go to the bank and see the manager, explain the situation. He'll know we're good for the money. It's just whether he'll waive the limits on cash withdrawals. I can also visit the building society and draw out the maximum they'll allow. I did think of talking to my accountant – he's a great friend and Emma's godfather – I'm sure he'll help or at least advise us.'

'That all sounds good. I think there's a reason Beecham only vandalised your car and not Margaret's and that's to leave you transport to make the exchange. Perhaps when we're finished here you can visit the bank? Once you have the money we'll mark it with UV ink. It's invisible to the naked eye, and we'll take note of the serial numbers. We're confident of catching Beecham. These things are standard procedure, okay?'

A nod from George signalled his agreement and Margaret managed half a smile. The couple appeared relieved to hand over the decision-making.

'Are you okay to visit the bank alone or would you like one of our officers to go with you?' Sam offered. 'A plain-clothed one.'

'No, I'll be fine. I'll ring Henry first, if that's okay with you, to put him in the picture and see if he has any suggestions.'

'Good. If Henry does agree to help, we'd like to meet him. I'll be off now – we'll keep in touch through Jenny.'

Samantha left the Porters' home and returned to New Middridge police station. The possibility of Beecham watching the house crossed her mind, but she felt it improbable. After his night-time exploits he'd probably be back with Emma, hopefully treating her with some basic humanity.

Back at the station Sam updated Paul and Layla and then took the stairs, two at a time, to see Detective Chief Inspector Aiden Kent.

'Come in.' The DCI invited.

'Sir,' Sam was fired up, she'd longed for something to break and now it had, 'our missing person case has officially become an abduction. Emma Porter's parents received a ransom demand from Simon Beecham, a letter in her handwriting and a burner phone on which he rang them. He's also visited them through the night and vandalised George Porter's car.'

'What's the man demanding?'

'He's asked for £200,000, which George Porter's currently trying to gather, and Beecham's given them until Friday when he'll ring back at noon. Beecham stipulated no police, but fortunately the Porters trust us and felt unable to do this alone.' Sam looked directly at her boss. 'I can't say precisely what we'll need until we have a drop point, although this man is dangerous, our resources will probably be stretched.'

'Whatever you need will be available, Samantha. Keep me up to speed, will you?'

Sam was delighted. The DCI was generally supportive and

it was good to know he was behind her – she couldn't wait to get out of his office and set everything in place.

CHAPTER THIRTY-FIVE

Simon was restless, prowling the upstairs room, the proverbial bear with a sore head. He'd always been impatient and Emma shuddered, recognising this as a signal of one of his dark moods which made her shudder. Tucked in the belt at the back of his trousers, the ever-present gun was visible from where Emma sat, fearful of moving. She'd eaten the food he'd brought and wondered what would happen next.

Each passing hour highlighted her inability to change this awful situation. Dare she ask Simon when he expected her parents to pay the ransom? Knowing a timeline might help to ease her mind – Emma's current tactic of not thinking too far ahead and not dwelling on the possible outcomes of her plight simply wasn't working.

'When will you collect the money?' she ventured.

A grin spread across Simon's face. He seemed to welcome the distraction of talking and the opportunity to alarm her even more.

'You're assuming *Daddy* will pay up, are you? You must think highly of your worth.' Simon laughed, successfully ducking the question. 'Are you getting bored? Perhaps we could make our own entertainment?' Simon stopped pacing and moved towards her, the look in his eyes leaving Emma in no doubt as to what he meant.

Instinctively she jumped up and ran towards the bedroom she'd been kept in earlier. Maybe she could barricade the door to keep him out – the thought of him touching her was repulsive. Simon was swift, grabbing her arm before she reached the door and twisting her to face him, his breath warm and moist on her cheek.

'Get off me!' she shouted. His response was to grasp her even tighter. Emma wondered if she could reach the gun, but by the time the idea entered her head her arms were in a vice-like grip and she was being forced back towards the sofa. If Simon managed to get her there, to lay the full weight of his body on top of hers, she would be at his mercy. Emma reacted quickly, lifting her knee as hard as possible. Satisfaction flooded through her as she found her sensitive target and Simon let her go, falling to the floor and groaning in agony.

Six steps saw Emma reach the door, a portal she presumed led to freedom. Almost falling down the stairs, she came to another door and managed to open it. Cold air hit her like a punch as she forced her limbs to move, suddenly aware that her feet were bare. Simon had not returned her shoes. Emma ran, taking only a moment to decide which direction to go – towards the trees, her best option for concealment.

Crossing the track in front of the house, she almost fell into the safety and shelter of the trees, quickening her stride when she heard the door banging behind her. Simon was already in pursuit and Emma knew his mood would be dark and angry. He'd want revenge for the pain she'd inflicted.

The undergrowth was icy. Fallen branches scratched at her skin as she ran farther into the trees, fear washing over her and doubt setting in as to the wisdom of her actions. As branches grazed her limbs, Emma was aware of the pain in her feet and the blood from her arms, but it only spurred her on, longing for safety and freedom.

Suddenly a gunshot rang out and Emma froze, wasting valuable time to turn round to see if Simon was in sight. Her breath came in short, shallow bursts and her chest ached with the effort of running. There was no sign of Simon, he must have fired the gun to scare her but now that she was still, the reality of her situation was apparent. The trees were denser than she'd expected, the light poor, which could work to her advantage, although which way to go was unclear. Having turned almost a complete circle, Emma was quite disorientated, unsure which direction she'd come from and how to proceed. There wasn't time to think, to catch her breath, as she heard Simon shout her name.

'Emma, don't be a bloody fool! You'll get lost out here – you'll freeze to death!'

It took only a second to decide that the option of freezing to death was preferable to going back to the house and she started running again, heading away from the sound of his voice. However, fate had other ideas and she tripped over a protruding root, painfully stubbing her toes as she sprawled on the ground. An involuntary cry alerted Simon to her whereabouts and before Emma could pick herself up he was standing over her, his red face contorted into an angry scowl.

Grabbing her by the hair, Simon yanked Emma to her feet, causing more pain and bitter disappointment that her bid for freedom had failed so miserably. He half dragged her back to the house seeming unphased that anyone should hear or see them, the isolation of his hideaway highlighting the utter hopelessness of her situation.

After hauling her upstairs, Simon made for the bedroom and yanked Emma around to face him.

'Don't try anything like that again because next time I'll kill you!' The fierceness of his words left her in no doubt that he meant them, and as if to emphasise his point, he smashed a fist into her face, the sound of crunching bone echoed in her ears before he flung her onto the bed, then left, locking the door.

Emma curled onto her side, semi-conscious from the excruciating pain in her face. Blood oozed from her mouth and nose and a tooth fell onto the bed. Her jaw felt like it was on fire, the agony at least taking her focus from the cuts and scratches on her limbs. She shivered, cold and wet. Mud stained the sheets, blood and tears soaked the pillow.

When Emma came around it was dark again with no way of telling what time it was, early evening perhaps, or the middle of the night – it made little difference. An attempt to move triggered pain in almost every part of her body, particularly her jaw. Remaining motionless seemed the best option, although she longed for water to drink and clean her wounds. The only way to get a drink or a trip to the bathroom was to alert Simon, so she decided to stay still and ride out the pain. Her head throbbed, dizziness and a raging temperature confused her as Emma drifted in and out of consciousness.

Through swollen eyes, Emma looked at her wrists, the source of much of her pain, and observed that the right one was weeping – an infection which needed attention. She almost laughed. Who would tend her wounds? Certainly not Simon.

The next time Emma woke, it was still dark – it could have been days later, and she struggled to open her eyes which were little more than slits, her left eye almost completely closed. Moving was still painful, but as she focussed on the black shapes in the room, a mug was visible beside the bed, or was she hallucinating?

Reaching for the mug, it was a relief to feel its solid shape in her trembling hand as she lifted it to her lips, sipping the water slowly, which was all she could do as she vowed never to take it for granted again.

CHAPTER THIRTY-SIX

How do you ask your bank manager for £200,000 in cash immediately? George's plight was at least shared by his friend and accountant, Henry Acres, who willingly came on board to help. A quick phone call after Sam left the house solicited the man's assistance and Henry made himself instantly available to accompany George.

'I'm only filling in tax returns and the tax man can wait for his money! Besides, I know the manager at your branch, we belong to the same golf club. Let me ring him and warn him we're coming. I'm sure he'll see us when he learns the gravity of the situation.' The two agreed a time to meet outside the Porters' bank in New Middridge High Street.

It seemed like an age since George was at this same bank with his daughter, yet it was less than two weeks earlier. He thought then that life had dealt them a cruel hand. Emma had been used and abused by Beecham, who stole everything she possessed – but it seemed a trifle in comparison now that his daughter's life was at stake. Emma was more precious than any possession he owned and he didn't know what he'd do if that bastard didn't return her to them.

Henry greeted his friend with a warm handshake and a concerned expression. 'George, I'm so sorry, you should have let me know sooner... bloody hell, you must be out of your mind! Whoever would have thought it? He seemed an okay sort of chap at the wedding.'

'We were all taken in. I'll tell you more later. Getting this money together's the priority. I thought I'd see what the bank can give me then go to the building society and take as much out there as possible.'

'Forget the building society, they only allow £500 a day maximum withdrawal and they'll take forever to get permission to bend the rules – the bank's our best bet. They have more flexibility. Look, I don't want to take over but I've been thinking on the way here and if there's any problem with getting the cash, I can raise a substantial part of it myself, probably half the full amount.'

George was stunned. 'I can't let you do that!'

'Yes, my friend, you can. Emma's my god-daughter and I love her like family. I've every confidence the police will find this bastard and we'll get our money back.'

'If we don't, I'll reimburse you every penny, Henry. It's very generous, are you sure?'

'Absolutely, now let's go inside and get this sorted.'

Nigel Best was on the phone and a smiling woman asked the two men to wait in a small room until he was free. The wait afforded George the opportunity to relate the events of the last couple of days and for Henry to reassure him that whatever the outcome of the next hour, they would raise the money.

'We'll stand more chance of getting it if we tell Nigel the reason for our need and the urgency. Is that okay?' Henry asked. 'We need to tell him the police are involved, it'll add authenticity.'

'Whatever it takes and, Henry, thanks. I feel better for

having you beside me.' George's eyes glistened with tears at the evidence of such friendship.

Mr Best was a portly man who put George in mind of Captain Mainwaring in *Dad's Army*, but his voice was soft and easy-going as he apologised for keeping them waiting – nothing like the bumbling sitcom character. Mr Best listened silently as the two men poured out their request and the appalling necessity for it, his expression one of total empathy.

'This is horrendous and I'm so sorry it's happened to you. I have a daughter and can only imagine what you must be going through. Don't let the money worry you – it can be arranged.' His slight smile and positive response brought relief flooding through George's mind. 'We normally receive cash twice weekly, ordered from our cash centre in Washington. It's an unusually high amount, but your accounts with us cover it, and as the circumstance is dire, I'm happy to request the full amount. I can also assure you of my absolute discretion. No one will hear about this matter from my lips. If the order goes in today we can have the money by close of business tomorrow. Will that do, or will coming back to collect it be a problem?'

Henry spoke up, and offered to coordinate the physical collection of the money, one less burden for his friend. 'It won't be a problem, Nigel. I'll be happy to take responsibility for collecting the money, and thank you.'

George could hardly speak. Such a weight had been lifted from his shoulders and he could have kissed the two men.

Henry followed George back to the Porters' house, where they told Margaret and Jenny what had transpired. Jenny seemed particularly pleased to be getting the money the following day; it allowed plenty of time before Beecham rang with instructions regarding the exchange, sufficient to get the notes marked and their serial numbers recorded. She suggested an officer accompany Acres to pick up the money, a suggestion he readily accepted. DC Paul Roper would be the man for the job.

'I'm fairly sure having the police involved oiled the wheels somewhat.' George turned to his wife. 'You were right, Margaret. I was stupid even to consider going it alone.'

It would be an agonising wait until Beecham rang again.

As the Porters comforted each other in the kitchen, Jenny took the opportunity to learn a little more about Henry Acres, glad he'd come forward to support his friends. It appeared he'd only met Simon Beecham once, at the wedding, not the best place to get to know someone's true character. But even then, Emma's new 'husband' had expressed an interest in Henry's business, suggesting they meet later for a mutually beneficial chat.

Such a meeting never took place, yet to Jenny it was another indicator that Beecham's motive in wheedling his way into the Porter family was one of self-interest. She wondered how quickly the man had realised he'd chosen the wrong family. The Porters were never going to be a pushover. And what would Simon Beecham have done if those plans hadn't been thwarted, if Diane Beecham hadn't appeared on the scene to accuse him of bigamy?

George and Margaret joined them in the lounge, mugs of coffee in their hands. They sat in comfortable chairs, feeling anything but comfortable – the clock chimed twice, 2pm – the next two days were going to be interminably long. Margaret maintained that waiting was one of the hardest things to do and no one argued with her.

CHAPTER THIRTY-SEVEN

'Emma! Wake up!'

Emma was in Portugal on her honeymoon – the sun was uncomfortably hot and sweat trickled down between her shoulder blades. She should be happy, yet a lump in her throat felt so big it threatened to choke her. It was a paradox – this ought to be the happiest time of her life – something was off-kilter. She couldn't breathe easily, even outside on the beach. Her senses warned her of water on her face but Emma wasn't in the sea – the brilliant azure sea she'd love to capture on canvas. The heat was stifling; she was so thirsty; her lips were swollen, caked with something – could it be sand? She wanted to drink but couldn't raise her body from its prone position, couldn't reach out her arm. Why? It was all so confusing. What was happening?

Sleep enveloped her again, a welcome velvety blackness whose embrace Emma yearned for, to be free from pain and the strange sense of foreboding, surely a nightmare.

'Emma, wake up!' The voice intruded into her oblivion, harsh and unwelcome. It was a familiar voice – an alarming one which invoked panic – a voice from which she wanted to run away yet her body stubbornly refused to move. Someone was pouring water on her face, roughly wiping away the dirt and then fiercely shaking her shoulders.

No, no!

An overwhelming desire to be left alone, to sink back into her dream and feel the sun on her skin, took over her being, to hear the waves lapping on the shore, to bask in peace...

Bare trees blocked her way, gnarled branches reaching for her, grabbing greedily at her skin to claw her back to that awful house. The trees moved, closing in on her while her feet sank into the mud, her soles scratched by the roots buried beneath. The darkness was cloying, a thick airless soup, its fingers extending down into her lungs, stealing her breath. And the heat almost blistered her skin – were the trees on fire? Is that why she struggled to breathe, why it felt as if she was melting?

'Emma!' The voice was distant but urgent, dragging her back to a place she didn't want to be. Her face was wet, hot. She gasped for breath.

'Emma!' It echoed through her brain, terrifyingly near yet distant. She heard a groan from somewhere deep within her own body, and everything went black again.

In the Porters' household, the day was dragging. Thursday. Emma had been missing since Monday evening; it was their longest week. Another night with very little sleep passed and another loomed ahead before this nightmare could be over. The couple skirted about one another, running out of words and not wanting to cause upset by saying the wrong thing.

For George and Margaret their fertile imaginations had

become a curse and neither dared to share the images which filled their minds, tormenting each waking hour. Their home, usually such a happy pulsating place, was transformed into a dark waiting room and neither occupant was sure exactly what the outcome of their wait would be.

CHAPTER THIRTY-EIGHT

In her New Middridge office, DI Sam Freeman nervously tapped her fingers on the desk – it was 7.30am on Friday – she'd been awake since 4am, adrenaline pumping through her body, fired up with anticipation of the day ahead.

It was dark when she'd arrived, the endless rain had ceased and the air was unusually mild for early November, which would hopefully be in their favour. Inside felt stuffy. Sam had already consumed two cups of coffee to calm her nerves. Not knowing how the case would pan out added a tangible tension to the mix of emotions the detective was experiencing. Well aware that this was the day when the Beecham case would be resolved, Samantha was cautiously optimistic about the result.

The office was quiet, almost eerie, and the room felt much larger than it did when filled with personnel, hollow without the sound of computers and constant chatter. Sam was itching for the working day to begin.

A tired-looking Jenny arrived, yawning as she walked through the door. 'Did you sleep here, boss?' she asked, shrugging off her coat.

'It feels like it. How were the Porters when you left them last night?'

'Tired, anxious, anticipating the worst – just as you'd expect. Will I have the pleasure of taking them the money this morning?'

'Yes, it should be ready and waiting with the custody sergeant.'

Henry Acres and Paul Roper had collected the money from the bank the evening before and taken it straight to the police station for recording the numbers and marking the notes with UV ink.

Jenny smiled. 'This will undoubtedly be the only time in my life when I'll have such a large amount of money in my possession!'

'Good job I trust you then. Four hours to go before the call.' Sam looked at her watch, the hands in the same position as the last time she'd looked. 'Enjoy the peace while you can. It'll be all systems go when we hear from Beecham. I just hope he gives us sufficient time to do all the necessaries. The trouble is, we don't know what that will be until we have a location.'

If Beecham insisted on George delivering the money within an hour or two of his call, their job would be much more problematic than it would be with more time. But at least they were reasonably sure he was operating alone, so he couldn't be watching the Porters' house simultaneously if he was at a drop point. Sam had discussed this scenario with DCs Roper and Gupta the day before, keeping Jenny updated with frequent telephone calls to the Porters. A brainstorming session threw up several possible scenarios, each considered and prepared for as much as possible. The reality was they couldn't plan for every eventuality.

Paul Roper and Layla Gupta arrived together, sharing a

private joke which prompted Sam and Jenny to exchange a knowing look. They'd long suspected that the two officers were in a relationship and wished them good luck if they were, but today wasn't the day to speculate on anything other than the job at hand.

'Morning, you two!' Jenny greeted them cheerfully while Samantha nodded in their direction. Computers were fired up and the two detective constables checked any overnight developments. Sam wasn't pushing for information as she would usually be doing, her mind elsewhere, so she was somewhat surprised when Layla suddenly yelped.

'Got him!'

The others gathered around to see what she meant as she proudly read an email from one of the garages she'd queried regarding possible purchases by Beecham.

'Village Motors have responded. They sold a used black Range Rover to a Christopher Simpson a week ago. He paid in cash and took the vehicle the same day, all paperwork was in order, and they sent me the registration number.' Layla beamed, clearly delighted with her find.

'Forged paperwork that will be.' Paul huffed, appearing disgruntled with the fact that Layla was the one to make the first breakthrough. He went back to his computer to step up his search for properties.

'Village Motors, where's that, Layla? I don't know it,' Sam asked. The DC looked again at the email. 'It's at Alston, a town on the A686 thirty miles from here.'

'Good work, now get on the phone to the garage owner and ask if he'll look at a photo of our suspect to see if he or any of his salesmen recognise him as Simpson.'

'Yes, boss.' Her head went straight down to find a phone number and she made the call within a minute.

'Paul, break off for now and get that registration number to ANPR will you, quickly, man.' Sam stared at him, expecting him to suggest Layla should do it. Samantha wasn't in the mood to be questioned and fortunately for Paul he did as she asked.

Within half an hour, the team had a positive ID on Beecham as the man who bought the Range Rover using the name Christopher Simpson.

'The garage boss sold Beecham the car himself. It's a one-man operation, and he's certain it's the right man, although he was wearing glasses and his hair was darker.' Layla took a deep breath and sat back, putting her hands behind her head and stretching.

'Right, if we get a hit with the ANPR, I don't want any approach made. We need Beecham on the move today. He has to think he's invisible until we get Emma back. Jenny, isn't it time you went to the Porters' house? You can tell them we've discovered he's driving a different vehicle, although there are no details yet. It might just encourage them to know something's going our way. I'll join you before noon when the call comes in and we should have all units ready to move ASAP when we have a location.'

Jenny left and Sam went upstairs to relate their latest find to the DCI. She'd keep in constant contact with her boss but was anxious to be at the house to ensure nothing untoward was happening there.

After giving the positive news to Aiden Kent relating to tracing the vehicle Beecham was using, Sam went over the operation's logistics, reminding the DCI that their needs might change radically once they knew the location and time of the exchange.

Kent looked at her over the rim of his glasses, and she felt like a little girl back in school. 'Hopefully, three units will suffice. We do have to consider the budget, Samantha. But if you're right about Beecham working alone then we should be able to tie everything up this evening. It'll be an excellent result.'

At least he didn't ask for it to be gift-wrapped, Sam thought, returning to her office downstairs.

CHAPTER THIRTY-NINE

9.45am. There were still over two hours to go until the expected call and the tension was building. When Jenny arrived to resume her duties as FLO, the marked money with her, George and Margaret looked washed out. After a long sleepless night they felt weak and tired, yet their senses were on high alert, anticipating the outcome of the day and the numerous problems and possibilities it could present. Jenny did her best to be pleasant and asked if she could get anything for them. No. There was nothing. They only wanted to have their daughter home safely, and the police were working hard towards that goal.

The mood in the house vacillated between optimism and despair. Margaret excused herself several times to go upstairs, returning red-eyed to offer yet more unwanted coffee. Jenny followed her into the kitchen where she put the large expanding nylon holdall down and kicked it under the table where she thought it wouldn't be a reminder to them all of what lay ahead. She silently speculated what she would do with such a massive amount – the possibilities were endless. Jenny had been surprised how much the money weighed and wondered what

Beecham would do with it. Then she chided herself – he wasn't going to get away with it, was he?

The Porters had showed little interest in the money when Jenny carried it into the house, their minds fixed solely on Emma. She believed they wouldn't be overly concerned if Beecham did get away with the money as long as their daughter was safely returned to them. A lesson perhaps in what truly matters in life.

Henry Acres arrived at the house just before 11am and Jenny breathed a sigh of relief at the prospect of someone to share the task of keeping the couple calm and positive. His presence somehow diluted the tension. While George and Margaret talked with their friend, Jenny moved into the hallway. It wasn't her job to spy on the family and they needed a degree of privacy to allow them to be themselves. Constantly having a stranger in their home could add to the strain they were already under, negating her purpose for being there.

It was a beautiful house, so different from where Emma had lived with Beecham. Jenny studied the paintings on the wall, all different, yet each painted with an eye for colour. They were stunning – images that prompted a desire to walk down the paths, open the distant garden gate and sneak a look into someone else's life, or follow the track through the wood and enjoy the birdsong and the numerous outdoor scents.

Emma was undoubtedly talented. These were commercial pieces which would appeal to many people. A twinge of something caught Jenny by surprise, a sadness for Emma's situation maybe, and a realisation of her responsibility. If she'd been religious, this would be the time to offer up a prayer for Emma Porter's safe return.

Samantha arrived at 11.15am, joining the family and her DS in the lounge. Her presence seemed to signal the beginning of something big and the tension became even more viscous.

'Is the phone fully charged?' Sam asked.

Jenny nodded. 'Yes, I put it on when I arrived. It's one hundred per cent.'

'Good. George, are you okay to answer the call?'

'Yes.' The reality of the situation left George with no choice. Sam couldn't offer to take the call for him as they were still hopeful Beecham was unaware, or at best unsure, of police involvement.

'I just wish he'd ring early so we can get on with it.' George's voice betrayed his anxiety.

'I know – and we've gone over this before. Remember, you must insist on speaking to Emma. He'll be expecting you to ask so she'll probably be with him when he rings. Ask him to repeat any instructions. We can't make any mistakes about the venue or the time. Once we have the relevant details, I have two units on standby at the station and someone will tail you at a distance. Depending on how far we'll be travelling, we may use a tag-team manoeuvre with the other units so don't worry if you lose sight of the tail. They'll not lose you.' Sam was all business, her manner instilling confidence. George nodded his understanding.

Coffee and sandwiches were on the kitchen table, untouched. Sam glanced at them.

'Perhaps you should eat something. We don't know what the next few hours will throw at us and being weak from hunger won't help anyone.' She led by example and took a ham sandwich she didn't want. The others half-heartedly followed her lead, all except Margaret who sat looking thoughtful.

'Can I go with him to get our girl?' Her voice, barely a whisper, cracked.

'I'm not sure that's a good idea.' Samantha understood the request. She'd feel the same and insist on it, hoping for the chance to scratch the man's eyes out. 'We need to keep a presence here in case of problems – an unexpected change of plan. Perhaps Mr Acres will stay with you?' She looked at their friend who dipped his head in agreement.

'Yes, of course, anything.' He turned and smiled at Margaret, who squeezed her eyes closed – a child not invited to the party.

11.55am. This was undoubtedly the edgiest moment of Samantha's career. The room was silent as the minutes slowly ticked away.

'What if he doesn't ring?' George blurted out.

'If he wants his money he'll ring. Please don't worry if he's a few minutes late. From what we know of Beecham he likes to be in control, to keep everyone guessing, and I'm presuming he'll want to play a few of his little mind games. So being late is something we should expect.' Sam hoped *late* would be no more than a few minutes. Looking at Margaret Porter chewing on her fingernails, she didn't think the couple could take much more stress.

Noon. All eyes were on the silent mobile phone. George stood and paced the room, his body stiff and his eyes darting to the phone every few seconds.

'Come on, man,' he muttered.

'Don't let him rattle you, George. That's what he wants. When you answer the call, try to remain calm and don't comment on the fact he's late,' the DI cautioned.

12.15pm – still no call. Now even Samantha was getting worried.

CHAPTER FORTY

Swirling waters made Emma dizzy. The heat was unbearable – the trees had shifted to the beach, growing at strange angles out of the sand, swaying gently in the breeze. And it was dark but she could feel the branches reaching out to her, grazing her arms, scratching her face.

'Emma, wake up!' A chink of light intruded into her darkness. 'Emma, come on, get up. Here, drink this.' Simon's voice.

No, no, leave me alone.

But she couldn't speak the words. Her lips remained closed, parched.

Suddenly water was pouring on her face, cold against the heat of her skin.

'Drink water, please?'

Again, the request was only in her head.

Simon was lifting her, sitting her up. Pain shot through her body, she ached everywhere and a wave of nausea swept over her.

'Emma, listen to me!' He was angry – she knew that tone only too well. 'I need you to speak to your parents, Emma.'

Simon had her attention. Emma struggled to find the strength to open her sticky and swollen eyes. The light dazzled, the darkness faded away. She lacked the strength to sit up and her mouth was so dry.

Suddenly Simon pushed her forward, stuffing a pillow behind her back. She screamed as white-hot pain shot through her shoulders and her face. He was holding a cup to her lips, water. Parting her lips was an effort but the liquid felt good. As it wetted her mouth, Emma coughed and it dribbled out. Simon put it to her lips again, and Emma managed to swallow this time.

Breathe, drink slowly. What's happening?

She lay back on the pillows, remembering where she was and wishing to sleep again.

'Don't close your eyes! You need to speak to your parents soon. Don't you want to see them, Emma?' Simon's voice was mocking. He knew she wanted to see them if only to get away from him.

Focus, Emma, think. If he wants me to talk to them, he must be going to let me go.

The thought gave her the strength to lift her head. Her eyes met Simon's. He looked at her with a sneer on his face.

'Good. I'm going to ring them now and you're going to tell them you're okay. That's all, don't try to be clever, right?' She nodded and reached for the cup in his hand.

'Okay, just a little more.' He allowed her another drink and as she lowered the cup, the gun came into her sightline. She'd almost forgotten about it, yet it lay on the bed close to her right hand. Simon saw her looking and picked it up.

'You don't have the strength.' He laughed. 'Just do as I've told you or you'll have a long time to regret it.' Then, raising the gun to Emma's face, he slowly stroked her cheek with the muzzle. It felt cold against her burning skin, simultaneously sensual and terrifying.

Would he really let her go when he had his money, or would he kill her?

Simon tucked the gun into the back of his belt. He was right. She didn't have the strength, yet her senses were returning. Emma was more aware and watched as he pulled a mobile phone from his pocket, not his phone but a cheap disposable one. He searched for a number.

'Remember, be a good girl.' He squeezed her shoulder to emphasise his words; the pain made her wince. The ringtone stopped and Emma strained to hear the voice on the other end. Simon stood up and moved away from the bed where she lay still propped up on pillows.

'Have you got the money? Good, now listen, this is what you're going to do...'

Emma's heart raced as she listened to the instructions for her release, the name of a town she recognised – and then the time – 11pm. Although she had no idea of the time, it was light outside which meant it would still be several hours until the meeting with her father. As these thoughts crept through her mind, Simon approached her and held the phone next to her ear. Tears pricked her eyes as she heard her father's voice.

'Emma! Are you all right?' He sounded desperate.

'Yes... Dad, please help me...' Simon wrenched the phone away and the call ended far too soon. The simple exertion of speaking those few words had exhausted Emma.

'Right, so now we just have to wait until dark.' Simon perched on the side of the bed again, looking at her in a way which made her skin crawl. Emma was suddenly grateful for the mud and dirt covering her body and the swollen face even though it hurt like hell. Simon didn't go near her, stood gruffly to leave the room and locked the door behind him.

CHAPTER FORTY-ONE

It was 12.23pm when Beecham finally rang, mind games, Samantha thought, but George didn't comment; he took down the details as instructed and asked to speak to his daughter. His hands were visibly shaking and Sam's heart went out to him. As the phone was on speaker, all those present heard Emma's feeble voice, five brief words but the fear in her voice was chilling, telling them as much as the words themselves. Beecham's final message was alarming, particularly for George and Margaret.

'If you try to fool me in any way, you'll regret it. I'll keep my end of the bargain and return your precious daughter – if I get my money – but if you mess me about or try to come after me, Emma will never be safe. I'll make sure you never sleep soundly again – you'll always be wondering when she'll disappear and next time, it will be for good.'

An uncomfortable silence lasted only a few moments, broken by Margaret who chose not to comment on Beecham's final threat.

'She sounded awful, ill and so afraid!' Margaret sobbed openly. Hearing her daughter's voice was almost too much to bear. 'And we have to wait even longer. Why couldn't he let us go now? We've got the money.'

'He wants the cover of darkness, Margaret,' Sam said, 'and he's chosen a place where there'll be people. Jenny, I know the name but haven't been there. Do you know Beacon Bridge?'

'Yes, it's on the A69 about six miles west of Hexham.' Jenny was already searching Google Maps. 'It's a small market town but with a thriving nightlife. Although little more than a large village it has more pubs per population than anywhere else in the North. It should take forty minutes or so to get there.'

'Right, I'm off back to the station to revise our plans. Jenny will stay here, George, and we'll be in touch as soon as we know how to proceed.'

Samantha was puzzled – this wasn't at all what she'd expected – a car park in a small market town. Most perpetrators would choose somewhere deserted, an old quarry or warehouse perhaps. What was Beecham's reasoning?

Sam's first stop was to the office where she gave details of the exchange venue to Paul and Layla, instructing them to find out as much about the location as possible. Next, she went upstairs to tell the DCI.

Aiden Kent was closely following the progress of DI Freeman's case and was up to speed. Expecting Samantha, he motioned to a seat as she entered his office.

'He's making us wait a bit longer, sir, but at least it gives us time to get things in place. The drop-off point is a town-centre car park in Beacon Bridge. DCs Roper and Gupta are on it as we speak. 11pm will be busy, chucking out time at the pubs, and I believe there are several in the vicinity. We'll have a detailed map soon.'

The DCI scratched his chin. 'I can understand his thinking. If the place is crawling with late-night revellers, no one will pay attention to him and perhaps he's hoping to get lost in the crowd. Has he been any more specific about where to park?'

'Yes, sir, Mr Porter has to turn right inside the car park and take the nearest available spot to the electric charging point. Now we have the details of Beecham's new vehicle we'll at least know what we're looking for and be able to follow him as he leaves the car park. I'll refine the plans now, and get back to you ASAP.' Sam was keen to return to the others to see actual maps of the area.

'Right, but we'll have to contact Northumbria Police to let them know we're operating in their patch. Do you want me to do it?'

'Yes, sir, thank you.' Sam stood to leave. A courtesy call to another force would come better from a senior officer and was one less thing for her to worry about.

Several maps of Beacon Bridge and the surrounding area were sprawled on the central table in the office, and Layla was studying them meticulously. She pushed the route maps to one side, the town centre one being of more interest. The car park Beecham specified was slap bang in the middle of the town, a long rectangular shape surrounded on three sides by public houses, six in all. A row of terraced cottages completed the fourth. A satellite image from Google showed two vehicular entrances, one at either end of the car park and a pedestrian opening on one of the longer sides. The boundary appeared to be a low railing; stepping over it would be easy, yet as it was unlikely Beecham would attempt to make his escape on foot, it shouldn't cause a problem.

Samantha, Paul and Layla pored over the maps looking closely at the surrounding streets to decide the best places to site their vehicles. Three cars would be deployed with two officers in each, communicating by radio. Then, having chosen the spots which would provide the best vantage points, they turned their attention to the routes into the town.

Paul didn't sound hopeful of finding Beecham with the available technology. 'We don't know which direction Beecham will be coming from and with those roads we won't pick him up on ANPR. There are hardly any cameras in the ten-mile radius of the town. However, if he's entering the area from further afield and uses a motorway, there's a chance we might pick him up – a slim one but don't hold your breath.'

Samantha nodded. 'It would be good to get a lead on where he's coming from, but we'll pick him up in Beacon Bridge at the drop after Emma is safely in her father's hands. If I can get a couple of extra officers as well as the six we have, we can put them outside one of the pubs – a couple of mates having a cigarette outside isn't unusual. If we go for the Red Lion, it's nearest to the charging point so they'll get a good view of George Porter's car.'

Samantha wanted to cover every eventuality. 'We won't approach Beecham until he leaves the car park, there are too many potential risks and we want him in the car with the money, so we may need to tail him until he's on the open road, then it'll be all systems go.'

'Have you cleared the overtime?' Paul asked. The extra men they would need to draft in could take an entire night shift out of New Middridge.

'Not yet. I'll see DCI Kent when I take him the final plan.' Sam grimaced – overtime budgets were always a contentious issue. Had Beecham chosen a daytime exchange more officers would have been available. 'The DCI's contacting Northumbria Police to let them know we're operating on their patch. Maybe they'll offer a few extra uniforms.' DCI Kent would have to sweet talk them for that to happen; each force guarded their budget jealously.

The three detectives went over the plans for a final time before Sam was happy to take them upstairs. 'We'll have a full briefing at 8pm. Layla, will you draw up a list of available personnel. You might need to use your charm on the duty sergeant and I'll broach the subject of overtime with the DCI. When we're all set up, have a break and something to eat, it's going to be a long night.'

DCI Kent had secured a car with two officers from Northumbria Police. 'They want to be in on things when such a serious operation is going down in their patch,' he explained.

Samantha wondered if they'd bill them for the overtime, it was more than likely but the DCI seemed unconcerned. She pushed to maintain the numbers they'd discussed earlier, the Northumbria bodies would be welcome extras and the DCI agreed. Samantha was now faced with a few anxious hours to fill, which would begin with a trip back to the Porters' house.

CHAPTER FORTY-TWO

Jenny answered the door, her face reflecting the tension within the house. Samantha paused to take a deep breath before joining the Porters and Henry Acres in the lounge. Sam's mood was solemn, the ultimate responsibility of someone's life depended on her getting things right; it was a salutary thought which spurred Sam on and held her focus.

5pm. Each occupant of the room was tired and anxious, worry hovering over them all like a dark and weighty canopy. Three pairs of eyes turned to greet the detective as she entered the room, expectancy on every face. With no attempt at pointless small talk, Sam sat and outlined the plans they'd put in place. Wide-eyed nods suggested approval as they listened patiently, a seed of optimism planted and watered with each word.

'Is it usual for another police force to join the operation?' Henry Acres asked.

'Not entirely, but as we're working on their patch they want some input, and this is the route they've chosen. But it's a good thing; more personnel at the location increases the odds in our favour.'

'And what *are* the odds?' Acres continued.

'I'm not in the habit of speculating, Mr Acres. I'm confident we've put in place everything possible to ensure a good result.' While mildly irritated at the question, Sam realised no malice or criticism was intended.

Margaret spoke up. 'We're so grateful, Samantha. There's no way we could have coped with this without you, so thank you both.'

'You're welcome, Margaret. We'll do our very best.'

6pm. Sam decided to bring Layla in to stay with Margaret, allowing Jenny to attend the rendezvous. She'd prefer her DS to be in one of the other vehicles rather than remaining at the house and was confident Layla would do an excellent job supporting Margaret when her husband left to take the money.

Telephoning the office to inform Layla of the change, Sam sensed disappointment in the DC's voice and knew she'd prefer to be where the action was but Layla didn't complain and set off immediately to take over the role of FLO.

As soon as DC Gupta arrived at the Porters' home, Sam knew she'd made the right decision. Layla's quiet interest in people endeared her to Margaret immediately. As the young constable gently posed open-ended questions, drawing the distraught woman out of herself, Sam and Jenny took their leave and returned to the station.

In the deli across the road from the station, the two women hugged large mugs of coffee, toasted sandwiches on the table in front of them. Both were hungry and demolished the food, needing the energy it offered.

'Thanks for bringing me in on this,' Jenny said. 'Layla's a natural. Did you see how she managed to take Margaret's mind off their situation? And she's genuinely interested in people.

Asking about Emma, her mother's favourite subject, was spot on. The baby photographs will probably be out soon and she might learn something useful.' Jenny stretched her arms and rolled her shoulders.

'Are you okay?' Samantha asked.

'Yes, it's been a long day. I'd usually be at home with my ready meal in the microwave and something mindless on the television. This is far more exciting, but a tad scary too.'

'Once the operation begins, you'll get a second wind and the adrenaline will kick in to keep us on the ball.' Sam smiled to reassure her DS.

8pm. The team had commandeered a conference room for the final briefing led by DI Samantha Freeman. Surprisingly the two officers from Northumbria had travelled down to join them. Paul Roper had expected them to join the briefing by a Zoom link but they'd chosen to come in person. Both were male officers. PC Steve Daley was out of uniform and accompanied DS Tony Finch. Paul remarked that things must be quiet in their neck of the woods, but they all knew the next few hours would change that.

The team members were partnered up, allocated a vehicle and given the location of where to park. If space was unavailable, the nearest available parking spot was to be secured. Next, the order of leaving was decided – Sam and PC Gary Cox would be in the lead vehicle – the local officers from Northumbria following, and Jenny and another two PCs would leave ten minutes later. Paul Roper with two more PCs would be in the final car tasked with discreetly tailing George Porter to the rendezvous. The men from the last two cars were the foot soldiers who would blend into the drinking crowd, ready to move swiftly.

Each team member was given a vest for protection, to wear under their civilian clothes, and a pair of night-vision binoculars were allocated to each car. Hopefully the binoculars would provide them with an advantage over Beecham, seeing him from a distance without being spotted.

Sam was confident she'd done everything possible in preparation, which she relayed to the DCI when he rang for an update at 9pm.

It was almost a relief when 9.30 arrived and Sam finally set off for Beacon Bridge. Gary Cox drove and she was pleased to be in a pool car – his legs would never have folded into her little Mini. She rang Layla to check all was well with the Porters – George would be leaving at 10pm, and according to Layla he was already in his coat with the money beside him, waiting for the off.

'Try to keep him calm. Tell them everything's going to plan from our end and he mustn't leave too early. We need everything in place before he pulls into the car park. Paul will be waiting to meet him en route and follow him to the destination.' She knew Layla would be all over this and in control, but it made her feel better to remind the girl. Sam needed to be doing something.

Twenty interminable miles. Gary Cox drove steadily. The roads were quiet, no one was venturing out on a dark November night. They would already be in a warm pub sharing a drink with friends or at home watching *EastEnders* or whatever. Gary tried to make conversation but all Sam would talk about was the case, probabilities and possibilities... he admired her focus.

The PC admitted to being familiar with Beacon Bridge,

recommending the George and Dragon for a good meal at a reasonable price, but the DI wanted to hear about the pub's location rather than how good their steak and hand-cut chips were. Gary answered her questions as well as he could.

Their allocated parking spot was the nearest to the electric charger in the car park and twenty-two minutes after setting off, they arrived. Gary reversed into a spot which Sam considered the perfect place then they breathed a sigh of relief and settled down to wait. They were first on the scene.

CHAPTER FORTY-THREE

George Porter couldn't remember ever being as afraid as he was that night, his legs were literally shaking and he wondered if he'd be able to pull himself together enough to drive. But there was no alternative. Beecham had specified that he and he alone bring the money.

Margaret's embrace almost crushed his ribs as he stood at their front door, feeling as a soldier might have done going off to war all those years ago, but the life at stake was his daughter's, not his own.

Manoeuvring the car along their drive, George narrowly missed the gatepost, swerving just in time to avoid the collision – how he wished he'd had a stiff drink but felt it unwise with a police officer in the house.

George knew the road well. Beacon Bridge was an attractive town where they'd often driven at weekends, lunching in one of the many pubs. He seemed to remember Emma setting up her easel and painting the view across the nearby river Nent one Sunday afternoon, but that was before she married Beecham, before this nightmare had thrown them all into turmoil. Silently George prayed to the god he'd neglected for many years but whose help and comfort he now desperately craved. Would tonight bring the miracle they needed?

After passing the junction for Eastgate on the A689, George was aware of a vehicle pulling out behind him, not close, but near enough to reassure him of a police presence and lighten his spirit slightly. At times he lost sight of the car, but it appeared again on straight stretches of the road, hanging in behind him, an encouragement to be strong.

The familiar car park was relatively full at 10.54pm as he pulled in and turned right, but George spotted a space three cars down from the electric charging point and pulled in. Six minutes to go. He was tempted to look around, to try to identify the police officers he knew were surrounding the car park, but he remembered Samantha Freeman's words, *Act as if you're alone, don't look for anyone.* Easier said than done. With his car vandalised, he was driving Margaret's Ford Focus and Sam had also said Beecham would know that and would seek George out.

11.04pm. Pub doors were swung open, light spilling over towards the car park, the noise level rising. George had stepped out of the car and was leaning on the boot, in full view, alert and terrified. He'd learned that Beecham would probably be in a black Range Rover, and George scanned the cars around him, hardly daring to move his head. Two cars fitted the description but they could have been dark blue or grey, it was impossible to tell. Conflicting emotions flooded George's body, primarily fear but also euphoria at the thought of seeing Emma again and having her back in his care. He hoped the man wouldn't play his stupid games again and make him wait even longer.

Emma was unaware of time as she drifted in and out of consciousness. In her more lucid moments, she knew she had a temperature and that her wrists were probably infected. An examination showed the swelling was getting worse and they were weeping too. Had Simon really meant to treat her so brutally? Was he punishing her for the way things had worked out?

When awake, Emma longed for the release of sleep or unconsciousness. Each time she opened her eyes she scanned the room warily, afraid Simon might be watching her and terrified of what might transpire in the next few hours.

When her captor did make an appearance, it was dark – night-time, although precisely what hour she couldn't tell. He wore a coat and a hat pulled low over his head. It was time, and Emma's heart surged. Attempting to lift herself from the bed, dizziness forced her down again, nausea washing over her.

'Get up!' he snapped.

She turned her head to look at him. Did he actually think she wanted to stay here? She tried again, tentatively moving her legs off the bed and struggling to lift her body. Finally in a sitting position, Emma knew she had to stand.

'Don't want to go home, eh? You'd rather stay here with me, would you?' Simon goaded her. Emma hadn't the strength to reply, to spit out the hateful words in her head. Instead, she channelled her energy into standing. Pain shot through her feet and she sobbed as old wounds opened up; she looked down at the mess of her swollen, bleeding feet.

Simon grabbed her by the arms and dragged her across the room. The agony made her feel woozy. She was afraid of passing out. When it became evident that Emma couldn't walk unaided, he put his arm under hers and half carried her through the lounge, dragging her down the stairs and outside into the cold fresh air. Shivering, Emma welcomed the light breeze and as Simon bundled her into the back of the car she almost smiled – she was going home.

A thick, scratchy blanket was thrown over her, accompanied by instructions to remain still and not make any noise. Simon ensured she saw the gun in his hand, but he had nothing to fear. She was in no state to make a run for it and curling up on the back seat with the blanket over her, Emma was in pain but the happiest she'd been for days.

Samantha Freeman was antsy. The team was in place, maintaining radio silence as instructed until someone had a sighting. 11pm had been and gone, each minute, each second, dragging as she forced herself to breathe steadily. The night-vision binoculars were brilliant. Sam scanned the car park and was amazed at how clear people's features were. There should be no problem spotting Beecham.

The foot officers had strolled over the car park before 11pm, reconnoitring the vehicles already parked. Sam was impressed with their merry appearance, they fitted in well with other late-night drinkers. The officers radioed in that there was no sign of Beecham's Range Rover as they were propping up the walls of the Red Lion, smoking and laughing. *Rhubarb, rhubarb?* she wondered. In a way, Beecham had made it easy for them to stake out the place. The cover he'd intended for himself served their purposes equally as well.

11.06pm. Sam almost jumped from her seat, leaning forward to get a better look.

'It's him!' she shouted and heard the rustle of activity from the other units. 'Oh, hell, he's in the Nissan! Not to worry, he's out of the car now, wearing a woollen hat and glasses but it's him all right.' Sam recognised the set of his jaw, the sloped shoulders. Having studied the man's photograph often enough, she could pick him out anywhere.

As the others in the team located their suspect, George Porter had also spotted him, and the two men were less than ten yards apart. They were talking together, and Sam was hopeful that they might be able to get in and grab Beecham when he inspected the money, which he was sure to do. But then – was Emma in the car?

Samantha watched for a few more seconds as Simon and George turned towards the Nissan and then she saw it. The light from a car's headlights caught the barrel – it glinted in Sam's binoculars.

'Hold everything... he's got a gun!'

CHAPTER FORTY-FOUR

The gun was an immediate game-changer. The operation was going down in a town-centre car park surrounded by people spilling out from the local pubs, heading for their cars and the risk of going in was too great. Samantha could only instruct her team to watch the scene play out before them, which reluctantly they did. Reverting to the original plan of following Beecham when he left the car park was the only thing to do, but even the parameters for that had changed. When a gun was in play, the armed response unit was drafted in and the case would be taken out of Sam's hands. A feeling of powerlessness settled over her as she was forced to watch the outcome, unable to intervene.

DS Tony Finch asked Sam's permission to call in the incident – it was on their patch and ultimately any decisions would be made by his senior officers.

'Okay.' Sam had no choice other than to agree. 'But we're going ahead with tailing him when he leaves, surreptitiously as planned.' Her mind was a whirl of possibilities until her attention was grabbed by Beecham and George Porter, who together were half carrying Emma towards Porter's car.

To the casual observer, she could have passed as a young woman who'd had too much to drink. Only on closer inspection could the awful reality be seen. Through Sam's binoculars Emma appeared dreadful, half-conscious and without a coat or shoes. Jenny was immediately on the phone for an ambulance while the others were forced to watch the drama playing out before them, uncertain of the outcome.

George seemed to be doing the heavy lifting. Beecham had one hand tucked in his pocket, undoubtedly holding the gun. They stowed Emma in the back seat of her father's car. Samantha was relieved that a helpful member of the public hadn't offered to assist – heaven knows how Beecham would have reacted to such interference. George, looking breathless and stooped, opened the boot of his car and pulled out the holdall filled with money.

DS Tony Finch's voice boomed over the radio. 'Boss, the AR unit is mobilising. They aim to set up roadblocks on the A689 east, and the B6277 south. It'll take time. Can we stall him in any way?'

A voice Sam didn't recognise replied. 'Not without alerting him – hold on, what's he doing now?'

Beecham was walking back to his Nissan. He didn't get inside. Instead, he leaned through the front door, bent over for a few moments and then suddenly hurried away, the bag still in his hand.

'What the hell?' Sam shouted. 'He's heading for the pedestrian gate...' She was getting excited, hoping the two officers on foot would follow at a distance and she was about to warn them to proceed with caution when the sky was suddenly lit up by a huge explosion and mayhem broke loose.

The Nissan was on fire, flames leaping greedily into the air while people nearby screamed and ran in all directions. Sam was temporarily blinded and lost sight of Beecham as her attention swung to the seat of the explosion, assessing the damage.

'Ring in a major incident!' she shouted over the radio, needlessly, as at least four officers were already doing so. Soon all the emergency services would be in attendance – Sam had lost control of the operation.

The priority switched to preserving life. Sam and Gary Cox ran towards the burning vehicle. 'Police! Clear the area!' she shouted to stunned onlookers. PC Cox had had the foresight to grab the fire extinguisher from the pool car and immediately tackled the blaze. Sam assessed the area, looking for casualties. A woman holding her arm and screaming with pain was attempting to get into her car, a few spaces down from the burning Nissan.

'No, please, get far away. It's not safe!' Sam ran to warn the woman, pushing her to a safe distance, afraid the fire would spread to other vehicles. Two men from the pub appeared with extinguishers and worked with Gary to get the flames under control while the rest of the team commenced evacuating the area.

When it appeared the situation was under control, Sam did a quick headcount of her colleagues; they were all there. Although pleased they were safe she was then furious. 'Where's Beecham! Did no one see him leave or follow him?'

The answer was negative. Their priority was to evacuate the car park, which they'd done successfully. Beecham had slipped away in the chaos – undoubtedly what he'd planned all along.

Leaving the team to keep back spectators and allow those fighting the fire some space, Sam hurried over to George Porter's car, which was thankfully parked at a safe distance from the burning Nissan. Emma lay on the back seat, semi-conscious, and Sam was sickened at the young woman's appearance.

'Shall I drive her to the hospital?' George looked dazed and in need of attention himself.

'No, ambulances are on the way. She'll get immediate attention from the paramedics who'll then take her to the hospital. I'm afraid Beecham's got away.' The DI expected an angry reaction but George seemed to barely register her words and nodded, his focus on Emma.

'Not to worry, I've got my girl back.' He stroked Emma's forehead. It was evident she'd suffered significant trauma. Sam wanted to speak to her as soon as possible, but it wouldn't be tonight. Emma was barely conscious.

'Why don't you ring Margaret to let her know you've got Emma, or would you like me to do it?'

'No, I'll ring.' George pulled out his phone, hands trembling and managed to find his wife's number. Sam could hear the cries of relief on the other end as he told her their daughter was safe. Wisely he didn't relate any further details, including the fact that he was waiting for an ambulance and Emma needed urgent hospital treatment.

Samantha moved away to make her own difficult phone call to DCI Aiden Kent. She pressed the phone to her left ear, covering her right with her hand to block out the noise. It was 11.40pm, late to make a call yet she knew the DCI would want to be kept in the loop.

How do you tell your boss that the evening has turned into a disaster movie? Sam stuck to the basics, telling him that Emma Porter was safe and with her father before relating the bad news – losing Beecham and the money and the explosion in the car park. The welcome sound of sirens filled the air, an ambulance first, followed by a fire engine and two more ambulances. Sam used the distraction to end her call and get back to the crime scene.

Within minutes Emma and George Porter were in the

capable hands of two paramedics, and Sam had one less concern on her mind. She turned to the shell of the Nissan where a very hot and sweaty Gary gave her a nervous smile. The fire was out, a result due to his quick thinking. The fire crew took over, dousing down the car to make it safe and avoid secondary fires.

Samantha took the opportunity to view the other nearby vehicles and assess the damage, which she was doing when Jenny caught up with her. Together they looked at the scene of utter devastation. Paintwork bubbled on the right wing of the closest car, with black spots where sparks had landed on the roof and bonnet. Other cars were spotted with burn marks, probably only three or four in total.

Jenny rubbed her eyes with her fists. 'Could have been worse.'

'Any casualties?' Sam asked.

'A woman with slight burns to her arms who's more shocked than injured, another woman who fell in her attempt to run away has a sprained or broken ankle. They're both being taken care of by the paramedics. Thankfully no one was seriously hurt. How's Emma?'

'She's with the paramedics too, and then off to the hospital. She looks in a bad way. Goodness only knows what the bastard's done to her!'

'Shame he got away but we'll get him, boss. I know we will.' Jenny squeezed Sam's arm before moving away to check on the rest of the team while Sam stared at the wreck.

DS Tony Finch appeared at her elbow, a man beside him whom he introduced as DI Derek Ogilvy, his boss. Sam looked at the newcomer, feeling completely exhausted. Bitter disappointment at how the operation had ended exacerbated her downward spiralling mood and was reflected in her face. Unsure if she should apologise to the Northumbrian DI, Sam stared silently at him, bewildered, waiting for the expected tirade of abuse.

His blue eyes twinkled as he smiled at her. 'Good work, detective.'

'But...' Sam waved her hand at the devastation around them, speechless.

'You've got your hostage back, I hear – and there are no dead bodies – in my book that's a result. Now go home and get some sleep, my team will sort out this mess and we'll speak tomorrow.'

CHAPTER FORTY-FIVE

Samantha Freeman stepped through her front door at 1.30am, weary, dirty and emotionally drained. She'd hung around the scene only long enough to speak to each team member, thanking and reassuring them that they would complete the job they'd started and bring Beecham to justice.

While Gary Cox travelled with Jenny, Sam left Beacon Bridge and headed back to New Middridge driving the pool car. Halfway home she stopped the car and wound down the windows to let the fresh air take away the stink of the fire. Putting her forehead on the steering wheel Sam finally gave way to her emotions and sobbed bitterly. It was more a release of tension than anything else – she certainly wasn't feeling sorry for her predicament – angry, yes – but she would take this as a setback, a blip in the investigation which wasn't over yet.

After five minutes, Sam continued on her way and soon found herself in Ravi's comforting arms.

'You shouldn't have waited up,' she said, glad he had.

'And if the boot was on the other foot?' He led her upstairs and pointed her toward the shower. 'You look bloody awful!' He blew her a kiss.

Catching sight of herself in the mirror Sam couldn't argue. Her face was smeared with soot, tear tracks dissecting her cheeks, a fact Ravi must have noticed, and her hair smelled of fire.

Five minutes under the hot spears of water went some way to restoring Sam to her usual self. She pulled on a pair of winceyette pyjamas and trudged downstairs where Ravi was making hot chocolate.

He looked her up and down. 'Nice!'

She smiled. 'Comfort jim-jams.'

Sipping the chocolate and eating a croissant smothered with strawberry jam, Sam told Ravi about the dreadful day she'd experienced. Her frustration and disappointment tumbled out as she berated herself, cursed Simon Beecham, and praised her team and colleagues from Northumbria Police. She broke off only once to call the hospital and enquire about Emma Porter. A nurse informed her that their patient was comfortable and sleeping, her parents both in attendance; Samantha expected nothing less.

'Feeling any better?' Ravi asked, picking a crumb off her cheek. Sam nodded and snuggled into his shoulder, grateful for his strength and support.

'If I wasn't so damned tired...'

'Sleep is what we both need; a few hours before the merry-go-round begins all over again. But just a bit of news from my end first – Jonesy, who's heading up the "presidential file", says things are even worse than they first thought. Johnsons have completed their internal investigations and it seems Beecham, or whatever his name is, has got away with far more than they originally thought. It could even be getting on for half a million.'

Samantha arrived at the station at 9am the following morning, late for her but early considering the circumstances. Bumping into Jenny in the car park, the two briefly discussed the previous evening's events and as they reached their office were not surprised to find it empty. Sam's desk was clear except for a note from Aiden Kent asking the DI to go to his office.

Jenny insisted on accompanying her upstairs for 'moral support' and knocked on the door, raising her hand to show crossed fingers to her boss. As they entered the room, the DCI looked up at the two women.

'Are you both okay?' His concern appeared genuine, relaxing the tension in Sam's shoulders as she nodded and smiled nervously. 'Sit down and tell me all about it.'

Sam summarised the operation's events from when they set off from New Middridge. Kent had been up to speed with all that had happened before then.

'It was going according to plan, sir, until the gun complicated matters. We were reassessing and consulting AR when Beecham leaned into the car and somehow triggered a fire, resulting in the explosion. He hurried off on foot which we hadn't anticipated, and with our team's focus on the mayhem he'd created and keeping the public safe, he got away. I took my eye off the ball, and lost him. I can only apologise.' She'd been the team leader, the buck stopped with her.

Aiden Kent looked directly at Samantha. 'I've spent half an hour on the phone with the DCI at Northumbria Police this morning and we're both of the same opinion – you're not responsible for this debacle, DI Freeman, Simon Beecham is. DCI Turner is as appalled with the man as I am; a complete disregard for public safety, it's disgraceful, almost an act of terrorism and the sooner he's caught the better. However, in such difficult circumstances, you and your team behaved appropriately and followed the correct procedure. I'd like you to pass on my thanks to your colleagues and if they're well enough to continue the search for Beecham, let's get on with it. Northumbria Police have offered any assistance we may need, so don't be afraid to ask for help. Now, if you're sure you're both okay, I'll not keep you any longer.'

Outside the DCI's office, Jenny lifted her hand for a high five and the pair allowed themselves a brief smile. It had been more a commendation than the ticking-off Sam expected, and it went a long way towards restoring her faith in herself. Anticipating a rollicking she felt was deserved or a lecture on budgets and what the fiasco would cost in monetary terms, it appeared her boss viewed it differently, as did Northumbria Police. The relief Sam experienced was enormous. Any tiredness left her body to be replaced with a new enthusiasm to catch Simon Beecham and bring him to justice for his ever-mounting crimes.

Paul and Layla were in the office when they returned, arriving together again it seemed, and the first thing to do was to hold a debriefing. Even with support from the DCI, Sam wanted to make sure they learned from the events of the day and that mistakes would be identified in the hope they wouldn't be repeated. Only after this could they get their heads buried into the task of finding their suspect.

A brainstorming session commenced immediately, fuelled by coffee and doughnuts. Several valid points were raised, but it wasn't long until Jenny became irritated by Paul's constant carping.

'Paul, if you say "if only" one more time, I will scream. We're all wiser with hindsight and it's not in the least bit productive to drag up the "if only" all the time.'

Paul defended himself. 'Yeah, but if we'd thought to search the streets beforehand, we might have spotted Beecham's Range Rover and expected him to leave on foot.'

'Yes, Paul, you're right, but Jenny's right too, no more "if only" please.' Sam felt like a mother sorting out her squabbling children but wanted the debriefing to be constructive, not degenerate into a blame game. Deciding they'd covered everything pertinent and beneficial, she finished the session. The work to find Beecham needed to begin again in earnest.

'Paul, did you ever find anything on the flat in the north end where Beecham lived before moving in with Emma?' Sam asked.

'No, I was distracted with other things. I'll get back to it if you think it's important.'

'It's a lead, and we're a bit short on those. Have another shot at it and see if anything turns up will you?'

Paul settled down at his computer, cursing the man; having to search everything in three different names tripled his workload.

Sam left the three other detectives to continue the search while she made her way to the hospital to see the Porter family.

CHAPTER FORTY-SIX

Emma Porter had been taken to Durham University Hospital, her father by her side and her mother joining them as soon as Layla Gupta could get her there. Sam parked in the crowded car park five minutes from the entrance and headed into the building.

When she reached Emma's ward she found George and Margaret alone in a side room, staring solemnly at an empty bed. For a second Sam panicked and thought the worst.

'They've taken her for X-rays,' Margaret explained.

Sam nodded, relieved, and sat beside the couple to wait. 'How is she?'

'Awful!' A sob escaped Margaret's lips and her husband put his arm around her shoulders, drawing her to him.

'But she's safe, love, and she'll get better.' He turned to Sam. 'We're very grateful to you, Samantha, and please pass on our thanks to everyone else who helped.' George's words were something of a surprise; she'd wondered how the Porters would react to the previous day's outcome – it had undoubtedly been a costly day for them – but it appeared getting their daughter back was paramount, losing the money secondary.

'Thank you, it wasn't the best outcome but I'm glad Emma's safe. Have the doctors been able to tell you much about her injuries?'

'She's very dehydrated and had quite a high temperature so they put her on intravenous fluids and antibiotics. They think her wrists are the seat of the infection. The bindings were so tight that her skin's broken in several places, and her feet are in a bad state too. It seems she tried to escape and being without shoes, her feet are cut and bruised. But the worst injury by far is to her face. The X-ray is to determine if her jaw's broken. The doctor says she's received quite a heavy blow and lost a tooth too. She can hardly talk...' George's voice, low and monotone, trailed off as he appeared to contemplate what his beloved daughter suffered at the hands of Simon Beecham, while Margaret turned her face away as if unable to listen to the words.

'How can one human being do such things to another?' he asked, though not expecting an answer for which Sam was grateful – she didn't have one.

'I'll need to speak to Emma sometime soon.'

'No! She needs rest,' Margaret protested.

'I know, but she may have clues as to where Beecham held her, even if she doesn't realise it, something she knows could lead us to him. Has she said anything at all?'

'No. I think she's traumatised, and they gave her something to calm her down. She's slept quite a bit.'

'And have either of you managed to sleep?' Sam didn't need to ask. The answer was visible in their faces.

'I don't think I'll ever sleep soundly again,' Margaret said. Her husband squeezed her shoulder, a weary sigh saying more than any words.

The sound of a bed trundling along the corridor signalled Emma's return. Prone on the crisp white sheets, she was manoeuvred back into the room. Sam was shocked by her appearance. The girl's wrists were bandaged yet the swelling was evident, and her feet were red, scratched and swollen with a white ointment slathered over them. Emma's cheeks seemed hollow, her face pale beneath the bruising and puffy as she looked at Sam with dull eyes.

'Hello, Emma, it's good to see you again.' Sam smiled but was unsure if Emma even registered her presence. After a moment she turned her head and mouthed, '*Hello.*' It was apparent the interview would have to wait. Samantha didn't want to add to the family's distress by insisting on questioning Emma while she was so ill. As she was about to say so, a doctor entered the room in a swish of white coat and energy.

'Hi, I'm Dr Ely.' He smiled widely. 'And you must be Emma's parents and her sister?'

'Oh, no, I'm a police officer, DI Freeman... I'll wait outside.' Sam stood to leave – Emma lifted her hand and reached for hers.

'No, stay, please.' Speaking was clearly painful, and Sam felt unusually emotional as Emma clasped her hand. She nodded and stayed still as the doctor carried on.

'The X-ray shows a single fracture to the lower jaw, right-hand side.' His eyes were on Emma. 'Painful, I know, but the good news is it's a clean break and shouldn't require surgery. It will heal naturally. You'll just have to be careful – keep off the toffees, eh? Painkillers will help, we'll give you some strong ones and the swelling should go down in a few days. Six to eight weeks should see you as good as new, and your dentist will be able to suggest something for the missing tooth, although not until the break's healed.' Emma listened with tears in her eyes, as did Margaret.

'The infection will soon respond to the antibiotics and we'll keep you in for a couple of nights' observation, then you can go home.' The young doctor would never know what his last two words meant to Emma and her parents.

When he left, Sam turned to Emma. 'I'll need a statement from you soon, when you're ready. For now, do you know where Beecham was keeping you?'

'A house... near woods... barn... conversion maybe?' Emma struggled to speak. 'We seemed to drive for ages last night, but I was a bit out of it.'

'That's great, Emma, thank you. I'll leave now – you have my number if anything comes to mind.'

Samantha left the little family and wondered why neither Mr nor Mrs Porter even asked about the money. In her book, this spoke volumes about the type of people they were.

Nothing significant had surfaced during her absence, and Sam felt the old frustration taking hold. Her instinct was to work tirelessly to bring the case to a close; the reality was that she couldn't push her team or herself too hard. In truth, they could be in for the long haul. Tracking Beecham down wasn't going to be easy and unless they got a lucky break, the case could drag on indefinitely.

It had undoubtedly been a stressful week and the team were still working even though it was Saturday. They needed a break. She watched as DC Paul Roper stretched and yawned, shifting in his chair and massaging the knots in his shoulders. It was lunchtime and Sam decided to send them all home.

'Get some rest, enjoy some downtime and we'll pick up again on Monday.' Although keen to press on, there was no argument, each team member recognised the need for space to recharge their batteries and very quickly the office was empty.

CHAPTER FORTY-SEVEN

A short weekend proved better than none, and the four detectives returned to New Middridge police station on Monday morning, refreshed and keen to pick up the threads of their investigation.

There was an early morning call from George Porter to say he was going to the hospital later that morning to pick up Emma. She was well enough to be allowed home and he sounded delighted. Samantha asked permission to call that afternoon to see if Emma would be up to making a statement. He agreed, Sam doubted if Margaret would have allowed her to visit.

After ending the call, the detective was still unsettled, longing for something more to do than harass her colleagues to search faster and dig deeper, so she went over the road to the deli to treat them all to some decent coffee.

On her return, Sam heard the excited chatter from the corridor and DC Roper was waving a piece of paper at her when she pushed open the door.

'Guess what? I think I've found another wife!' His eyes sparkled with excitement.

'Explain?'

'I've been concentrating on the flats near North Park. The only likely ones were two blocks of council flats, so I asked for a list of tenants and low and behold in number six, there resides a Mrs Lily Beecham!' Paul looked expectantly at the DI as if waiting for a pat on the head.

'Could be a coincidence – the same name.' Sam tried to curb her excitement; surely the man couldn't have another wife lurking in his past? 'Is she the only occupant?'

'Yes, the flat's solely in her name; she could be another ex?'

'Paul, don't look so crestfallen. There's no way I'm *not* going to check this out. Good work, detective! Jenny, grab your coat.'

New Middridge police station was fairly central to the town and it took less than twenty minutes to drive to North Rise flats. Jenny chatted throughout the journey, speculating on whether this woman could be connected to their case. Was it likely they might even find the man himself?

Number six was on the ground floor, the door flanked by two large dustbins, one for rubbish, one for recycling and neither smelt particularly fragrant. Not great kerb appeal but there appeared to be no other space to keep them and the other flats had the same problem. Jenny rapped on the glass-panelled front door. No one answered, so she knocked again.

'All right, keep your hair on!' a voice shouted from inside. The door was opened by an elderly lady on a walking stick who peered out from a narrow gap, a chain preventing it from opening fully. The woman looked them both up and down. 'Yes?'

'Lily Beecham? I'm DS Jenny Newcombe and this is DI Samantha Freeman. Could we come inside to talk to you for a few minutes?' Jenny held her ID close enough for the woman to see and was rewarded with the door opening wide enough for them to follow her inside.

Lily wasn't as grumpy as her initial bark suggested, and as she made her way slowly down the narrow passage she apologised for the mess. 'You'll have to take me as I am, pet. I don't manage the chores as well as I used to.'

'No problem, Mrs Beecham. Thank you for allowing us in.' Sam took in the small flat. It was typical of most council properties, the economy of space being the chief priority with tiny rooms and not too solid walls – they could hear music blaring from the next-door property. It was, however, reasonably clean and tidy despite Lily's apology. Sam had seen much worse, and they often joked that it was better to wipe your feet on the way out in some of the homes they visited.

Once settled in the lounge, the two detectives squashed together on a tiny sofa, Lily Beecham offered them a toothless grin.

'What's this all about then?' she asked. Lily's age was difficult to determine. She could have been anywhere on either side of seventy, her stooped body and lack of teeth making a judgement difficult.

'We're looking for a man called Simon Beecham whom we think could help us with an ongoing investigation, and we wondered if he was a relative?' Sam rummaged in her bag for a photograph.

'Simon's my son!' Lily beamed proudly. 'He's abroad at the moment though, something to do with his work, and I'm afraid I don't know when he'll be back. You think he can help you out do you, pet?'

'Yes, we'd hoped to contact him as soon as possible.'

'Sorry, love, but I don't know when he's coming back. He's often away – goes all over the world for his firm, he does, not that they appreciate his efforts, mind you, and they only pay him peanuts. Poor lad, I try to sub him when I can although the pension doesn't go as far as it used to, you know?'

'When did you last see Simon, Mrs Beecham?' Sam asked, smiling at the woman.

'Oh, a couple of weeks ago. I can't be sure exactly – the days all run into each other for me now. I don't get out much – arthritis, you see.' She patted her knee with a gnarled hand.

'And where did you say Simon works?'

'He's with some big pharmaceutical company, in sales but he does so much more. They put on him something shocking, expect him to work such long hours. He's based in Durham most of the time.'

'And is Simon married?' Jenny was keen to hear the answer.

'Goodness me no, he's always been shy with women. I suppose he's still young enough to settle down, yet with all the hours he works I don't know when he'll find the time to meet a nice lass.' Beecham's mother smiled wistfully.

'And does Simon live here with you when he's not travelling, Mrs Beecham?' Although Lily seemed more than happy to talk, Sam felt a little guilty at probing for information.

'Only occasionally. I think the company has a place where he stays in Durham but like I said, he works away a lot and sometimes I don't see him for weeks on end. But he's a good lad is Simon, always turns up to visit when he can. What is it you want to ask him about then?' Lily was finally showing some curiosity.

'It's a case we've been working on recently involving a young woman called Emma. Has he ever mentioned anyone of that name to you at all?' Sam was deliberately vague.

'No, as I said he doesn't have much time for girls.'

'And what about Simon's father? Can I ask if he's still around?' Sam wanted to move things on.

'A waster that one – the only decent thing he ever did for us was to get himself knocked down and killed coming out of the pub one night – had a skinful as usual.' Lily sucked on her gums like she had a bad taste in her mouth.

'Oh, I'm sorry, when was that?'

'Years ago, pet. Simon was only fifteen and we lived in Felling at the time, but we didn't miss the beggar. He hadn't much time for either of us and was a bit too handy with his fists an' all. Thought women were only on this earth to do his bidding, he did, the sod! Poor bairn was sometimes scared out of his wits, yet thought the man was a god at other times. Not how a little boy should see his da, for sure. Good riddance to him I say.' Lily folded her arms across her chest, then, as if dragging herself back to the present, asked, 'Shall I tell Simon to get in touch with you when he gets back?'

'Thank you, Mrs Beecham. That would be great. You've been very helpful. We'll leave you in peace now.' Sam and Jenny stood to leave.

'But you're welcome to a cup of tea, pet, if you've time?' Lily offered.

'It's very kind but I'm afraid we have somewhere else to go. Thanks again, Mrs Beecham.'

On the way out of the room, Sam noticed a small silver-framed photo of a teenage Simon, smiling for the camera. She wondered if he was already on the way to becoming a narcissistic psychopath even then.

CHAPTER FORTY-EIGHT

Jenny vented her feelings as they left Lily's home. 'Can you believe the man? Who's the real Simon Beecham – his mother's existence certainly put paid to the story he made up about living in care, and there's the Felling connection too. The poor woman's been taken in just like his wives and Emma. I feel sorry for her; the old dear's heading for quite a shock.'

'Lily's account certainly shows him up for what he really is. Even she doesn't know the man. And you're right. Her world's going to be shattered when we finally catch him.'

'And his father sounded a case too, a misogynist bully. Is it any wonder Beecham's like he is?'

'Introjected values,' Samantha said, her eyes on the road while listening to her sergeant.

'Pardon?'

'Introjected values – the values children absorb from those around them, generally parents or caregivers who mould our way of thinking. Beecham may have been scared of his father, but he would unconsciously learn from him and soak up his ideas and standards. A child still loves and admires a parent no matter how badly treated they are, and Beecham Senior's values have been passed on to his son.'

'Shame we can't arrest the father too then,' Jenny mused. 'But all those lies Simon tells. It must be like keeping plates spinning on poles. I don't know how he manages.'

'Yes, it all increases our knowledge of Beecham but still doesn't help us find the man.'

Sam dropped Jenny at the station to update Paul and Layla on the latest developments while she drove on to the south side of town to the Porters' home.

The area was in complete contrast to where Lily Beecham lived; leafy streets, if a little stark in November, neat grass verges and not a dustbin in sight. The houses were, without exception, well maintained, not least the Porters' into whose drive Samantha turned, mentally preparing herself for questions she may be unable to answer.

Emma lay on the sofa under a quilt, looking only slightly improved, a little more colour in her cheeks perhaps but still swollen around her jawline. The area around her eyes was almost black; bandages covered her wrists and her feet poked out from under the quilt, covered with short cotton socks. Margaret fussed over her daughter and offered tea to their visitor.

'That would be lovely, thank you,' Sam said.

'Feeling any better?' she asked Emma when they were alone.

'A little – sorry about the funny talking.' She spoke out of one side of her mouth, the other too swollen to move, and her words were a little hard to interpret.

Samantha smiled. 'Are you up to giving me a statement? We can stop any time you wish.'

Emma nodded and the detective took out her notebook.

'Do you remember what happened after you left work last Monday evening?'

'I didn't get very far before something covered my face – a sweet smell, like nail-polish remover, and everything went black. When I woke up, I was alone in a strange house with a bag over my head and my hands tied behind me. I knew Simon must have taken me – and then he came back.' Emma's voice was breaking at the memory.

Sam waited to give her time, the thought of what this girl suffered served to enthuse the detective's quest to find Beecham.

Margaret appeared in the doorway with a tray in her hand. Putting it down, she turned to Sam. 'Do you have to do this now? She's only just got home.'

'It's okay, Mum. I want to do it, to help find the bastard.'

Sam moved on to more practical questions. 'Can you remember anything about the house, Emma? Anything at all which might help us locate it?'

'I think it was a conversion, a split-level house. There were beams but it was modern, quite beautiful really. I only saw the upstairs rooms, a kitchen lounge and a bathroom. And he locked me in a bedroom when he went out. I did manage to get outside once. Simon tried...' Emma glanced at her mother and appeared to change what she was about to say. 'I hit him and ran out into the trees, but I had no shoes on and fell. He dragged me back inside. He has a gun – it went off a couple of times.' Emma became anxious at the memory of the gun and Margaret gasped.

Sam continued. 'We know about the gun, Emma. What you say about the trees is helpful. Did you see any other houses nearby or a road perhaps?'

'No, no houses or road, just a track between the house and the woods. He said no one would hear me if I screamed.' Sam nodded encouragingly and Emma managed to continue. 'I think I must have been delirious after the episode in the woods.

Everything was muddled up in my mind, and I couldn't even tell if it was day or night. The next thing I remember clearly is Simon shaking me to wake up so I could speak to Dad on the phone. Then I was in Simon's car and we drove for a long time. Suddenly it was like being in Hell with the fire and everything.' Emma's head fell back on the cushion prompting her mother to begin fussing again. 'I'm fine, Mum, really.'

'And how did you get your injuries, Emma?' Sam asked.

'Simon's fist...' Emma glanced at her mother's shocked expression and stopped, clearly not wanting to elaborate in front of her.

George Porter entered the room and looked directly at Samantha, an inquiring look which the detective answered with a shake of her head. He sat and smiled at his daughter.

Emma turned to Sam. 'Can I ask you something now?'

'Of course.'

'Simon said something about me being third time lucky and I didn't understand what he meant.'

George addressed Samantha apologetically. 'We haven't had a chance to tell her what you found out.'

'That's fine. We've discovered a few other things since Saturday, which I can tell you about if you're up to it?'

Emma nodded, her eyes wide in anticipation.

'Diane told us she was Simon's second wife, not his first.'

'What?' Emma couldn't quite manage a shout.

'He was married to someone called Angela when they were both very young. We traced her to a house near Felling, Newcastle, and she was very helpful. They divorced within months, and she's now happily married with a family.' Sam paused – Emma's eyes willed her to go on. 'Today we also traced the flat where we thought Simon might have lived before he married you; it's a council flat which we visited this morning and where we met Simon's mother.'

'His mother!' Emma looked horrified. 'But...'

'He told us he grew up in care and had no family!' George finished his daughter's sentence, shock etched on his face.

Sam gave them a moment to process this latest deception. 'Lily Beecham is a widow. Simon was fifteen when his father died in an accident. Lily appears genuine and has no idea where her son is. Currently, she thinks he's abroad for work and that he's employed by a pharmaceutical company in Durham. We think he's used her address when it suited his purpose, and he's clearly far from honest with her. She has no idea he's ever been married.'

'How the hell can he get away with all those lies? Does she know where he might be hiding – she could be covering for him,' George said. It was a logical assumption.

'I'm fairly sure she's telling the truth. It appears Simon's used her over the years and every other woman in his life. I'm sorry I've nothing more concrete to tell you but we *are* working hard to find him and your money. Jenny and two DCs are at the station now searching records and trying to discover his whereabouts. We're not giving up.' It was the best Sam could offer, and before she left, the family expressed their appreciation for the team's efforts.

Margaret apologised as she saw the DI out. 'I'm sorry I was a bit sharp with you earlier.'

'No problem, you've all been under a huge strain. It's understandable.' Samantha smiled at her before going back to the station. Her little Mini could probably find its own way there.

CHAPTER FORTY-NINE

Jenny greeted her boss as she entered the office. 'How's Emma?'

'Still bruised and swollen, the psychological damage will take the longest to heal. I really need to see her alone. I think she's keeping some things to herself, trying to protect her mother.'

Jenny raised her eyebrows. 'What? You think she might know where he is?'

'No, nothing like that. I mean those injuries and what Simon did to her. Emma chose her words carefully because Margaret was there – it's possible Beecham raped Emma, but I didn't feel it appropriate to push the issue. It's still very raw.'

'Poor kid, thank God she's safe now. So, what's next, boss?'

'We plod on. The all-ports alert still stands and if he takes the Range Rover onto any major roads, the ANPR will pick him up. Leave Paul and Layla to continue the searches, we've got a mountain of reports to get stuck into and we don't want our Northumbria colleagues to think we're not on the ball.' The thought of reports didn't appeal to either of them, but it was a necessary evil, so all four officers remained at their desks for the rest of the day without any significant breakthrough.

Samantha took time out only once to speak on the phone to DI Derek Ogilvy in Northumbria and offer their help in the clean-up operation. He declined, precisely what she'd hoped, insisting that the best help they could give was to catch the madman who'd caused such mayhem. Derek confirmed that the only casualties were the woman with the burns and another with a sprained ankle. They were treated at the hospital and then allowed home.

It was a miracle no one else was injured, although many would be traumatised by what they'd witnessed. Vehicle damage was another story but the police involvement consisted mostly of allocating crime numbers – the insurance companies would take care of the rest. DI Ogilvy dismissed her apologies and joked that he'd given the reports to his sergeant, suggesting she did the same.

Sam thanked the DI for his understanding and ended the call before telling the others to go home and rest. The work would continue in earnest the following morning.

9.30am, Tuesday, and DC Paul Roper's phone rang. The team had all been in the office since 8am and the buzzing was a welcome distraction.

Jenny rolled her head to relieve the kinks in her neck. 'Time for coffee, methinks. Shall I go over the road for the good stuff?'

Sam's face brightened at the thought and she reached for her bag. 'My treat!' She gave Jenny a couple of notes yet before the DS could leave the office, Paul frantically waved his arms in an effort to attract her attention. He ended his call, barely able to get the words out quickly enough.

'That was an estate agent in Hexham.'

'He sold Beecham a house?' Jenny asked hopefully.

'No...' Paul paused, looking from Sam to Jenny.

Sam frowned. 'Spit it out!'

'He had a man on the phone this morning wanting to sell a house – a Mr Christopher Simpson – the estate agent remembered the name from my earlier call and thought I might be interested!'

'Go on...'

'The house in question is near the village of Falstone, twenty-five miles north-west of Hexham, a remote property inside the Kielder Forest Park.' Paul beamed like a schoolboy.

It sounded hopeful, the location was certainly a possibility and the name was correct. It was unlikely to be another Christopher Simpson; this was their best lead so far.

'What did you tell the estate agent to do?' Sam asked.

'Nothing, for now. I said I'd get back to him. He's made an appointment to meet the vendor and value the property tomorrow. It was only afterwards that the name clicked and he rang me.'

'Good, get him back on the phone and tell him not to talk to anyone about this and if he hears from this Mr Simpson again to let us know if there's any change in the arrangement.'

Paul moved away to make the call.

'Boss, it's here on Google Earth if you want a look.' Layla had been tapping away on her computer while Sam and Jenny peered over her shoulder. The house was certainly isolated and as Layla zoomed in closer, they were amazed at the detail visible on the screen. Could they be the trees into which Emma had run attempting to escape? 'It's dated last year but the area shouldn't have changed much.'

'Can you get in any closer?' Sam asked.

'No, it's good, just not that good.'

'What are the chances of two Christopher Simpsons living in a remote forest area, both with Range Rovers? We've got him. We've bloody got him!' Relief and excitement flooded Sam's body. She lifted her hand and high-fived Jenny and then Layla. Paul joined in the euphoria.

'The estate agent's happy to oblige, quite excited to be helping the police, although I didn't tell him any details. Beecham's appointment is at 11am tomorrow. With a bit of luck, we'll have him by then. And guess what, the house has a name – The White House! Talk about bloody pretentious. It has to be Beecham.'

Sam asked Layla to print off a copy of the Google Earth picture and ran upstairs, holding it as if it were gold, to see the DCI.

Relating the estate agent's call and the evidence of the photograph, Aiden Kent was soon convinced they'd found their man.

'It'll have to be an Armed Response operation. When did you want to make a move?'

Sam checked her watch, 10.20am. 'Tonight, sir. There's time to pull an operation together and it would make sense to go in after dark, the element of surprise? And if he's putting the house on the market, he's planning to move on. We've got an all-ports alert but the man is a serial alias user – he could still get away, the Porters' money with him.' Sam was gabbling, she knew but was so keen to get on with an arrest that any delay would be totally unacceptable.

Kent smiled. 'Okay, you've persuaded me. I'll get on to AR and arrange a meeting ASAP. Could you ring the DI at Northumbria? It'll have to be a joint operation.'

Samantha ran down the stairs to tell the others they were on for that night.

'The DCI is contacting AR – Beecham's possession of a gun

means they'll have to go in first. We also need to speak to Northumbria Police. It's on their patch, so a joint operation is the way forward.'

The excitement in the room was palpable. New energy enthused their previously tired bodies and minds; there was no question that all four detectives would work through the night and Sam would assign all three to be in the field, they deserved as much.

DI Derek Ogilvy was delighted to hear from Sam so soon. 'Well done. I thought this one would drag on, you've certainly put in the groundwork and it's paid off. Let me know when the briefing is. I think I want to be in on this one myself.'

Sam ended the call and breathed a sigh of relief. It was all coming together and would hopefully soon be over.

CHAPTER FIFTY

The full briefing was at 3pm that afternoon. Armed Response left the detectives in no doubt that they were in charge of Operation Kielder, and as Sam listened to their plan, she was grateful for their skill and professionalism. It was a relatively straightforward operation for the AR team – only one suspect and one handgun. What was more, the suspect was most probably confident his location was unknown; his level of vigilance was assumed to be medium to low.

Six armed officers would approach on foot; the pathway to the house was an unadopted road, therefore little more than a track. All vehicles would be left a hundred yards from the target. Sam and her team were solemnly told they would need to remain well away from the house until given the all-clear to enter. It was fine by her; she was happy to leave it to the experts even though the thought of seeing Beecham again and physically putting cuffs on the man gave her a guilty rush of pleasure.

A rendezvous point was determined, and assembly at the agreed location would be 2.30am, half an hour before entry to the house – it couldn't come soon enough for the New

Middridge team. DCI Kent was in attendance at the briefing with DI Derek Ogilvy and his sergeant from Northumbria Police.

When the meeting was over and each team member was acquainted with their role, timing and positions, Sam's team returned to their office, buzzing with anticipation and impressed by the AR officers' efficiency. It then became a waiting game; frustratingly, there was little more they could do but grab something to eat and try to relax.

Driving time from New Middridge to Falstone was approximately one hour twelve minutes and Sam decided they would leave at 12.30am, allowing extra time for unforeseen circumstances. They took three pool cars and two PCs with the four-strong team. DCI Kent was to be kept informed at every step of the operation. They would all go without sleep that night.

A clear night smiled upon them. The temperature hovered around zero with a touch of ground frost and a half-moon providing welcome extra light. They travelled in convoy with two officers in each car and radio contact, yet little to discuss.

Samantha and Layla were in the lead car, the atmosphere crackling with anticipation. Layla had never been involved in an AR operation and constantly asked questions about her boss's experience working with them. Sam answered, wanting only to concentrate on the current operation, but the DC needed to learn, so Sam tried to be patient.

On arrival, contrary to thinking they'd be first on the scene, they found the AR officers already in position. Two of their team had been on reconnaissance since midnight, watching the property from strategic points in the woods. A report informed them that all lights in the property were extinguished at 12.30am.

Assuming Beecham was asleep and if the situation remained static, they decided to bring the entry time forward to 2.30am. Sam hurriedly rang DCI Kent to inform him of the change and then listened to the AR officers' preparations with awe. Each one was in full protective armour, 'suited and booted', they referred to it, with night-vision optics and what they informed those less knowledgeable in such matters were Heckler and Koch G36K semi-automatic firearms.

Waiting had already played a massive part in this investigation and as the officers stood around in the cold night air a frisson of excitement kept them warm. It was simultaneously exhilarating and frightening, and Sam comforted herself with the knowledge that the AR team regarded their suspect as low risk. Her mind raced ahead to the point when she'd be called into the property to make the actual arrest, and a shudder of anticipation ran through her body. It was a task she relished.

With only minutes before the appointed time, they received instructions to return to their vehicles. The AR team clustered together in a last-minute conference – it was reminiscent of a huddle of football or rugby players – but this wasn't a game and much more dangerous.

The New Middridge detectives watched the AR officers move into action, creeping along the road in a semi-crouched position with great stealth and remarkable silence, still with a fair distance to cover but on high alert from the outset. Then, finally, the black-clad figures disappeared into the night. Sam made another call to DCI Kent, probably the last until they could call with the news that Beecham was safely in handcuffs.

Anxiety levels rose when the team was out of sight. There was always an element of doubt, and Sam still bore in mind the car park fiasco in Beacon Bridge, praying this night's outcome would be more successful. She possessed a radio the AR leader had given her and knew radio silence would be maintained until they breached the property, barring any problem.

It seemed to take forever. Sitting in the car was a hard ask; even pacing the rough path would have been preferable. Paul Roper gnawed at his fingernails. Layla and Jenny sat in silence, hardly daring to breathe, let alone talk, while Sam's eyes were searching for any movement, her ears alert for the slightest sound.

A cloud covered the moon. The darkness intensified as did the mood of those left behind waiting. With no light from the moon or street lighting, the velvet blackness was a rare sight to those who lived in the town. It was like a dense blanket enfolding them in another world, but a tense edgy world, unlike their everyday reality. They all strained to hear. Surely the team should be at the house by now and any sound would carry easily in the stillness of their surroundings. Only an owl hooted – until suddenly a distant crash – and then shouting.

It must have been less than a minute, although it felt like ten, before the radio crackled to life and Samantha finally got the command to proceed. They switched on their car engines and sped up to the house where Beecham had been hiding.

CHAPTER FIFTY-ONE

The White House was lit up like a carousel, the front door wide open, battered down by the team. In their line of work they rarely knocked. An AR officer stood guard outside, his weapon over his shoulder.

'Upstairs! All's clear, ma'am.' The staccato words sounded like honey, welcome as spring and Samantha's heart leapt to think the case was finally coming to a close.

Two doors led off the immediate hallway, one on each side of a central staircase which all the New Middridge officers took two at a time. Light flooded every space, revealing a modern luxurious home, possibly one converted from the bones of a barn. The room they entered was a beautifully furnished lounge. Sam's eyes were immediately drawn to an open doorway where she could see the backs of four of the AR officers leaning over a bed.

'Don't move a muscle!' one of them shouted at the figure on the bed. Tactfully, DI Ogilvy and his sergeant allowed her team to go forward, hanging back so they could make the final arrest. Sam moved forward until Simon Beecham came into view, his hands behind his head, prone and confused on the bed. A smile forced its way onto Sam's lips as she moved to the side of the bed to let him see her clearly.

Beecham's hard green eyes glared up at her. Sheer hatred was conveyed in his stare. If there hadn't been four burly officers with guns trained on him, she was in no doubt he'd take pleasure in physically attacking her. But he was powerless, cornered in his lair, and Sam took great delight in staring him out.

'Cuffs, ma'am?' An officer handed her a pair. Sam ordered Beecham to stand slowly and place his hands behind his back while she snapped on the handcuffs. Jenny was at her shoulder, as Sam finally had the pleasure of arresting the man for abduction, extortion and fraud, and to read him his rights. Several other charges would follow but for the moment these would suffice.

Beecham was marched forcibly down the stairs and into the car where her two PCs would drive him to New Middridge to spend the rest of the night in the cells.

'We've had a sweep of the premises and there are no booby traps. It appears the only weapon is this handgun,' the AR team leader told Sam, offering her the gun which was safely inside a plastic evidence bag. 'Are you okay if we get off now?' He had the satisfied expression of a man who knows his job's been well done.

'Yes, thank you, we'll take it from here. I appreciate your help and please thank your team for me.' Sam pulled herself up to her full five foot two inches and offered her hand to the officer who shook it enthusiastically. She followed him downstairs and instructed her two PCs to return to the station, with Paul and Layla following. She and Jenny would stay. They both wanted an initial look around before leaving. Derek Ogilvy stayed back too, his interest keen, and Samantha reminded herself that although this was her arrest – her case – they were on DI Ogilvy's patch.

Firstly, Samantha rang DCI Kent and related the mechanics of the operation and its successful outcome, praising the AR team's efficiency and that of their colleagues from Northumbria Police. She imagined him dropping back into his warm comfortable bed and falling straight to sleep, a contented man.

Pulling on gloves, the remaining officers started a search of the property.

Jenny whistled. 'This is quite some place. I wonder what it's going on the market for?'

DI Ogilvy laughed at her wonderment. 'More than you'll ever earn.'

Beginning downstairs they entered the two large rooms, one equipped as a gym, the other housing a full-size snooker table and a laundry area at the far end.

'Wonder who he expected to play with,' Jenny pondered. The rooms were pristine, sparsely equipped and presented more for show than to be used. However, a closer inspection of a wall cupboard revealed something more sinister; a can of petrol and five glass bottles. Jenny lifted the can and shook it, it was full and a pile of rags was stuffed behind it.

'Petrol bombs?' She looked enquiringly at Samantha, whose mind was processing the find. The initial report from the scene at the car park suggested an accelerant was used to set Beecham's Nissan alight. Could it have been a petrol bomb? But what did he need the rest of it for?

They moved upstairs to the living quarters and into a long open-plan lounge with huge windows. It seemed unusual to have the living accommodation upstairs but was probably to make use of the views which in daylight must be spectacular. A modern kitchen at one end made Jenny sigh. 'I think I'm in the wrong job.'

'Hey, look where his ill-gotten gains have landed him, a cosy cell in the nick and a long stretch at Her Majesty's pleasure to come,' Sam reminded her.

Three bedrooms and a bathroom completed the living accommodation, the master suite being the room where they'd discovered Beecham. One of the smaller bedrooms held a single bed, stripped to the mattress. Sam guessed Emma had been imprisoned here as the third room was empty. Even without sheets, there'd be plenty of Emma's DNA in the place to gather as evidence. They'd get CSI officers there at first light.

After an initial scout around, the detectives searched drawers, cupboards, and anywhere where evidence of Beecham's offences could be hidden. The fraud squad would undoubtedly want to search the house for themselves as soon as the CSI were through. They'd be looking for a paper trail, evidence for their case.

Jenny took the master bedroom, finding a suitcase packed and ready to go – and a familiar large holdall. 'Looks like he had travel plans, boss, and I've hit the jackpot too!'

Samantha was beside her instantly, smiling as she recognised the Porters' bag. Strangely in the excitement of the arrest, she'd almost forgotten about the money. Unzipping the flap, it appeared to be all still in place – there'd hardly been sufficient time for the man to go on a spending spree.

'I should probably ring the DCI again but I'll let him sleep and tell him tomorrow.'

In a drawer in the lounge, Sam discovered Beecham's passport. In fact, there were three passports in each of his aliases and an airline ticket to the Dominican Republic for Friday of that week. It was in the name of Christopher Simpson.

'It appears we were just in time.' Derek Ogilvy was at her shoulder.

Sam shuddered, realising how close they'd cut it. If

Beecham had succeeded in leaving the country, it would almost certainly have been a major operation to get him back; the Dominican Republic was one of the countries which did not have an extradition treaty with the UK.

DI Ogilvy yawned. It had been a long day and was essentially Wednesday morning. Sam took the hint and asked Jenny to bag the paperwork they'd found while she bagged the passports. They also took a laptop and two phones they'd discovered.

As they left the building, Ogilvy's sergeant secured the door that the AR officers had battered down, and they finally left 'The White House' to go home for a few hours of well-deserved sleep.

CHAPTER FIFTY-TWO

DI Freeman was back in the office at 9am on Wednesday. She'd arrived home at nearly 5am and as she climbed into bed held no expectations of sleep. Ravi stirred, turning to ask if it had all gone well.

'Like clockwork. Suspect in custody, money retrieved, no hiccups.' She smiled, snuggled into the warmth of his chest and promptly fell asleep.

'Good girl,' Ravi whispered and the next thing she was aware of was her shoulder being gently shaken as he said, 'It's eight o'clock. Do you want to get up?'

Sam flung the covers back and jumped out of bed. The events of earlier that morning instantly flooded her mind and a frisson of excitement ran through her body. A quick shower and she was on her way out of the door with Ravi, updating him on events and promising to knock off early that evening so they could go out to celebrate.

The rest of the team had yet to arrive, so Sam used the quiet time to call Emma Porter. Details of Operation Kielder hadn't been shared with the family – armed response activities were executed on a need-to-know basis. Now Sam was free to share the news that Beecham was finally in custody.

Margaret answered the phone and after minimal pleasantries, Samantha asked to speak to Emma. When Sam relayed the operation's salient points, Emma appeared quite overcome at the news.

'Really?' was all she could ask.

'Yes and we recovered the money, which looks untouched. We'll have to hang on to it for a while as evidence, but you can pass on the good news to your parents.' Sam was delighted to be sharing this positive outcome. It had been a harrowing case – hopefully this conclusion would go some way to bringing an end to their nightmare.

'Where was the house?' Emma was bound to have mountains of questions.

'In the Kielder Forest Park. Look, today's going to be a bit full-on but I'll come out to see you later this afternoon and you can ask your questions then. Is that okay?' Whether or not Sam would have all the answers she didn't know, but a face-to-face meeting was more appropriate and by then the family would have had time to process the news.

'There is something I didn't tell you before, something Mum and Dad don't need to know.' Emma's voice dropped to a whisper. Protecting her parents still seemed uppermost in her mind. 'Simon told me he would punish them, that they would pay with more than money. For some reason he seems to hate them. Do you know what he could have meant?'

Samantha immediately thought of the stash of petrol in The White House, the bottles and the rags, and was convinced then that Beecham intended to burn down their home – the house they'd refused to let him use as collateral. Perhaps the attack on their car had been a warning, the man flexing his muscles to show his strength.

'I think I might know what he was planning but he's safely locked up now, so please don't worry. We'll talk about it later, all right?'

'Yes, that's fine, and Sam – thank you!'

The relief in Emma's voice was thanks enough and the detective was grinning as she made her way upstairs to the DCI's office, knowing he'd be anxious to hear every detail of Operation Kielder.

'Great work, Samantha – it came together beautifully. Well done!' Praise indeed from DCI Kent. 'I've already had fraud at Aykley Heads on the phone wanting to know when they can have a crack at Beecham. I agreed this afternoon around three, will that fit in with you?'

'It'll work, yes. But, to be perfectly honest, I'm not sure how Beecham will play this one. He likes to be in control, yet he's lost the higher ground entirely. He must realise this but he could still clam up. I'm fairly sure he'll want a solicitor and whether he'll own up to his crimes or choose to make our lives difficult remains to be seen.'

'Surely the man knows the evidence is overwhelming.'

'It is, sir, and whatever happens he's going away for a long stretch which I consider to be a good result.' Sam allowed herself to feel smug, but only for a minute as she was keen to get downstairs to see her colleagues and then interview Simon Beecham.

Jenny, Paul and Layla were sharing a joke when she joined them. It was good to hear laughter; their working environment had been strained for too long recently. Four coffees from the deli stood on the table beside a tray of huge pastries calling out to be eaten. Sam helped herself, needing the sugar rush.

Jenny greeted her, licking her lips from her pastry. 'Hey, boss, get any sleep?'

'A couple of hours... you?'

'About the same – good result though, eh?' She looked tired but exhilarated. There was nothing like adrenaline to keep sleep at bay.

'Absolutely, and now we get to interview him. Any news as to how he's been behaving?' Sam looked at the other three.

'The duty sergeant says he's been no trouble, very quiet. He must have plenty to think about and has already asked for a solicitor – stipulating it should be a man.' Paul chuckled. 'Someone's on the way, due any time, so I think we should be good to go at about eleven.'

'Great stuff, Paul. Have you spoken to your estate agent yet? We don't want him visiting the house only to find the CSI all over it.'

'Just about to do it.' The DC hurried off to make the call.

'Right, Jenny, let's decide how we'll play this.'

For the next twenty minutes the detectives huddled around Sam's desk planning the interview with Beecham, although aware that much depended on whether or not the man decided to talk. A no-comment interview was a strong possibility.

Beecham's new solicitor, Ian Wallace, was a small man, almost as wide as he was tall, with a bald head and heavy thick-lensed glasses which kept falling down his nose. He'd been in consultation with his client for forty minutes before the detectives entered the interview room and appeared to have copious notes on his legal pad.

Simon Beecham sat beside the man, dressed in a paper body suit, an improvement on the shorts and T-shirt in which he was arrested. However, with his body at an angle facing the wall, it appeared he had no intention of participating in the interview. The room was warm and Sam opened the window, not wanting them to nod off during the proceedings. Jenny switched on the tape and verbalised the date, time and the names of those present.

Sam shuffled her papers, pausing for a moment before speaking. 'Mr Beecham, you were arrested earlier this morning on charges of abduction, extortion and fraud. How would you like to plead?' She looked directly at their suspect who remained turned away, deliberately avoiding eye contact. It was no more than she expected. Beecham's chin was raised in an arrogant manner, his jaw stubbornly set with his mouth firmly closed.

'My client has asked me to speak on his behalf, DI Freeman.' Wallace pushed his glasses further up his nose and squinted at his pad. 'He is prepared to plead guilty to the charges against him and would ask for another incident be taken into consideration – a historic incident.' Wallace glanced from one detective to the other before clearing his throat and continuing. 'My client wishes you to know that in 1987 he was driving the vehicle which struck, and subsequently killed, his father.'

EPILOGUE

Ten months later

Viridian, cobalt, sap – Emma carefully stippled the three shades of green watercolour paints onto her latest picture, absorbed in getting the balance exactly right. Stepping back, the satisfying intermingling of colour prompted a rare smile. A few dots of gold to represent the sun filtering through the canopy of trees, and it would be complete.

Painting had become Emma's escape, the only time she truly became herself again. Perhaps it was a somewhat reclusive occupation, but time passed quickly during the execution of her pictures and wasn't time the great healer?

Of course, there was unlimited support from her parents, emotionally and financially, and being in their company was the salve Emma needed to heal. It worked both ways. Although George and Margaret wanted their daughter to move on, they too needed to step back in time and take up the role of protectors again as they had throughout her childhood.

Two major events loomed on the horizon of Emma Porter's life, serendipitously, both scheduled for the same week in early September. The first was the sentencing hearing for Simon regarding her abduction. It was ten months since that particular nightmare had unfolded, undoubtedly the worst period of her life and one which would be indelibly seared in Emma's memory, perhaps forever.

Without a viable option, Simon had pleaded guilty, negating the necessity of a full-blown trial in which Emma would have been the chief witness – and the unwilling focus of publicity.

Simon was already in prison. The CPS in their wisdom decided to proceed immediately with the charge of bigamy, which was heard within a couple of months of his arrest. Beecham was subsequently sentenced to five years imprisonment. While safely ensconced at Her Majesty's pleasure, they could process the more complicated cases of fraud, aggravated abduction and the manslaughter of his father.

Sam had broken the news of Simon's confession regarding his father's death to an astonished Porter family. They thought they were beginning to understand the depravity of the man and the depth of his wickedness, but this final revelation was incredible. Sam explained that the decision to confess after so many years was a rather prudent one. As he would be serving time for the more recent crimes, a further sentence would run concurrently so why not get it out of the way too? The CPS eventually accepted Beecham's insistence that he intended to injure his father, not kill him. Any attempt to prove premeditated murder after such an extensive time-lapse would be near impossible. The fact he was a minor at the time was also in Beecham's favour.

At the bigamy hearing in January, Emma sat between her parents and listened to Simon's solicitor pleading mental health problems and a deprived background as mitigating circumstances. It took George every bit of self-control not to stand and speak his mind.

The next hurdle would be sentencing for abduction. Emma decided not to attend this hearing. She'd had enough of Simon Beecham and wished to avoid another ordeal that would undoubtedly play on her emotions and inhabit her mind on those dark days and nights which still plagued her. Samantha had been an absolute rock in the last few months and Emma would prefer to hear the verdict after the event from her.

DI Freeman made sure nothing was left out of her meticulously put-together case, wanting to throw the proverbial book at Beecham. Simon stood to answer charges of aggravated abduction, unlawful imprisonment and possessing an unlicensed firearm with intent to injure. There were also charges relating to the debacle at the car park and the fraud case to consider at this same hearing.

After his surprise confession, a charge of manslaughter was added to the mix. The CPS certainly had their work cut out in this case. The charge of abduction would carry the longest custodial sentence, but sadly the jail time Simon served for each offence would run concurrently.

Emma spent the day upstairs in the attic room she used as her studio, losing herself in creativity. Late in the afternoon, Sam and Jenny arrived with the news that Beecham had received twelve years for aggravated abduction, eight years for fraud and only fifteen months for manslaughter; as expected the sentences would run concurrently.

Sam acknowledged it as a good result. Emma was ambivalent, wishing they could have added the jail time together to keep Simon locked away for many more years. One consolation was that the judge, concerned at the diversity and callousness of his crimes, recommended he serve at least the longer term of twelve years before being considered for parole.

The Porters thanked DI Freeman and DS Newcombe profusely, impressed with both women's ability and dedication and feeling eternally indebted to them for reuniting them as a family.

George and Margaret offered to take their daughter out for a meal, an occasion which would seem almost celebratory, but the last thing Emma felt like doing was celebrating. So instead, they stayed at home, and Margaret put the kettle on.

After her ordeal, Emma found it impossible to return to the surgery where she'd previously worked. Too many memories and the tangible fear of stepping out of the door combined to make returning no longer an option. Her employers offered an extended period of absence, but she declined. It was time to move on, shake off the past, and begin a new life.

The second significant event in Emma's week was to be an exhibition at New Middridge Town Hall. She'd made tentative steps to turn her passion for painting into a career and had already completed two commissions for oil paintings of clients' houses. She'd happily have accepted the commissions without charge if she had other employment. George was guiding his daughter in the ways of business, and Emma was currently a self-employed freelance artist, not yet earning enough to pay tax, but that was no hardship.

Success continued in the form of the invitation to exhibit as one of six local artists, and a whole wall was available for her to fill with work of her own choosing. Such excitement was a much welcome distraction in the Porter household. Simon Beecham was relegated to history as they turned determinedly to the future. An exhibition would be the perfect vehicle to kick-start Emma's career and banish the ghosts of the past.

Late at night, during last-minute preparations for the exhibition, Emma's eye was drawn to the wooden box in the corner of her studio. It was stacked on top of a drawing pad and a few other bits and pieces which her father had retrieved from her 'marital' home. She'd had no desire to look at them before, wanting no reminders of that dreadful time. Now Emma acknowledged she needed to face that part of her life to end it permanently.

Tears filled Emma's eyes as she turned the pages of her sketchbook. She could barely remember creating those images, but she understood what they were and their significance. During a period when she'd felt so very alone and afraid, with no one to talk to, she'd expressed her feelings in this sketch pad; it was her release, her escape.

Staring at the awful ugly charcoal house, Emma's tears flowed freely, cathartic tears. She remembered how she'd felt smudging the charcoal onto the paper, drawing what she couldn't verbalise, a dark depressing house which was *her*. Her life with Simon. The shadows the house cast were long and far-reaching but, as her tears fell, the image blurred and distorted.

Emma closed the pad and tucked it under her arm, knowing precisely what she needed to do. Carrying it downstairs she slipped quietly into the garden, careful not to disturb her sleeping parents and made her way across the dark lawn. The fire pit was uncovered with just a few ashes from its last use still visible in the well. Emma tore the image of the charcoal house from the sketch pad, pulled a box of matches from her pocket and set the corner alight. Holding it over the pit she watched as the edges blackened and curled, and as the flames took hold, she dropped it into the pit.

A smile spread across her face as she witnessed her old life, the most painful of times, crumble into ashes, greedily devoured by flames.

Emma stood tall, turned her back on the charred remains and headed purposefully back towards the light.

THE END

A NOTE FROM THE AUTHOR

Thank you for reading *The Charcoal House*. I hope you enjoyed the story.

One of the many delights of writing fiction is building a character, particularly an evil one. Simon Beecham fits perfectly into this category. A vain narcissist devoid of empathy for his fellow human beings, Simon's pride and belief in his superiority are startling traits. Surely no one can be this egotistical?

Another pleasure in developing evil characters is to find a way to bring them down, to allow good to triumph over evil. Simon's downfall illustrates absolutely that pride comes before a fall.

To read more of my work, please visit my Amazon author page, Facebook author page @gillianjacksonauthor, follow me on Twitter @GillianJackson7 or visit my website, www.gillianjackson.co.uk.

ACKNOWLEDGEMENTS

My thanks as always to my husband and family for their love and support during the hours I spend writing. And to the team at Bloodhound Books for their amazing help in getting this book out into the world. Each book is a collaboration, I get to do the good bits; inventing characters and weaving plots, they work on the polishing and presenting. I truly appreciate their dedication, professionalism and guidance throughout the process.

A NOTE FROM THE PUBLISHER

Thank you for reading this book. If you enjoyed it please do consider leaving a review on Amazon to help others find it too.

We hate typos. All of our books have been rigorously edited and proofread, but sometimes mistakes do slip through. If you have spotted a typo, please do let us know and we can get it amended within hours.

info@bloodhoundbooks.com

Printed in Great Britain
by Amazon

24063763R00162